MW00627307

CLUBBED TWO
Anxiety, Anger, Activism

Maureen,

Enjoy the Club!

Robert A Karl

Robert A. Karl *March 2022*

Self-published by the Author

First Edition: January 2022

ISBN: 978-1-7365181-5-1

Cover Art: Alejandro Mesurado (Instagram @mesurado.art)

Cover Design: Nirkri (fiverr.com/nirkri)

Dedicated to anyone and everyone
touched by the AIDS pandemic.

PROLOGUE

In 1976, Joey used his inheritance to move to Philadelphia and open Club Sanctuary, the biggest and hottest gay nightclub in PA. Hanging out in a city park one night, he met Henry, a young, intelligent and ambitious African-American gay male.

Together, they built a solid relationship, a solid business and a commitment to serve as a resource to the LGBTQ community. Friendships were formed, obstacles were overcome and the club expanded as Joey and Henry moved from having a casual relationship to developing a strong emotional bond resulting in marriage. Though not recognized legally, their commitment to one another grew stronger as they struggled to provide a club environment that was open to all segments of the community.

Just as they began to feel a degree of success in their ambitions, a fatal blow was struck as the AIDS pandemic began to decimate their friends and customers. With the cause of the illnesses still unknown, with no treatment and no cure, the LGBTQ community was just beginning to understand the magnitude of the struggle they faced.

The story continues here as Joey narrates the stories of diverse, interesting and entertaining characters in the queer community during the 1980s and early 90s.

ONE

"You don't want these books, son," the man behind the counter told me sternly. I stood there, frozen with embarrassment, wondering how to convince him that *Yes, I did want those books*. I wanted them more than anything in the world at that very moment. I took a minute to wipe the sweat from my palms, trying to think of an answer. Looking down, I saw that my hands were trembling, a sure sign of my extreme state of anxiety. I also felt my erection, hard as a rock just a minute ago, shrink into the suddenly uncomfortable stickiness of the wet pouch of my white briefs.

I had just spent the better part of an hour, carefully and closely checking out the merchandise I wanted. No, it was more than a want. It was a need. Just yesterday, I had found a section of this strip mall bookstore that seemed to be calling my name. I stood at a distance, watching the guys who were lined up at the shelves of neatly-arranged magazines, casually thumbing through the pages that I dared not touch. A few feet from the magazine racks were two rows of stands holding paperback books. But not just any books. No, these were special, in a special all-male section of the bookstore.

Titles like *The Pirates' Good Boys*, *The Wet Boys of Summer*, *What Cowboys Do In the Dark* and *Beach Boy Bingo* caught my youthful eyes. I walked by those titles as slowly as possible, wanting to reach out and grab a book, but not daring to touch any of them, worried that I might be seen by someone. I knew I wasn't supposed to be here.

As I approached the magazine area, my mind was racing at the sight of those delicious temptations. I was close

1

enough to see the titles, in blaring headlines. *The Demigods*, *Bicep Boys, Young Treasures*, *Secrets in the Sand*, *On Lifeguard Duty*. They were carefully positioned by the store's staff so only the titles were visible. You had to actually pull one from the shelf to see the full cover, and then to see the forbidden photos on the inside pages.

I was especially intrigued by the title *Bicep Boys*. I wasn't exactly sure what biceps were, but I knew that if the boys in that magazine had them, then I wanted them. I wanted them so much that it hurt.

All of them under the sign that made me very nervous.

"Must Be 18 Years Old to Purchase," it screamed at me.

I was 13 years old. Well, 13 and a half. For me, that meant I was practically 14. *Wasn't I?* But I was small for my age and a late bloomer, having just recently started going through those bodily changes. Little tufts of hair in strange places. A bad smell under my arms if I didn't wash thoroughly. And on the bumpy bus ride to school every weekday morning, there was a hardness in my pants that I could not control.

Recently, I had to start holding my blue canvas duffle bag, used as a bookbag, on my lap, instead of placing it on the floor like usual, trying to hide the bulge that was clearly visible between my legs. It didn't escape my notice that some of the other boys in my class had recently started doing the same thing. My best guess was that we were all having the same reaction as our bodies were bouncing in the seats of the bus. Every 13- and 14-year-old boy, trying to hide their erections, caused by the incessant bouncing of the school bus as it stimulated our youthful bodies. And who knows what each one of them was thinking? Having an erection can cause some funny thoughts, you know.

2

But back to the bookstore. The first day I found that forbidden area, I just observed. I was nervous and scared. But there was no way I could unsee what I now knew to be true. There were actual documents…books, magazines and who knew what else that showed exactly what I was interested in seeing. Young men in various stages of undress, in sexy poses and looking at the camera in a way that convinced me that those guys in the photos wanted…ME! Yes, I was young and foolish enough to think that those models actually wanted to have sex with me. Crazy, right? And even if they didn't want me, well, there was no doubt in my mind that I wanted them.

I spent some time in the bookstore that day moving between the all-male section and the straight, but still-smutty section. There were lots and lots of magazines featuring bare-breasted ladies that drew no interest from me. However, I thought I should pretend that I liked those pictures, in case anyone was watching me. I felt the need to be very discreet about my true desires.

I was on a mission for sexually explicit materials. Although I was a good student in school, reading at an advanced grade level, those classics of literature in the other sections of the store were not on my mind today. I was being cautious, hoping to distract anyone from thinking that I was...well, I was still working on what I was exactly.

I spent more time than I really wanted to, looking at the *Playboy* magazines and others featuring full-breasted females, pretending that I was interested. If anyone was watching, I was determined to make them think I was just another horny straight teenage boy.

I was sure that I was succeeding in hiding my motives. In this area of the bookstore, no one made eye contact with anyone else. All eyes were either glued to the magazines, the books, or staring blankly into space. I got the feeling that everyone was in some way embarrassed to be there. I was no exception.

At some point, I had to drag myself out of the store. I had to be home for dinner. Homework had to be completed. But my mind never left the store. That was all I could think about, trying to figure out a plan to get what I wanted. And of course, I just couldn't get those images out of my head. Those gorgeous young guys. The titles of the books and magazines. I was too scared to open any of them, so it was left to my imagination to wonder what adventures were described inside those pages.

There was a pause.

A VERY long pause.

"What happened next, Kurt?" The question came from Danny, a member of the group, who was literally sitting on the edge of his seat, listening to the story.

"My name isn't Kurt. It's Kirk, you asshole! Why can't you get that right? It's written plain as day here on my nametag!" Kirk made an exaggerated gesture, pointing to the tag on his shirt, then pulling his shirt away from his body to make his name more clearly visible.

I watched the interaction between Kirk and Danny with interest. I wasn't sure, but I thought I detected sparks between them. No, not sparks of resentment or dislike for each other. Sexual sparks. I considered the possibility that Danny was just trying to get some attention from Kirk, especially when I saw how intently Danny's eyes watched every move Kirk made as he told the story from his youth. I laughed quietly to myself, picturing Danny

4

drooling at the sight of the blonde hunk who was replaying a scene from his past life here at the Center.

And who am I? My name's Joey. I'm here at the Center today with my friend Bobby, who asked me to accompany him for moral support. Insatiable, lustful Bobby, who nudged me hard in my ribs when Kirk pulled up his shirt, exposing his taut abs. At that sight, Bobby let out a sigh, perhaps a little too loudly. *Oh well, I guess Kirk is probably used to guys staring at his abs. His upper body looked like one of those statues of the Greek and Roman gods you might see in a museum.*

The counselor coughed, getting everyone's attention. "Do you want to continue today, Kirk, or let it go till next week?"

"No, I'm good. I can keep going and tell you guys what happened the next day when I went back to that bookstore."

Kirk continued speaking to the group of men gathered in that tight circle, describing his next trip to the bookstore in search of gay materials.

"It was all I could do to get through the next school day. Listening to those teachers drone on and on about whatever. On most days, I'd be fairly interested. But not that day. All I could think about were those dirty books with alluring titles that I just knew I had to read.

The Pirates' Good Boys, *The Wet Boys of Summer*, *What Cowboys Do In the Dark* and *Beach Boy Bingo*. I mean, c'mon, Beach Boy Bingo…that's a game I knew I wanted to learn how to play!"

The men in the group laughed, but I also noticed that Danny, the one who seemed to like Kirk, never cracked a smile. Instead, he was just staring at Kirk, licking his lips, edging closer to the edge of his hard, plastic chair. I thought Danny might jump Kirk's bones right there on the floor, in the middle of the circle of guys.

Kirk clapped his hands at the mention of *Beach Boy Bingo* and continued, "I had told my Mom that I'd be late coming home from school that day. Gave her some shit about trying out for the Drama Club. You know, just starting 9th Grade, being a freshman, you gotta get into some of those extracurriculars. So she believed me, no problem."

"But of course, there was no Drama Club tryout, at least not for me. I got my skinny ass right on that school bus after school, got off at that little strip mall and practically ran those two blocks to the store. I don't even think my little dick had time to get soft after the bus drive before I was back at the store, this time ready to score my books."

Danny was licking his lips when Kirk mentioned his dick, and I saw him grab his crotch suggestively, not caring if anyone else in the group noticed or not. He only had eyes for Kirk.

"My plan was to walk right into the store, grab what I wanted and head for the checkout. But as soon as I got to the all-male section of the store, I froze."

"You were actin' like a pussy," Danny muttered under his breath.

"I was fuckin' 13 years old. I was scared," Kirk replied. Danny was mad at himself for saying anything. He figured it was a mistake to make fun of the guy he wanted to have sucking his dick later on.

"I headed for the magazines first. I already knew what I wanted. *The Demigods*, *Young Treasures* and *Bicep Boys* were at the top of my wish list. I had to squeeze between two much taller and heavier men to reach my goal at the magazine rack. Of course, they were taller and heavier because they were actually mature men. But I knew we had a common interest. Anyway, I had to stand on tiptoes to reach for the mags, my fingers just within reach of those luscious demigods. But my hands were slippery with nervous sweat, so my first reach for *The Demigods* magazine ended up with nothing."

"Did that really happen or are you makin' that shit up?" This time, it was my friend Bobby who was doing the interrupting. I looked at him sideways to try to silently tell him to cool it, but Kirk wasn't about to be denied his chance to tell the story his way.

"Who's tellin' the story, you or me?" he shot back at Bobby.

"On my second try, I finally had that bad boy in my hands. Then I imitated the guys around me, trying to casually leaf through the pages, while my heart was beating so fast I could feel it thumping in my skinny chest, and my dick was about ready to explode right there in the store, without a touch."

At that, Danny let out a small moan, and sweat was visible on his brow. He looked exasperated, because this story was clearly getting to him, but he had to restrain his impulses while they were all in the group meeting. He shuffled nervously in his seat, and again he mumbled, this time saying, "Go on. Go on. Tell us what happened next."

"I leafed quickly through the pages, barely able to believe what I was seeing. Page after glossy page, nothing but the most beautiful images I had ever seen. Young men, teenagers really, flexing their biceps, pumping out their chests, many of them gleaming with sweat…and of course, the money shot, where I could see their packages wrapped tightly in those little cloth straps that barely hid anything. As I fondled the pages, packed with those glossy photos, I stared at the images with wide-eyed wonder, thinking that the guys in the photos looked glossy too, glossy with sweat as they gazed at one another, posing while dressed only in those tiny, sexy posing straps. I couldn't take my eyes away from those luscious bulging straps, feeling the heat in my own pants."

The entire group was silent as Kirk continued describing his teenage adventure in the bookstore.

"Of course, in those days, complete male nudity was forbidden in a magazine. Same for showing pubic hair. Each model could show his round, smooth, hairless ass, but dicks and balls were not to be seen. I was forced to use my imagination, and it transported me to a place where every one of those guys had the absolutely perfect, large, bulging, veiny dick that I could practically taste right there. All of these guys were smooth, silky smooth, and I wanted them to rub those smooth bodies all over me."

"And as much as I loved those male photos, I was just a little disappointed that not one picture showed a dude with a boner. That's what I was dying to see!"

Danny moaned again, a little more loudly this time. My friend Bobby practically broke my rib jabbing me.

"I held the magazine tightly to my chest and reached for the next object of my desire, the magazine titled *Young Treasures*. My clammy fingers could barely move the pages. I kinda thought I might get in trouble for ruining the magazines with my sweaty hands. But somehow, I opened the pages and felt my dick jump at the sights inside. Young treasures, indeed! And while every photo I had seen in *The Demigods* had been of white guys, *Young Treasures* included images of Black guys too, giving me a glimpse of something I had never seen before. Fascinated, I stood staring at those photos for what seemed like too long, forgetting that I still had to pay for them. Then I grabbed a copy of *Bicep Boys*, leafing through it quickly, wondering what a bicep looked like. I didn't see anything out of the ordinary, though what I saw was exactly what I was interested in. Boys, boys and more boys, in sexy-ass poses, looking so strong, so masculine, so handsome that I wanted to shriek with joy!"

Even I was getting a little hot listening to Kirk's story. You could hear the excitement as he re-lived this episode in his mind, sharing his secret with all the other men in the group.

Kirk continued, "Forcing myself to snap out of my reverie and back to reality, I headed for the paperback section. I tried to be casual as I strolled over to the all-male section, hoping that the other customers would continue to ignore me. I was on a quest, and I refused to let anything like fear stop me this time."

Kirk stopped to take a drink from his water bottle. During that brief pause, Bobby whispered to me, "Anything like that ever happen to you? Were you looking for queer porn when you were a teenager?"

"I'll tell you about it some other time," I whispered back, as Kirk started to speak again.

"I knew the titles I wanted, but I had to make sure the stories were what I was expecting…what I was hoping for. You know, if it wasn't filled with page after page after page of smutty gay sex, then I wasn't gonna be interested."

Another interruption occurred, and I began to wonder whether Kirk would ever be able to finish the story. Danny, the one who most clearly had the hots for Kirk, took his half-filled water bottle and rolled it across the floor, so that it landed directly in front of Kirk, and then somehow, seemingly like magic, the bottle spun around so the capped top was pointing directly back at Danny.

"That's it!" Danny screamed, jumping up from his chair. "I won Spin the Bottle and now you gotta kiss me, Kurt!"

Although the group members were apparently used to these kinds of antics from Danny, some of them were becoming annoyed. The leader of the group session got up from his chair and quietly stood directly behind Danny, firmly placing his hands on Danny's shoulders and began massaging his tense muscles. Almost immediately, a change came over Danny, a look of relaxation, giving me some hope that maybe Kirk would be able to finish before the end of the hour.

"Dude, if you call me Kurt one more time, I'm gonna shove somethin' right up your ass to get you to shut the fuck up!" But Danny didn't even seem to hear Kirk. His eyes were rolling into the back of his head as he fell under the trance of the deep massage.

Kirk went back to his story, leaning forward in his chair and lowering his voice, almost to a whisper.

This dude knows how to do an effective presentation, I thought.

"So, I get to the paperback section and damn, I can't find any copies of *What Cowboys Do In the Dark*. And you better believe I had a pretty good idea what those cowboys might be doin' to each other, though I was really hopin' to read all about it."

The grin on Kirk's face as he thought about that was striking. Even now, it was clear the thought of that book turned him on.

"I looked around and saw that there was a whole stack of *The Wet Boys of Summer*, so I grabbed one and started skimming as fast as I could. Inside the book, I saw words and phrases like 'Fuck my tight hot boy ass' and 'suck my throbbing horsemeat cock' and 'lick my asshole, prettyboy.' Oh my fuckin' god, I had never been so turned on in my life!"

"Dudes, I was shaking with excitement, but I managed to hold onto my three prize packages while I desperately looked through the books for that special, magical title. Yes! There it was! *Beach Boy Bingo*!"

"Once again, I thumbed through the pages, looking for the rules to play bingo with the boys on the beach. I read this passage, 'Down on your knees you fuckin' cocksucker, the older boy told the teen as he pulled at his throbbing, pulsing dick that needed to escape from his tight speedos.'

Then I flipped more pages, totally unaware of my surroundings, forgetting where I was, quickly reading, 'Rubbing his massive meat against my tight puckerhole, I felt his strong hands pulling my ass cheeks wide open, while his friends watched from a distance.'"

Kirk was staring off into space, looking a little like he had somehow transported himself back to that bookstore of his youth. He continued, his words tumbling out of his mouth, as he told the story he was sure the group was enjoying.

"I could feel all the blood in my body rushing to my face, turning my pale skin beet-red. The rest of my blood seemed to be filling my teenage dick to the brim; I felt like my cock was bigger and thicker than it had ever been, even more so than when I played with it incessantly under the covers of my bed. At that young age, I had already filled so many socks with cum that by the end of the week, I was often out of clean socks to wear before laundry got done."

"Quickly scanning the pages before I made a final decision about this book, I read these lines:

'I felt the boy who was behind me groan wildly as he fucked my asshole like a wild beast, thrusting, moaning, thrusting, moaning…till I felt his jizz being released from deep inside his nut sack, traveling the length of his uncut, throbbing cock, spilling his hot streams of silky sperm so deep in my ass that I could almost taste it. At the same time, the boy in front of me leaned back and howled like a dog, thrusting his hips toward my face, forcing his dick deeper and deeper down my throat, not caring that I was gagging, as he fed me his pearly rivers of manly milkiness.'"

I swear my jaw almost dropped to the floor as I listened to Kirk tell this part of the story. I doubted that any dick in the room was soft, since this was a group meeting for young, gay men…and though it wasn't meant to turn into an orgy, I could imagine that actually happening. I mean, Kirk had every one of us horny as fuck by this time.

But…another interruption.

"You really expect us to believe you remember all those lines from the book? Aren't you just making this up as you go along?" All eyes turned towards Nico, another member of the group, as he brought us back to reality with his question.

"Dude, believe whatever you fuckin' want," Kirk replied. "But think about how many times I read those books. Is it so hard to imagine that I remember it exactly?"

"After reading those parts of the book, I decided it was fuckin' perfect. Exactly what I needed to learn all about how to please the other boys."

"That's what I was thinking as I headed to the cash register. Between the three magazines and the two paperback books, I figured I was just about set for life."

The group leader, still massaging Danny's shoulders, interrupted this time. "Just two more minutes, Kirk, so let's wrap this up. We want a little time for refreshments after the sharing session."

Kirk quickly continued the story.

"I had to wait behind a couple of guys before I got to the head of the line. And that's when I heard those terrible, frustrating words that I told you when I started telling you about my experience."

"You don't want these books, son."

"Sir," Kirk asked the leader, "Can I just have a few more minutes to finish up? I want everyone to know what happened after I left the bookstore."

Nodding, the group leader granted permission for Kirk to continue.

"The last thing I expected was for the dude at the register to tell me I didn't *want* those books. Because of course, that wasn't true. *He* didn't want me to have gay books and magazines. *Society* didn't want me to have them. The truth is, I wanted them with every fiber of my being. I wasn't prepared to answer him, but I did blurt out, 'Yes, I do want them', pushing my money on the counter towards him.

He didn't take the money. He pushed it back at me. He took my precious books and mags, the objects of my lustful desires, and placed them under the counter, then motioning for the next customer to come forward.

So I left the store, more dejected than I had ever felt in all my 13 and a half years. I was dragging myself out of the store, shoulders drooping, eyes clouding with tears, with no plan for what to do next. My dick had gone from rock hard, dripping with wetness to a tiny little cocktail hot dog loosely hanging between my legs."

The group leader coughed, signaling that the story needed to end there, but Kirk went on.

"Okay, I can't go into detail this week, but I just want to let you know that after I left the store, I was sitting on a bench across from the store, waiting for the bus to take me home. But what happened next surprised even me. As I sat there, a lonely freshman in high school, desperately lonely and horny, one of the well-known, popular, handsome seniors in our school came over and sat down beside me."

"Here, I think maybe you want this," he said, handing me a brown paper bag.

"I was shocked. *What the fuck is he doing?* I thought. Besides being sad and dejected, now I was *nervous* too. But I was also curious, so I opened the bag, reached inside and started to pull out the contents."

"No," the older boy told me. "Don't take them out. Just look inside. I know what you were doing."

"Holy fuck!" I said as I peered into the bag and saw each of my treasures there, the objects of my perverse and perverted teenage desires, apparently a gift from this guy who was clearly out of my league. I mean, he had to be 17, maybe even 18 years old!

All of my selections were in the bag. *The Demigods, Bicep Boys, Young Treasures, The Wet Boys of Summer* and *Beach Boy Bingo.* I wanted to jump up and hug this guy, but I stopped myself, realizing I didn't know what to do. So, I started stammering,

"Hey, thanks man…what the…I mean, how did…I mean…I don't even know what to say. Here, let me pay you for these," I finally said when able to speak a complete sentence.

"Nah, that's okay," he told me, shaking his head and winking at me. I suddenly noticed his features. Tall, handsome, body of a jock...no, wait...the body of a Demigod!

"I left a note in there with my phone number," he told me, referring to the bag filled with gay goodies. "But don't ever call me unless it's an emergency. And I want you to meet me at 8 PM tomorrow in the park. Only call me if you can't get out of the house to meet me. And make sure that you're wearing clean underpants when we meet."

Kirk stopped speaking. The silence in the room was heavy, almost unbearably so.

"Thanks, Kirk," the group leader said matter-of-factly, as if nothing phased him, not even the possibility of a client telling the story of losing his virginity.

"Everyone's invited to stay for some refreshments. But only about 20 minutes. We all have to be out of the building before I have to lock up at 5."

I looked over at Bobby, unsure of our next step. "You wanna stay for the cookies and lemonade?" I teased.

"It's kinda polite to stay and socialize for a few minutes," he replied.

I took the hint and walked over to introduce myself to Nico, who was standing alone, looking a little lost...and very handsome in my eyes. Though I wasn't looking for a sexual connection, I was always interested in making new friends. As I introduced myself, I watched Bobby make his way over to talk with Danny, the one who had kept interrupting Kirk.

"Hey, I'm Joey," I said, offering my hand to Nico. "This is a pretty cool group you guys have here."

Nico smiled, introducing himself and shaking my hand vigorously. "Yeah, thanks to the Sarge over there," he explained, nodding in the direction of the group discussion leader." If it wasn't for him, gay veterans like us would just be left to fend for ourselves. And let me tell ya, it can be brutal out there."

"Until Bobby told me about this group, I didn't realize there were gay veterans," I said, stupidly forgetting all about Stephen, the gay naval officer I had met before he was transferred to San Francisco, taking my bartender Lonnie with him.

As we chatted, Bobby and Danny both walked over to Kirk.

"Sorry about that bullshit I was givin' you earlier, you know, during your speech and all," Danny explained. "I didn't really mean anything by it. You know how I get…a little crazy sometimes." Danny's head was hanging low, but also checking for any sign from Kirk that he had been forgiven.

"It's okay, babe, I already know." Kirk knew that Danny liked him, and he also knew that Danny had the grace of a third-grade boy trying to impress a little girl in his class when it came to courting Kirk. To hear Kirk tell it, he was going to force Danny to prove he was worthy of his attention…and his dick.

"Let's get some lemonade before we get shut down," Kirk offered. Both Bobby and Danny made a move to help Kirk, but he raised his hand, making a motion for them to stop.

"I'm pretty fuckin' sure I can get over to the table all by myself," Kirk grunted, pushing the wheels of his chair and gliding over to the refreshment stand.

I was watching and I couldn't help but wonder what had happened to Kirk. Were his injuries so serious that he had to spend all his time in a wheelchair? Would that be a permanent condition for him?

A few minutes later, Bobby and I were in the parking lot of the non-descript building at 4th and Race Streets, in the Old City section of Philadelphia, heading for Bobby's car. There was a small sign identifying the basement office as the location of the Veterans Service Center. Today was my first visit, being asked to accompany Bobby because his boyfriend had a small part in a production of Les Miz at the Walnut Street Theatre, and the Sunday matinee was at the same time as Bobby's meeting with the Gay Veterans Alliance. The GVA was totally off the radar of the military establishment. Sergeant Reynolds would probably have been court-martialed if anyone in the military brass knew that he was allowing gay vets to meet at the Service Center. Even though they had fought in the war just like other veterans, gay veterans were never a topic of discussion in the military. At least, not as far as any of us knew.

TWO

I had a lot of questions for Bobby about what had just happened. But I had to hold those till later. It was just a short drive to the apartment I shared with my husband, Henry, in Society Hill Towers. A five-minute drive down Second Street and I was home, ready to start preparing for the big party at the club tonight.

Alejandro, one of the Board members at Sanctuary, the biggest, hottest and gayest club in all of Philly…no, in all of Pennsylvania, had been planning for tonight for months. It was the first Sunday Night White Party, which would become an annual event, held on a selected Sunday in the month of July. And no, a White Party had nothing to do with race, my dear. It was all about the outfits…the more glamorous the better…but everything, and I do mean everything that was worn had to be white!

This year's event was being held on Sunday, July 25, 1982.

When I got home, I greeted Henry with a warm hug and a kiss. After we got married on Christmas Day, 1980, our love had only grown stronger. In my mind, Henry was perfect in every way. He supported me when I needed it, and he challenged me to grow when he recognized that was the right thing to do. He never let me slack off when it came to supporting our gay community. As the owners of Sanctuary, (and yes, Henry became a co-owner with me when we got married, even though our union wasn't recognized as legal in the eyes of the state of Pennsylvania), we felt a responsibility to not only entertain, but to provide resources for the community when needed.

And the last 18 months or so of wedded bliss did nothing to diminish the sexual attraction between us. We fucked all the time and we fucked everywhere. It would be difficult to find a spot in our fancy, spacious Society Hill Towers apartment that hadn't been touched by our hot, sweaty bodies during a steamy and passionate sexual encounter. And during these 18 months, Henry had learned how to satisfy his desire for dominance and my desire for submission in ways that might make a lot of gay men blush. Or maybe not.

Three weeks ago, Henry brought home a gift for me. More accurately, gifts for both of us. He wasn't shy about spending money, since the club provided us with a steady stream of what seemed to be an endless supply of cash. And, he wasn't one bit shy about keeping our love alive with all sorts of little gifts and surprises.

Two boxes were placed on the coffee table in the living room, next to the glossy fashion magazines and hardcover photo books. "Sit down," he told me, his voice deep, hypnotic, commanding.

I did as I was told without thinking, without question. As our relationship grew, it had become apparent which one of us was dominant, and the other was obedient and submissive.

"You can open this one first, though don't think it's for you, babe. It's all for me." He sounded like he was boasting, for some reason, proud that he owned whatever was in that big black box.

He handed it to me, placing it in my lap, as he squeezed tightly into me, wrapping his arm around my waist with his strong left arm. The lid of the box said "Pleasure Chest" which I recognized as a leather/sex toy shop located in the basement of a brownstone on Walnut Street. "That's where you bought me my first cockring…the leather one with the metal studs!" I exclaimed, in a voice that I thought was probably just a little too high, a little too girly.

"Good thing you remember, my little puta,"[1] Henry growled, his lips so close to my ear I could feel his hot breath. *Damn, he still knows how to get my dick going…and how to get my ass wet*, I thought.

"Oh, so now I'm your puta," I teased. "I thought I was your perrita." [2]

I only knew enough Spanish to know he was talking dirty to me, so I used words I knew he had called me before. Though Henry is Black, he has some Latino blood in him. His paternal grandfather was from the Dominican Republic, and Henry grew up speaking both Spanish and English at home. However, without constant practice, much of the Spanish he had learned was long forgotten at this point.

The box was heavy. "What's in here, babe? Like a thousand cockrings? Two thousand?" Henry gave me a look of displeasure. I knew that I needed to be more serious about what was happening. "Ok, I'm done with the jokes," I whispered, my voice suddenly dry and hoarse.

As soon as I removed the top of the box, the smell of fresh leather filled the room, strong, pungent, and most of all, manly. It reminded me of the smell that always hit me when I went to The Hole, the part of our club dedicated to the leather community. Henry was giving me a stern look, but I was pretty sure that he was smiling on the inside, pleased with himself and hoping that I'd be pleased as

---

[1] Puta - Spanish for bitch

[2] Perrita - Literally, a small female dog. Used here to mean a bitch

20

well. However, I also knew that the time for jokes was over.

I reached into the box, pulling out a leather harness. It was heavy, so I knew Henry meant business. This was no toy. The leather straps were thick and included metal studs made of gleaming chrome. I held the harness by the shoulder straps and saw that there were two other body straps, designed to encircle the chest and waist. Metallic rings held all the pieces together. Buckles would be used to firmly attach the harness to Henry's body.

"Sniff it," he told me.

I looked at him, hesitating for a moment. He didn't like that.

"Sniff the fuckin' leather!" he commanded in his deep, booming, authoritarian voice. With no further delay, I started to sniff the leather straps, inhaling that intoxicating aroma of real leather.

"Lick it, puta!" No hesitation this time. My tongue felt the smoothness of the fine-grain leather, with the combination of the erotic scent and the intoxicating taste making my dick jump.

"Now stick your tongue through one of those rings."

Submissively, I obeyed, then feeling Henry's strong Black hands taking a firm hold of the back of my head, guiding my face to within an inch of the hard bulge in his tight-fitting jeans. He started guiding my head up and down, forcing me to lick his crotch.

"You like that, babe?"

I nodded my agreement.

"Okay, bitch, I like gettin' you all worked up in a sweat," he sneered, pushing my face away. "Get the next piece outta the box."

I admit that I was excited by what was going on. Henry knew what I liked and how I liked it. He had no doubt

21

that, when it came to sex, he could be as dominant as he wanted to be and he'd never hear any complaints from me.

The next piece was an extension to the top harness. This part had a metal ring where Henry could insert his cock, having it firmly supported and that could also apply tension to his balls if used properly. A circular piece would go around his lower waist and the final strap would go between his legs, tight inside his ass cheeks, almost like a black leather thong.

"Bitch, you already know what to do. Don't act so fuckin' innocent and stupid," he scolded me, as I started sniffing, then licking the second piece of expensive leather.

Henry could not only sense my excitement; he could see it. My dick was straining to be released from my clothing, feeling suffocated inside my tight purple bikini briefs, with my skin-tight jeans making it even more difficult to find a comfortable position.

"Open your pants and pull your dick outta that little girly bikini I know you're wearin'! But that's all. Don't touch it or you won't like it when I throw a glassful of ice water on it to calm you the fuck down."

I was moaning with desire at that command, fumbling with my jeans, finally unbuttoning them with my shaking fingers, then pulling my throbbing cock out of my bikini, which had a tell-tale spot of sticky wetness in the pouch.

Henry, who had been standing in front of me, sat on the sofa, legs spread wide, and firmly guided me off the sofa and down onto the hardwood floor. "Kneel right there," he told me, pushing me in the direction where he wanted me, right next to his left leg. "I'll show you the rest of my stuff."

Before digging deeper into the box, Henry took hold of my hair, which was just barely long enough for him to get a handful. His grip was firm but gentle. But if I had resisted, I already knew he wouldn't hesitate to use his authority to be sure I did as he wanted. Pulling me by the hair, he placed my chin on his leg, my nose so close to his manhood that I could have caught his scent, except for the unmistakable scent of the fabric softener I used when I washed his jeans for him. That was the first time I ever felt sorry about my overzealous efforts at doing the laundry.

I hoped Henry would unleash his dick, but no such luck. As I knelt at his side, my throbbing cock bouncing with every breath I took, Henry reached into the box and pulled out a pair of black leather gloves. "Oh yeah," he murmured, admiring the fine work of the smooth, velvety leather. "We're gonna have some fun with these, boy."

He laid the gloves on his leg, just above his knee, and then reached for the back of my head, giving my hair a little tug, indicating that he wanted me to lift my head. Opening my mouth just a bit as I did so, Henry took two fingers of his right hand and gently inserted them into my waiting, eager mouth.

"Don't suck, just hold them in there."

Henry already knew that would drive me crazy with desire. I wanted to suck...suck on anything...but that desire was denied to me. At least for now.

In and out...in and out...in and out. So slowly, so deliberately, so demanding and dominating...Henry slowly pushed those two fingers into my mouth and then back out, daring me to defy him and start sucking.

"Good boy, yeah, you're a very good boy," he whispered into my ear, bending closer so I could feel his hardness against my cheeks through the rough denim of his jeans.

Pulling his fingers from my drooling mouth, he reached down between my legs, lightly brushing the pink head of my cock, so close to exploding that I was shaking. He rubbed some of my spit against the swollen tip, opening the tiny slit with his fingers, mixing my saliva with my dripping pre-cum. I couldn't keep the moans from escaping my lips, knowing that Henry was well aware of the effect he was having on me.

"Get up!" he suddenly commanded.

My legs were weak and shaking as I struggled to rise to my feet. He bent me over, so my head was close to the floor, my ass over his lap, my bikinis still covering my hard cheeks while my rock-hard dick was caught between Henry's legs.

I smelled the leather of the glove before I could taste it, as Henry forced me to take the glove in my mouth.

"This oughta keep you quiet, little boy," he teased me, as I felt his other hand pulling my underpants down, exposing my most vulnerable spot to Henry's lustful eyes. Now using both hands, he spread me wide and spit loudly into me. I could feel the spit dripping inside me, while some dribbled down the side of my leg. Gasping, I felt one finger enter me, probing me, pushing deep inside. Then, a second finger slid deeper inside, invading my privacy and making me squeal.

I admit it, I was enjoying this intimate moment with my husband. Henry knew how to turn me on, and he always found new and exciting ways to keep us satisfied sexually.

With a sudden jerk, Henry lifted me totally off his lap, holding me in the air, dangling me like a toy, like a puppet. He started to put me on the sofa next to him, but his one bare hand was slippery with sweat, and he almost dropped me. I opened my mouth in surprise, a little shocked at the sudden feeling of falling, and the glove dropped from my mouth to the floor.

"Don't worry, babe, I got more of that for you," he whispered in my direction, as he regained control of my body and sat me on the sofa next to him. "But I wanna save that for just a little later. Now I want you to open up your gift."

He handed me the box, but didn't relinquish control immediately. "I hope you like this!"

The package was black and pink and said "Victoria's Secret." I had no idea what that was. It seems that a new store had just opened in the Gallery Mall, and Henry wanted me to have something from that shop.

"Go ahead, you can open it, sweetie."

"Thank you, my King!" I replied. Now, Henry had never asked me to address him as "My King," but I knew he liked it. It always brought a beautiful smile to his handsome face. Especially when I addressed him with that term of utmost respect and love when we were out in public. This time, he grabbed hold of his crotch, taking hold of his still-erect manhood through his jeans, and told me, "That's the way I like it!"

Opening the box, I was surprised…no, I was shocked at the contents. Three pairs of women's panties. One red, one pink, one black…all three sheer and lacey and delicate. Three bras. Again, one red, one pink, one black. Each had a beautiful lacey design embroidered on the front of the cups. And three of what I think are called babydoll nighties. Colors to match the panties and bras. Little bows in complementary colors.

Just looking at them, I knew they would be short...very short. I guess that was the idea, to allow the pretty panties to be seen peeking out from beneath the hem.

I gave Henry a questioning look. Now, we both knew I was submissive. I had even been known to shop in the women's sections of various stores, occasionally buying ladies' pants, tops and even shoes. But it had never even crossed my mind to buy lingerie, let alone wear it for Henry. I thought he liked seeing me in my tight, brightly-colored bikini briefs. Men's bikini briefs. With a pouch for my junk.

"Take these off, babe," he commanded, tugging at my tight briefs. "I wanna see you all dolled up. You know you're my baby doll, right?"

I don't know what came over me, but the first time putting on a pair of women's panties awakened something in me. Not that I wanted to be a female, or thought that I was a woman, but I was trembling with excitement as I pulled them up, finding it impossible for the panties to contain my erection, really barely able to hold my smooth, hairless nuts.

To be honest, when Henry forced me to dress in those panties, bra and babydoll, it felt like a freeing experience. I felt like I would no longer be confined to expressing my fashion sense mostly in men's clothing. It suddenly dawned on me that I had the freedom to wear anything I fuckin' wanted to wear.

Henry pulled back to get a full view. "Oh my fuckin' god," I heard him say. "You are so fuckin' sexy and beautiful! Put the rest of the outfit on, then go stand over by the wall and let me look at you."

After Henry helped me with the bra, and I completed the outfit with the nightie, I heard his breath quicken. It didn't escape his notice that my dick was emitting a steady stream of thick, sticky precum, a long string of it dangling in the air as I walked over to the wall, then slowly turning around, bending ever so slightly when my back was to Henry, giving him a full view of my round, firm, fleshy cheeks now covered with the pretty lace of the pink panties.

"In the bedroom. Now!"

I didn't have to be told twice. I knew what Henry was about to do. He was going to have me in any way he wanted. And I was willing to give him anything and everything because I loved him and I adored the way he could surprise me with gifts like these.

In the bedroom, I positioned myself across the bed on my stomach, instinctively spreading my legs wide. Henry stopped at the stereo, turning on the radio, which just happened to be playing "Love's Theme" by Barry White and The Love Unlimited Orchestra. Grinding my hips to the sensual beat of the song, Henry climbed on top of me, first grinding into the wetness of my ass cheeks before turning me over, grabbing the right cup of my bra, and forcing my mouth open with his tongue. This was about to be the best fuck we ever had.

**

"Oh my god, even my dick is hard!" That statement was met with a moment of silence, followed by screams of laughter from our group of friends. That's because it was Georgie, the lesbian member of the Board of Directors of Club Sanctuary, who just said her dick was hard. I couldn't stop giggling.

I could tell that Henry was pleased. The smile on his face gave everything away. He took my hand and placed it between his legs. Even in public, he was okay with displays of affection, allowing me to press my hand against his hardness, here in front of our friends. He leaned into me and kissed me hard.

"Okay you two, let's not get carried away. That was a great story, Joey. Very entertaining and uplifting, if you get my meaning." Ernest was now speaking. Ernest, better known as BaeBae, the Black Queen of All Queens, the best drag performer in Philly and the most-wanted makeup artist in the tri-state area.

BaeBae always spoke in a sultry whisper, doing her best to disguise her masculine voice. She was determined to one day transition to a full-fledged female, but she was still far from that goal. Today, as a guest at our Board meeting, held in a booth at the South Street Diner, she was dressed elegantly, as always. In drag. In full makeup. Wig. Earrings. Bracelets. A short black cocktail dress. And shoes with stiletto heels, shoes to die for. Crossing her legs under the table of the booth, always a commanding female presence, though she had been born into a male body.

Georgie was wearing a tailored women's suit, in a summery fabric, lemony-yellow with light green detailing. She liked to push the sleeves up above her elbows, displaying dozens of bracelets, and today was no exception. However, in place of her signature men's tie, she wore a stunning pearl necklace that looked like it had cost a small fortune.

As for me, I was decked out in tight black jeans, with the designer label "Gloria Vanderbilt" stitched on the back pocket. Yes, they were made for women, but that didn't stop me. I was fashion-forward and proudly strutted around in those skin-tight symbols of luxury. The jeans were paired with black docksiders…no socks, of course. My shirt was a plain white tee, worn untucked, long enough to cover my ass, so I was careful to tuck one part of the shirt to allow my designer jeans to be easily recognized. A loose-fitting black vest was worn over the tee shirt, completing the look except for three gold chains of various lengths and an expensive gold watch.

What was I wearing under those jeans? No comment.

Just kidding. I always have a comment. You probably already guessed it. Earlier that day, Henry watched with unabashed excitement as I pulled on the bright pink VS panties to wear under my jeans. Never missing an opportunity to display affection, he pulled me close to him, reaching inside the back of the panties, always interested in exploring the hotness that could be found back there.

"No time to play, coño,"[3] he said in a voice that was more of a moan of desire. I felt his breath against my rock-hard manhood as he lovingly kissed the mound inside the panties. "We gotta get ready for this brunch today."

"Can I tell you something, sweetie?" I asked Henry.

"Anything, babe. Whatsup?"

"You know I'll do anything for you, if you seriously want something from me."

"Yeah, I know. You've already done some crazy stuff to please me. I like that about you. No, check that. I *love* that about you."

"Well, I'm glad I can make you happy. And you know sometimes I can be a little bit girly and feminine. But you also know that I'm not a queen, not really. And as much as I love to roleplay and wear girly things…well, I don't want to be like that all the time. Like right now, these

---

[3] coño - Spanish for cunt

panties are killing me. There's no room for…for my manly parts."

Henry started laughing so hard, one of those contagious laughs where you can't help but join in.

"Honey, I know," he told me. "I like when you act like a bitch, but let's be honest. I fell in love with a man. I'm not tryin' to turn you into a woman. Now understand, the roleplay is awesome. I love it. But you never have to wear anything or do anything unless you're completely comfortable with it."

This is one reason why my love for Henry was so strong. If he wanted to, he could dominate and control everything about me…about us. But that wasn't his style. He was so incredibly generous and understanding in times like this. I just looked at him and sighed, pulled off my pink panties, and hugged him tightly, actually starting to grind into him and feeling my erection coming on strong.

"I wish we had time for me to show you just how manly I can be," I whispered into his ear. I was a little surprised at how much he was smiling at that statement.

But he was right. We were in a rush. So I grabbed a pair of blue and white Calvin Klein bikini briefs, with a built-in pouch to support my cock and balls comfortably, out of one of my underwear drawers, and hurriedly finished dressing. And yes, you heard that right. I love underwear so much that I have several dresser drawers devoted to storing them.

Not to be outdone fashion-wise, Henry was dressed in what were probably the most expensive clothes of anyone in our small group. Black and white checked dress pants that clung tightly to his waist, accentuating his round, muscular butt cheeks. They flared at the bottom, with very wide cuffs, in the style of the day. His shoes were made of the finest Italian leather, imported of course. Prada, if I remember the brand correctly. No socks, of course.

His all-white silk collarless shirt was exquisite, showing off his muscular physique and contrasting beautifully against his dark Black skin. Worn with several of the top buttons undone, his chest looked magnificent as his nipples pressed firmly against the soft, stretchy fabric. His only jewelry was a pair of diamond earrings, defying the convention of men usually only having one ear pierced.

Glancing around at the other customers, I was well aware that our group stood out from the crowd. But earlier in the day, when Henry asked if we should plan for brunch at one of our usual gay hangouts, I told him that I had such a deep craving for comfort food. Any of the diners in Philly would have fit the bill – the Melrose, the Penrose, the Oregon Diner. "Pick one, please."

Since the South Street Diner was within walking distance of our home in Society Hill Towers, it was an easy choice for Henry to make.

"What's the big idea you have? How can I help? What's my part in all this?" BaeBae asked.

"Okay, so there's a reason I told you that story about me wearing panties for the first time," I answered, grabbing Henry's crotch even more tightly as I got excited about what I was ready to tell the group.

"You all know we're having a White Party in a few weeks. Now listen, I know I'll never be a true Queen, like you, BaeBae, but just for one night, I wanna go out to the club in full drag. Totally white outfit, of course. And I already know I need help if I'm gonna make a good impression. That's why I need *your* help," I said, nodding in BaeBae's direction. She nodded back at me knowingly,

31

acknowledging her appreciation that I recognized her expertise in this area.

"You think of a name yet, darling?"

"As a matter of fact, I have. I wanna be known as Miss Joey X-Drag-a-Vaaaahnza!" I answered, dramatically emphasizing the last two syllables in my selected name.

Everyone at the booth was smiling, nodding their approval. "Darling, that's brilliant. I love it!"

I basked in the approval I had just received from the most glamorous Queen in Philly.

"When are we going shopping and what's the budget?" BaeBae asked excitedly. She knew it would take a lot of work to transform me into a glamorous drag queen, but she also knew without a doubt that she could do it.

"Right after we finish brunch," I told her. And just on cue, the waitress, looking a bit like the waitress character on TV who was always saying, "Kiss my grits,"[4] appeared with our meals.

I was more than ready to dig into my western omelet with a side of hash browns, while Henry was set to devour his blueberry pancakes, fried eggs, French fries and whole-wheat toast. Georgie was watching her carbs, so she settled for a small fruit salad and a bottle of Perrier. BaeBae's plate of French toast topped with powdered sugar and strawberries looked so enticing that I was tempted to sneak a bite of it, but I didn't dare.

Instead, I asked her about her fee.

"Don't even think about it, girl," she told me. "This one's on the house. But don't expect it to be free all the time. If you decide to make a habit of going in drag, my

---

[4] "Kiss my grits" was a phrase commonly used by a waitress character named Flo on the 1970s TV show, "Alice."

assistance will cost you, my dear," she said, batting her eyelashes and waving her hands in the air.

"But I do have a request." She was looking directly at Henry as she spoke.

"Henry, my dear, do you remember back when you were a regular at Sharkey's?"

I remembered Sharkey's clearly. It's a gay club with an almost completely Black clientele, located in a basement storefront in North Philly. That was where I had seen BaeBae for the first time, the first night when Henry and I had met.

BaeBae shifted her focus to me. "You know, your hubby there used to be a regular at Sharkey's. I also saw him hangin' with the Black guys. Till *you* came along, that is."

I wasn't sure if she was upset, angry or what, so I started to speak, feeling that I had to defend myself.

"Hush, child!" she admonished me, with a wave of her hand, glittering with green sparkle polish. "I'm just stating a fact. I have no problem with Henry being with a white boy. I've had a few myself, so I know what it can be like."

She started laughing loudly, and we all joined in. I felt a sense of relief wash over me, knowing that I had just received the approval from the most royal of all the Queens in Philly.

Henry re-directed the conversation back to what BaeBae wanted. "You had a request?"

"Yes, darling. Some of the regulars at Sharkey's are beginning to fall ill. You know what I mean. This sickness, this, well, I still don't even know what to call it, but I know it's spreading. And some of the boys up there need help."

33

She paused for a moment, glancing around the group of us at the booth, wondering what reaction she'd get from us.

"We already know we can't count on any outside help, so we're planning to help ourselves as much as we can," she continued. Our first mission is to be sure that everyone, and I mean everyone, has enough to eat. And not junk food. Good, nutritious food, to keep up our strength and maybe fight off whatever the fuck this disease is."

Everyone at the table nodded approvingly, even as we began to feel a tinge of remorse that we were eating so well.

"The group is called Sons of Oko. You know, the African god of the harvest. So instead of paying my fee for turning you into a queen extraordinaire, I'm asking for a donation to the Sons of Oko."

Georgie was already reaching into her purse, taking out the Club Sanctuary checkbook and quickly writing out a check for $1,000. She signed the check and handed it to me for a co-signature. I didn't have to think twice. I was happy to have the resources to help, handing the now-valid check back to Georgie. Before she handed it off to BaeBae, Georgie took a brand new hundred-dollar bill out of her wallet and handed both the check and the cash to BaeBae.

"We got you," Henry assured the Black Queen. "And I know you need money, but you're gonna need more than that. So, I'm volunteering to help in any way I can, any way you need me to help. Cooking, cleaning up the kitchen, delivering meals, anything. You hear me?"

I never saw BaeBae tear up before, but her eyes were watery and red. "Thank you, darling," she told Henry.

"And I don't just mean me. Joey and I are partners, in all parts of our lives. When I volunteer, he volunteers with me. We're a package deal," he stated firmly, squeezing my hand tightly under the table. I nodded my assent, ready to join with Henry in every endeavor.

Looking back and forth between Henry and BaeBae, I explained that I was 100% in favor of helping.

"But maybe it won't get that bad. Maybe this thing, this disease, will just be a fluke and go away all by itself."

I tried to sound brave, to sound convincing, but I had the feeling that no one believed what I had just said. No one thought it would just disappear. But it's also true that no one at our meeting that day could imagine just how bad it would get.

THREE

For the last two months, the ad campaign had been running strong. Fliers were pasted all over Center City Philly, with the highest concentration in the Gayborhood, of course.

The fliers had a dark red background, with an androgynous figure pictured dancing alone in the center of the sign. The figure had a black outline filled with white.

In huge letters, centered at the top, came the command:

DRESS IN WHITE

In smaller letters below the dancing figure was the location, Club Sanctuary, our address in the warehouse district and the date of the party, Sunday, July 25, 1982.

As the date approached, the excitement was building in the community. I could feel it. Everywhere I went, I heard people talking about it. And of course, there were plenty of rumors. For example:

"I heard Elton John will be there. But he refuses to only wear white. He's gonna be dressed in one of his most outrageous outfits, in rainbow colors, the White Party be damned."

"The Village People are going to perform. Can you picture them all in white? I mean, c'mon, what biker boy wears a white uniform?"

"Did you hear about the White Party? Liza is coming down from New York, bringing along the hottest guys who hang at Studio 54. She wants to wear white, but she told her friends that her nails just have to be emerald green. Divine Decadence just like in *Cabaret*!"

"My cousin's best friend's hairdresser lives in New York. He went to see Cher in that Broadway play. Oh, I forget the name. Something about Jimmy Dean, I think," he said, referring to Cher's Broadway hit *Come Back to the 5 and Dime, Jimmy Dean, Jimmy Dean.*

"Anyway, Cher's assistant who takes care of all her wigs was getting his hair done at my cousin's best friend's salon and guess what he heard? That Cher is gonna be at the White Party at Sanctuary. And guess what else? Right after this play, Cher is gonna retire so this is the very last chance that people will have to see her!"

I laughed when I heard the local gays chattering like that. They had no idea who would be there. But that didn't stop them from having their own opinions.

I knew that some people were planning to wear grand outfits. Like me. Not only a grand outfit, but I was also planning a grand entrance. This was going to be my debut in full drag. I was pretty sure I could do it once. After that, well, I wasn't planning to become a full-fledged member of the drag community, but I already knew that just about anything is possible.

I had given myself completely over to BaeBae to design everything for that night. Hair, makeup, jewelry, shoes and all the other accessories. And the dress.

Yes, I said it. The dress. Miss Joey X-Drag-a-Vaaaahnza would be wearing a dress, out in public, for the very first time. I wanted…I needed it to be perfect!

When I met BaeBae to plan the outfit, I already had a few ideas. First, I considered doing a Fay Wray imitation, but a Gay Fay Wray, with King Kong chasing me around the stage while I sang a song. Which song? No idea, yet.

Or, I thought I'd make a cute Raggedy Ann doll. Red hair, freckles, blue dress with a white apron. Again, no idea for a song.

And my third idea was Bette Davis. At least for this one, I knew the song to perform. "Bette Davis Eyes" by Kim Carnes. But I had to admit, I didn't know how to make myself look like Bette Davis.

When I told BaeBae about my ideas, she looked at me with a mix of dismay, sympathy, and disgust. When I tried to describe the look to Henry later that night, he was laughing so hard that he had tears in his eyes.

"I think she felt sorry that I could have such stupid ideas," I told Henry, joining in the laughter. I never had a problem recognizing when I had a silly idea, especially this time, after BaeBae had set me straight.

After I finished describing my three possible choices, BaeBae sat in front of me, looking intently into my eyes. I think she was scanning for any sign of intelligence.

"Darling," she began, reaching across the table, taking hold of my hand and gently stroking it, as if trying to calm a wild beast. "When you told me the name you had chosen, I had high hopes for your vision. To say that I'm disappointed would be just barely scratching the surface of the depths of my complete lack of respect for your most ordinary choices."

"First, you think you want to be chased around the stage by a giant monkey. No."

"Second, you want to flop around the stage like some limp-wristed queen or even worse, a limp-dicked queer with gigantic freckles and red hair. Like that Farkle Family[5] on TV? No."

My heart was dropping into my stomach. I was trying to impress BaeBae, which I could see wasn't happening.

---

[5] The Farkle Family was a sketch featured on "Rowan and Martin's Laugh-In" during the late 60s to early 70s.

"I will give you some credit for choice number three, Bette Davis," she said, raising her eyebrows. "She is an icon and that song is catchy. But I've seen far too many queens doing that one already. We want you to stand out, right, girl?"

I was disappointed but tried to hide that fact.

"But let me assure you, my dear," BaeBae continued, "that I, the Queen of All Queens, would never allow Miss Joey X-Drag-a-Vaaaahnza to appear foolish in her debut. Here, let me show you."

She pulled a sketchbook out of her very large purse and began flipping pages.

"Come and sit next to me," she said gently, as if trying to coach a scared pup out of a corner. "I won't hurt you. I already know you belong to that fabulously handsome husband of yours."

We both smiled at the thought of Henry.

I was in awe at the designs being presented to me. It was apparent that BaeBae had spent a considerable amount of time planning, sketching, and listing materials that would be necessary for each of the three possible looks. When I saw the final presentation, I leaned back, smiled, sighed, and quietly said, "Oh my god. I want that. I want to be that."

A smile slowly crept across BaeBae's face, for the first time during our meeting.

"Honey, maybe there's some hope for you after all. That's the perfect look for you. And when you see it for real, I promise you that you're going to love it!"

***

All over Philly, from the Great Northeast to Queen Village, from Germantown and Mount Airy to

39

Brewerytown, from Bartram's Garden to the Gayborhood, members of the LGBTQ community were preparing for the White Party at Sanctuary.

"You know you can't wear that. It isn't even white!"

Blaine looked disapprovingly at his roomie's choice of an outfit for the party.

"I know," David replied, upset with himself. He just wanted to wear a pair of summer white baggies and a white athletic shirt for a very casual, yet still sexy and fashionable look. But money was tight, very tight, and David only had clothes that were, to be honest, well-worn. To the extent that his white A-shirts, all of them, had developed a yellowish tinge.

David had hoped it might escape the notice of Blaine's eagle eye, but that wasn't going to happen. And if Blaine noticed, it was clear that this shirt wasn't going to be good enough to wear to Sanctuary. Not on the night of the biggest party of the year.

"Come on, let's head out to Goldberg's Army/Navy store before they close. We always find something there. And they sell the cheapest underwear in town. You can at least invest in a pack of new A-shirts," Blaine said with an encouraging look.

***

Some people just don't like to cooperate. Lemon and Lime, as they called themselves, were anti-establishment intellectuals. Trying to find a niche to distinguish themselves from all the other anti-establishment types out there, they had decided to oppose what they disdainfully called the "gay agenda." If the elite members of Philly's gay society favored something, then Lemon and Lime were opposed. No matter what.

A few months ago, they had formed a society, a fraternity. Known as NEG, No Elite Gays, they had incorporated using the Greek letters Nu Epsilon Gamma. And by incorporating, I mean that they had hung a sign on the front door of their shared studio apartment announcing themselves as:

Ν Ε Γ

Living in the middle of Center City Philly, in a roach-infested third-floor walkup at 12th and Spruce Streets, they planned to recruit disaffected young gay men into their frat. They wanted to rebel against what they saw as certain members of the LGBTQ community looking down on other members.

For the night of the White Party, their initial plan was to hold a counter-party, calling it the Anti-White Party. But they ran into all kinds of problems with that plan, including having nowhere to hold the party. Instead, they decided to crash the White Party at Sanctuary, defiantly refusing to wear white, and hoping to attract some notice.

They needed to attract some attention. Three months after they initially formed their group, the entire membership consisted of just those two, Lemon and Lime.

***

Carl and Karl were also getting ready to attend the White Party. Those two had a lot in common, besides their first names. I got to know them one night that was particularly slow at Sanctuary. They were the only two on the dance floor for about an hour, dancing with youthful abandon with no regard for the fact that no one else was on the dance floor. It was still early in the evening, as far as the after-hours clubgoers were concerned, so I was happy to at least see someone dancing.

They were fashionable, in a college-student sort of way. Khakis worn with loafers, a casual shirt, and a sweater worn with the arms tied in front were their usual club attire. For a little flash, they might wear earrings or even a touch of lipstick.

The night I met them, I went over and introduced myself when they took a break from dancing and headed to the bar. I ordered a round of drinks and started talking to them, finding them to be an absolute delight. They were always having fun and came up with some of the silliest, craziest ideas I had ever heard.

They took particular delight in their shared names. They also had developed a vocabulary where the word Karl (or Carl) could be used in some unconventional ways.

When I bought that first round of drinks, (I was slurping down vodka tonics, while Carl had a vodka martini and Karl had a Long Island Iced Tea), Karl took a long sip and in a loud voice proclaimed that his drink was KARLICIOUS!

Being somewhat drunk myself, I thought his pronouncement just a bit bizarre but also funny, so I joined in.

"My drink is FUCKING KARLICIOUS!" I shouted.

Not wanting to miss out on the fun, Carl stood up, raised his martini glass, and screamed "This is CARLIFFIC," then after downing the rest of the drink, he threw the glass onto the floor with all his might, only to see it fall unbroken, which was not his intent. Undeterred, he walked over to where the glass had stopped rolling, lifted his leg, and stomped on the glass with all his might. All the while, he was screaming that everything in his world was "Carliffic." Once, twice, his foot came down on the glass till it finally smashed to pieces on the third try. The look of triumph on his face as he returned to join us at the bar was precious. Or maybe it was Carliffic.

I thought it was the most fun thing that happened the entire night. After that, I noticed that Karl and Carl were regulars at Sanctuary, and they were always carrying on like that, just having a good time.

A week before the party, Carl happened to mention to Karl that he was looking a little...chubby. Karl was mortified. He was not about to go to the most fashionable party of the year, only to be looked at as a "fatty."

Of course, there was nothing wrong with Karl's weight. That was just Carl's way of playing on his insecurities. Something that happens all the time, actually way too much if you ask me.

Karl's reaction was to immediately go on the "cabbage soup diet." I kid you not. For the entire week, Karl ate nothing but cabbage soup, three times a day.

I won't even mention that Karl wished that it would be called "kabbage soup." Those two just never stopped with their carrying-on.

For the White Party, they had decided to dress alike. They wore long, baggy white satin basketball shorts over white long johns that went down to their ankles, almost reaching their white Jordans. Their tops were oversized plain white tees, which they decorated with those name tags that people wear to meetings and conventions. One said, "HELLO, My Name is Karl," and of course, the other one said, "HELLO, My Name is Carl." Holding hands, they headed to the party, where they expected to have a Karliffic time.

During the party, Karl was happy that his tummy looked slim and trim after eating all that cabbage soup. Right after the party, he knew he'd be at some greasy diner or pizza joint, scarfing down as much food as he could handle, or more.

***

The Fast Philly Bears were one of several gay motorcycle clubs whose members were regulars at the leather/levi bar at Club Sanctuary known as The Hole. On the third Friday of every month, they hosted a party there, always drawing a big crowd. And by big, I do mean a large number of guys, but I also mean that a lot of the guys were BIG as in Big Hairy Bears. Of course, they'd bring their cubs with them, who were mostly younger guys who wanted to join the club. They ranged from smooth-faced, innocent-looking young twinky boys to men with some meat on their bones.

The Fast Philly Bears held an important distinction among the other local MCs (Motorcycle Clubs). They had two female members. Yes, you heard me correctly. Two lesbians, both proven as expert riders, had been admitted to the club. This caused some controversy, both within the club and among other gay motorcycle clubs. Most wanted to keep the clubs exclusively male.

The final decision had been made by the club President, known to everyone as Cap'n Clyde, the biggest Bear in the club. He had the stereotypical look of an old Bear – big paunch hanging over his belt, long beard, even longer hair, and a face that seemed to be frozen in a permanent growl.

But his politics were super-liberal, progressive and he was determined to fight for equal rights, especially for members of the LGBTQ community. He couldn't reconcile that philosophy with excluding females, especially lesbians, from the club. And that's how Ivy and Lizzie had earned their colors and partied and rode with the Bears.

When the Bears heard about the White Party, they were interested, but they faced two obstacles. If they weren't dressed in the accepted dress code of leather and/or Levis, they couldn't head over to The Hole later on in the night. And they did want to dress in white, in keeping with the spirit of the party over at the main club.

So Cap'n Clyde went to meet with Sir Cody, the head bartender and chief enforcer of the rules at The Hole.

Cody listened intently as the Cap'n explained his dilemma, taking a minute to consider his decision.

"I don't see a problem," Cody said in his low growl of a voice. "After your members leave the White Party, in whatever outfit they decide to wear, they can just strip down to their jockstraps, and then you won't violate our dress code here. Any problem with that?"

Clyde thought about that for a full minute. He knew that jockstraps were a regular part of the uniform for his members, whether they were the biggest Bears or the smallest cubs. Except for two members, of course. Ivy and Lizzie weren't known to wear jocks on a regular basis. At least, not as far as the Cap'n knew.

"Thanks, Cody, problem solved," the Cap'n stated, firmly shaking his friend's hand.

At the next regular club meeting, Clyde explained the agreement to his members. They'd be free to wear any kind of white costume to the White Party, but they'd have to strip down and just wear jockstraps to go over to The Hole later. And no one would want to spend the entire night at the disco side of the club. It was expected that everyone would eventually make their way over to The Hole.

"What about you guys?" the Cap'n asked, looking directly at the two lesbian members.

Lizzie made a face as if to say she didn't care to be singled out like that. She started to say something, but before she could get started, Ivy just stood up, opened the button of her jeans, unzipped a little, and lowered the jeans just enough to show what she wore underneath.

"I don't think that's gonna be too much of a problem," she said, showing the wide band with the red stripes that everyone in the club recognized as the waistband of a jockstrap.

The other members started laughing and clapping. Not at the women, but with them. A few of the members found some respect for them for the very first time.

"Okay, it's settled then," Cap'n Clyde announced as they continued with other club business that had to be discussed.

***

Two days before the party, BaeBae was meeting with me for a final fitting and to review the makeup I'd be wearing. As she was applying various shades of eye shadow for testing purposes, she informed me that things seemed to be getting worse in the Black gay community with this new disease that had started going around.

"What can we do?"

BaeBae replied that she had an idea to help support the Sons of Oko, who were trying to support men who were getting too sick to take care of themselves.

That's why, when BaeBae and I arrived at the entrance to Club Sanctuary, on our way into the White Party, we were greeted by four Black men who were collecting donations to support the Sons of Oko.

I was dressed in a simple white outfit, pulling a small suitcase that contained everything I needed to change into my costume for my drag debut. I sighed with desire as I looked at these young hotties.

Dressed in tight white Levis that showed every curve of their asses, with deep bulges in front that could barely contain their manly parts, I confess that I was staring, possibly even drooling just a bit. Shirtless, they wore white vests, exposing their muscular pecs, their dark taut nipples and washboard abs. The look was completed with each one wearing a white bow tie, expertly wrapped around their necks, looking impeccable.

Although their skin tones ranged from dark ebony to caramel to a light tan, I loved the contrast of their clothing against their skin.

"Oh BaeBae, this was a great idea!" the one named Jeremy called out as we approached. Everybody's giving us money for the Sons. And wait till you get inside. You won't believe some of the people who already showed up tonight!"

And so we entered, clutching hands tightly, into the blinding light of the White Party.

FOUR

GLAM!

That was the first word that crossed my mind when I entered the club into a sea of white.

Although it was fairly early, the club was already packed with swarms of people. At first glance, everyone was wearing white. Success! A wave of satisfaction washed over me as I considered the possibility that we had brought together all these members of the queer community not only for a party of epic proportions but also to raise awareness and funds for those who were in need. I also somewhat selfishly thought that these people had gathered for my drag debut, but that was just a fleeting thought.

Henry, my beloved partner, was at the entrance to greet me and BaeBae. He took my hand and the three of us proceeded to make our way through the crowd to the room where I would be transformed into Miss Joey X-Drag-a-Vaaaahnza.

There was so much to look at that it was all a bit overwhelming. Though I have to admit, my focus was actually on Henry. He hadn't told me what he was going to wear tonight, and I was so pleased to see him wearing white jockey briefs, white socks, and his very cool white high-top Chucks. Nothing else.

Just like the lithe, muscular, tight bodies of the Black men outside who had been recruited by BaeBae to collect funds, Henry's beautiful Black skin provided such a stark contrast to the white outfit that I was enthralled.

And one thing about Henry. He was always horny. Always. So I wasn't really surprised to see him starting to get hard, right there in public, right in the middle of the crowd at the White Party, as he walked along beside me. Knowing that my man was still that turned on at the thought of me brought a smile to my face and warmth to my heart, as well as a stirring in my pants too. By the time we reached the changing room, Henry was fully erect, stretching the thin cotton of his little briefs almost to the breaking point.

I heard the comments as we walked past groups of chatty queens.

"That bitch gonna get some *bicho grande*[6] in about a minute," one Latino queen sporting a pocketbook across his chest smirked.

"*Leche, leche, leche!*"[7] clucked another.

I didn't mind. I knew Henry was hot. And at the moment, walking through the crowd with his big dick getting harder with each step just made him look even better and more desirable. I liked that guys noticed us. And I knew I looked good too. Besides, I had my wedding ring that I could flash in front of anyone who tried to get too pushy.

As BaeBae went to work, helping me transform into my character, the party in the main disco was going strong.

The Fast Philly Bears had about 25 members show up at the party. After much discussion and debate, they had decided to wear their usual leather and levi gear, none of which involved wearing white. However, in the spirit of the event, they each had wrapped themselves in a white sheet, tossing one end over the shoulder, in something resembling a Roman toga. At least, that was the intent. Some wore the look more effectively than others. Ivy and Lizzie had cut holes in their sheets to allow their heads

---

[6] bicho grande - Spanish for big dick
[7] Leche literally means milk but here refers to cum, sperm

and arms to be freed, covering their normal costume of jeans and leather jackets adorned with the club logo. Some thought they looked a little more like ghosts than Roman Senators, but really, it was the intent that was more important than the actual results. They wanted to join in the spirit of the White Party.

Many of the guests wore everyday outfits that were all white. Some looked like John Travolta in the hit movie *Saturday Night Fever*, sporting a white suit with a black shirt and shoes. Others wore sailor outfits, building on the image of members of the US Navy as a gay fetish. Of course, there were a few nuns in white habits, tennis players in white shorts and tees, and a threesome in matching white speedos.

Others were more extravagant, with costumes that surely took time, thought and effort to create. I remember seeing someone dressed as a butterfly, with intricate wings that were tinged with colorful glitter against a white background. I laughed when I saw the albino giraffe dancing with the white bunny rabbit, resembling the Mad Hatter character.

And speaking of hats, Harry the Hat, a well-known character in Philly's gay society, was wearing a white top hat, about twice the height of a regular top hat, adorned with strings of pearls and white netting that apparently had caught a few fake goldfish during the trip to the club. In reality, the goldfish were of the cracker variety and the other side of the netting on Harry's hat featured tiny origami swans constructed of red paper, standing out starkly against the white background. All sorts of shiny baubles and glittery shapes were also randomly attached to the hat, making it beautiful and funny and outrageous at the same time, which was Harry's intent. At any and every gay event, you could count on Harry the Hat to showcase a hat guaranteed to get your attention.

I didn't notice it at first, but Harry had attached a blue light on the top of his hat. Suddenly, I heard what sounded like a siren as the light started flashing and Harry began screaming, "Attention Kmart shoppers, attention Kmart shoppers!"

Then he started handing out drink tickets to anyone nearby. He had purchased hundreds of tickets at the door, good for a free drink from the bar, and a crowd soon followed his every step, just waiting for the "Blue Light Special" and free drinks from the always adorable, always funny and always outrageous Harry.

Above the blaring music, I heard him calling out to his friends, "Hail, Mary!" which was his signature line. Shortly after I first met him, I asked him about that.

"Oh, Mary," he told me. "You know that I know every queer in Philly. And they all know me. Or, at least they pretend to know me."

I smiled, knowing what he said was true.

"Well," he continued. "I can't possibly remember the name of all those bitches, so I decided long ago just to call everybody 'Mary.' It's just so much easier that way."

I couldn't argue with his logic, so I just went along with it.

And saying 'Hail Mary' just makes it a little more gay, don't you think?

I had to admire his style, which obviously got him what he wanted. Every time I saw him, he was surrounded by young twinkies who adored him. And of course, they were just his type.

Another legend was in attendance that night. Heaven Himself. He was in the news when he petitioned the courts to allow him to legally change his name to Heaven

Himself. It wasn't that he was so self-absorbed that he considered himself heavenly. Though many, who didn't actually know him, made that assumption. No, Heaven was determined to make a name for himself as a model. But not any model. He had moved from Philly to New York and became a darling of the modeling world, being the first and perhaps only male to walk the high-fashion runways in haute couture women's clothing, while fully maintaining his appearance as a cisgender male. In other words, he didn't try to look like a female. He fully embraced his maleness, though it would be a stretch to call him masculine. However, he achieved a level of fame that few models ever attain. And here he was, dressed in Yves Saint Laurent, with a high neckline, exaggerated sleeves and broad shoulders on a tight-waisted gown that fell midway between the knees and his feet. Wearing no makeup and a typical male haircut, he created a stir among the crowd as he mingled, talking with old friends and meeting new fans.

I was almost finished dressing when Henry came rushing back into the dressing room, after spending some time out in the crowd. "You won't believe that crowd out there," he told me. "And don't say I didn't warn you, but Sylvester's in the house!"

"Sylvester? You mean the singer, right? The one that sang "You Make Me Feel" is in the club?"

"The one and only! And wait till you see his outfit. Totally his style and totally on point. He looks like royalty!"

"Henry, he *is* royalty!" I shouted, almost knocking BaeBae's hand out of the way as she applied the finishing touches to my makeup. "I wonder if he'll agree to perform for us tonight?"

Henry left, still clad only in tighty whiteys, white socks and white Chucks to see if he could make those arrangements.

Meanwhile, Lemon and Lime, the ones who felt the need to be different in any way possible, were in the crowd at the party, looking for others who might be of the same mindset. Lemon had dressed in a green outfit and of course, Lime was wearing yellow. Anything to be contrary. Henry passed by them, shaking his head, as they were talking to a potential new member of their fraternity, who had come to the White Party also dressed in mostly green – a green paisley shirt, green neckerchief and fake green emerald jewelry.

"If you want to join our frat, you need a fruit name," Lime was hurriedly explaining. "Who would you be?"

The guy thought for a moment, hoping to impress his new friends.

"Grape. I wanna be the Grape."

"Cool, I like it," agreed Lemon. "But what color grape? Purple, red, or green?"

Again, the guy paused, taking a sip from his green apple martini.

"Definitely green," he decided. "I'll be the Green Gay Grape."

Lemon and Lime doubled over in laughter. "Perfect! Try saying that three times really fast!"

Throughout the night, whenever they felt the need for a laugh, they would start shouting, mispronouncing the new boy's name as "Green Gray Grape" or "Geen Gay Gape" or occasionally combining them all into a chant that was almost impossible to say correctly three times in a row. "Green Gay Grape! Geen Gay Gape! Green Gray Grape!" constantly breaking into hysterical drunken laughter with their new friend/frat brother.

While Henry was working his way through the back bar, looking for Sylvester, he stopped dead in his tracks.

"He's no ventriloquist and I'm no fucking dummy!"

Henry knew that line and recognized the voice instantly. Then he heard the cackling laughter, followed by laughter and applause from those who had gathered around to watch this impromptu show.

"I fuckin' can't believe it. That's Wayland Flowers and Madame here at our White Party!" Henry exclaimed to no one in particular.

Everyone knew Wayland and Madame. I first saw them perform on TV back home at my father's house. I was just a kid, watching one of those old variety shows, called *The Andy Williams Show*, with my father, when Wayland appeared on the screen with his ingenious puppet, Madame. I didn't understand most of their jokes, but my father was laughing like a kid at Madame's antics. I sat there, wondering how it was possible to be watching a puppet on TV whose nose was so clearly done in the shape of a penis.

Later that night, after my debut drag performance, Henry and I had a short chat with Wayland. Although the chat was completely with Madame, because Wayland stayed in character throughout the evening. He had a way of always making Madame the center of attention. They were on their way to Provincetown, MA, where they'd be headlining at the Madeira Club for the rest of the summer. Always up for a party, Wayland had heard about the White Party at Sanctuary and decided it would be fun to attend, make a few new friends and perform a little show. Of course, both Wayland and Madame were dressed appropriately in white outfits, joining in the spirit of the party.

Henry and I promised to catch his show if we could make it to Provincetown that summer. However, we already had other travel plans, so we couldn't make a firm commitment.

At exactly 1:30 AM, DJ Thunder stopped the music. He replaced it with the beat of a drum.

Thump! Thump! Thump! **Thump! Thump!**

Slowly at first, then getting faster and faster. The audience cleared the dance floor, not knowing what to expect, but ready for anything.

Then, the first few notes of the song were played, bringing the audience into a near-frenzy in just an instant. Bouncing up and down, it seemed like the entire building was shaking from the heat and passion of the crowd.

Thunder knew how to work the crowd. He had mixed the start of the song to last longer than usual, perfectly timed to coordinate with my grand entrance as Miss Joey X-Drag-a-Vaaaahnza.

When the opening notes to my song started, I began my descent towards the dance floor. Henry had hired a contractor to construct a platform that was now being lowered from the ceiling, after I had positioned myself in the center of the stage on the building's second floor.

Although we had practiced many times, my legs felt wobbly as I made my way towards what I hoped would be my adoring audience. Just as the platform reached eye-level for the club's patrons, DJ Thunder switched the song to the portion with those famous lyrics.

The song, of course, was the hottest of the hot hits of 1982, "Fame" by Irene Cara. The entire audience sang along as I began my lip-syncing, doing my best to be as dramatic as possible.

I was draped in a huge, white cape, made of some synthetic fur and covered with shiny white and silver rhinestones. The attached hood shielded my platinum blonde wig from view...at least for now.

I never felt as much love from a group of people as I did at that moment in time. The scene was wild, chaotic, crazy. People were handing dollar bills to me, throwing them in my direction, leaving piles of bills on the floor. Luckily, some of the barbacks were ready to scoop up the bills. Not that I'd be keeping any for myself. That money was already designated to support the efforts of the Sons of Oko, the HIV support group that had been formed to help those already in need.

As the song faded, I was blowing kisses to the crowd, bowing profusely and waving at my friends. I saw Henry watching me, beaming with pride, and I felt my heart bursting with more love for him than I could have ever imagined. This night would never have happened without him.

If anyone wondered about my outfit, in that outlandish hooded cape, they didn't show it. The audience was still cheering, dancing, and calling for more as I pranced around the stage, then coming to a dramatic halt exactly in the center.

DJ Thunder knew exactly what to do. He waited until I had set myself properly, cocking my head at a wicked angle, clutching my microphone. My fake microphone, of course. Even if I did sing, no one would be able to hear me.

With a dramatic flair, I tossed the cape to one of the nearby barbacks, while one of the others quickly brought a chair, a cane and my hat to the stage.

The crowd grew silent as I started to lip-sync the words to the "Theme from Cabaret" in the magical voice of the one and only Liza Minelli. If anyone had any doubts, they now completely understood my outfit.

I wasn't dressed in the lavender gown worn by Liza while singing the song in the movie. Instead, I was in an exact replica of what was worn on the album cover, the outfit she wore while singing "Mein Herr" in the movie.

BaeBae had done an excellent job, re-creating the look but transforming all the fabrics from black to white.

White bowler hat. White lace choker around my neck. White bodysuit. White garter belts. White stockings. White platform boots.

And my wig was styled just like Liza's hair, which I adored, but of course, it was blonde. Very blonde. Platinum blonde.

All that white contrasted sharply with my paste-on nails, painted in glittery green. Decadent, of course. Just like in the movie.

The costume paired with my make-up gave the illusion that I was shimmering on the stage. By the middle of the song, the queens in the audience began singing along with me. I almost felt like crying.

As I was approaching the grand finale of the song as well as the end of my act, I was feeling oh so glamorous.

Did you ever hear that performers on stage can't see their audiences because of all the bright lights beaming into their eyes? So, when you see some superstar waving and smiling at the crowd, they're really doing so blindly. It could be anyone or no one in the audience being waved at.

Well, that wasn't true for me on my small stage. I could see everyone. Every smiling face. Every person singing along with me. And just when I thought I was going to make it through the entire song without making any major mistakes, I saw him in the crowd.

For one second…two seconds…three seconds…which is an eternity during a performance, I stood frozen in my tracks. Of course, the song continued playing while I stood there looking like a damn fool.

But what I saw had caught me by complete surprise. There, in the middle of the audience, stood Kirk, the guy from the VA Center who had told the story about trying to buy those gay books and magazines.

He was standing on his one leg, with his wheelchair behind him, and I saw that he was crying as he sang the words about life being a cabaret. Beside him stood my friend Bobby, the one I had accompanied to the meeting at the Veterans Service Center. On Kirk's other side, I noticed Alejandro, one of the Board members of Sanctuary, though I couldn't tell if he was there by design or if it was just coincidental.

Both Kirk and Bobby were dressed in casual white summer outfits, but Kirk had the hem of his right pant leg pinned above the knee, keeping the cuff out of his way. It was only then that I realized that his right leg had been amputated at the knee.

After those three seconds of being frozen in time, I came back to Earth and realized that I was in the middle of a performance. So I continued, but I couldn't see anyone else in the audience. I was singing to Kirk and Bobby. No one else.

At the end of the song, the crowd was screaming, still throwing money, calling for an encore. Henry rushed up to me, gave me a huge wet kiss in front of the crowd, handing me the biggest bouquet of white roses that I had ever seen. Luckily, he was there to hold me up as I left the stage, overcome with so many emotions that I was unable to properly process them at that very moment.

As Henry and I left the stage together, all sorts of friends and fans crowded around us, oohing and aahing and offering their congratulations. I couldn't be sure if anyone had noticed that I lost my place for a few seconds while I was "singing", but I did notice that most of the compliments being thrown in my direction were for my outfit rather than for my performance.

I spent the rest of the night on the dance floor, mixing my drinks with my usual dose of Quaaludes, flying high, feeling the vibes of the night and enjoying the sense of community that I felt so strongly that night.

But I clearly remember being held in Henry's arms as we watched the amazing performance by Sylvester, totally impromptu, near the end of the night. That man was a true superstar in every sense of the word. Everyone in the club admired and adored him. Including me.

***

Henry and I got home from the club around 5:30 AM. That wasn't unusual for us. Our lives were spent at the club, so late nights were part of our usual routine.

That night, I was numb. I was glad that we had taken a taxi home, so we avoided what would have been a long walk. Henry was still dressed in his white briefs and I was in my drag outfit, but the driver paid us no mind. The taxi drivers who waited outside our club were used to all sorts of antics and so we had no trouble getting a ride.

"You want a nightcap?" Henry asked me, heading for the liquor cabinet.

"Sure, darling. Make it a gin and tonic, please."

While Henry made the drinks, I went into the bedroom to change. Although I looked glamorous, it felt good to get out of the costume. That bodysuit was tight, sometimes in the wrong places.

I came out of the bedroom wearing only a pair of white briefs, just like Henry. However, mine were my favorite brand, one that had a special design called a kangaroo pouch. Instead of opening from the side, like most men's briefs, these opened from the top, just like the pouch of a mother kangaroo.

Henry smiled, staring at me, as he handed me the drink and sat down next to me.

"I see you're up for some fun, and I do mean UP," he joked, seeing my growing erection.

"Does little joey wanna come out and play?"

"You know my little joey ain't really that little!" I protested, going along with the joke.

"But first, I have to tell you something," I said, getting serious for a moment.

"What is it, babe?"

"I had so much fun tonight. It was great putting on the show. And it was fun to dress up too."

"Okay then, what's the matter?" Henry asked quietly.

I looked at him directly, making sure he was paying attention, since he was starting to rub my legs and reaching for my ass, which I knew from experience would make him distracted.

"I don't wanna disappoint you, but I just don't think I really want to be a drag queen. I know that's what you want…"

"What? What makes you think I want you to be a drag queen?"

"Henry, you bought me all those feminine things from Victoria's Secret. The panties. The bras. I figured you were telling me to dress like a girl."

60

Henry tried to remain serious, but he leaned into me, pushing me down on the sofa, and started laughing as he wrapped me tightly in his strong arms. He kept laughing as he gently kissed each of my erect nipples, then sucked each one a little harder.

Then he sat up. "Honey, I love you so much. I love you the way you are. Dressing you up in panties and a bra was just a way for us to have some fun. Nothing more. Nothing less."

"So, you don't want me to be like BaeBae? Wearing dresses out in public, performing in shows?" I asked.

"Joey, if you want to be a drag queen, I would love it. But not because I want it. I'd love it because that would be you expressing yourself the way you want. But no, I'm not trying to get you to act in any special way. But I do want you to feel secure enough to try things out, just like you did tonight."

I felt so relieved to hear those words from my husband. So supportive. So loving. I felt valued and appreciated. And horny.

"I see little joey is looking for some attention," Henry said, eyeing my growing bulge. "And I'm feeling a little adventurous too!"

Henry gently pushed me onto my back, making his way to a favorite body part, my rock-hard hairless nipples. His tongue left a trail of wetness as he made his way downward. I was throbbing as I could feel his hot breath through my briefs, as he began to suck and nibble at my hardness through the white cotton cloth of my now-wet underwear.

Using his hands to spread my legs open, I fell under his spell, following his silent directions, opening myself to his oral pleasures. Lifting my hips, I sighed as he tugged at the waistband of my kangaroo undies, releasing my little joey from its bonds.

With one gulp, he swallowed me whole. He was an expert at this, cupping my swollen balls in one hand, stroking the bottom of my shaft with the other hand, and using his lips and tongue to suck, twirl and flick at my erection, hungrily taking my precum in his mouth.

Then I felt the familiar grab at my ass, and I knew he was looking to enter me with his ever-growing rod.

"No," he whispered, "Not like that this time."

He quickly stood and removed his briefs in one swift motion. My cock was fully erect, pointing towards my face as I lay there on my back.

"Like this, babe, but be gentle at first."

Then I watched as he squeezed a small amount of lube from the tube that he pulled from a nearby drawer, opened his legs wide, and slathered the lube on his hot, waiting hole.

He positioned himself above me, grabbing my dick and pointing it towards the sky, towards the entryway to heavenly bliss, and lowered himself onto me, gasping lightly as my cockhead made its entrance.

My head was exploding as Henry bounced up and down on my now-dripping pole. Henry was almost always the Top and this turn-around brought me to a frenzy. He squeezed his ass muscles each time he lowered himself, gasping with pleasure as I watched his dick swinging wildly in front of my face. Moaning, grimacing, grunting, he stroked his hardness, making it stretch to its full length of 9.5 inches of man-meat. I grabbed hold of his ass, guiding his movements. Up, down, up, down, up, down...Faster…faster…faster! My balls drew up close to my body, and I felt like I couldn't hold off any longer when Henry grunted loudly, shooting hot jets of creamy cum all over my chest, my neck, my face. Three seconds later, my dick exploded inside Henry, filling him with several jets of my creamy goodness. Gasping for breath, Henry laid against me, hugging me tightly, kissing my lips, tasting his own sweet cum juices as our lips locked together.

The perfect ending to our White party night.

***

The Green Gay Grape spent his first night at the Nu Epsilon Gamma frat house later that night, which in reality was a studio apartment on Spruce Street. He was more surprised than he should have been when he first walked in and saw several wooden paddles hanging on the wall.

As soon as they entered, Lime locked the door behind them, and both Lemon and Lime moved quickly to grab hold of the Grape, pulling a hood over his head, then grabbing his wrists, tying them behind his back.

The Grape was then pulled blindly onto the bed, feeling his pants being pulled down and his ass lifted into position.

Lemon and Lime each held a paddle, looking lustily at the Grape's luscious round ass, pants down around his knees, with his green satin bikini briefs covering the object of their desire.

Lemon whispered in the Grape's ear, telling him what to do. The Grape said what he was told to say.

"I am not an elite gay!" he said, and then felt the first light tap of the paddle against his ass cheeks.

"Louder, bitch!" Lime said, smacking his ass again, just a little bit harder.

"I am not an elite gay!" SMACK! Lime spanked the Grape hard enough that Grape was feeling a little regret and wondering exactly what he had gotten himself into.

"I belong to Nu Epsilon Gamma, No Elite Gays! Say it!" came the command from Lemon as he tugged the Grape's briefs down. exposing the new boy completely to the veteran members of the fraternity.

The Grape obeyed, hollering, though his voice was muffled by the hood still covering his head.

"I belong to Nu Epsilon Gamma! No Elite Gays!" followed by a loud, sharp, WHACK! as Grape felt the sting of the paddle.

Lemon and Lime were getting into a frenzy, and it wasn't long before Lime lost control, tossing all his clothes on the floor, spit into his hand, and using only his saliva for lube, plunged his hard cock deep into Grape's manhole. Bareback.

"Safe sex is for suckers," Lime muttered, as he arched his back, digging deeper into Grape's ass, then watching as Lemon stripped quickly, lifting the Grape's hood just enough so he could force his cock into Grape's mouth, and then Lemon and Lime watched each other get serviced by their new boy.

As Grape got spit-roasted, his cock jumped at the feeling of having two big hard unsheathed cocks inside him at the same time, and he heard Lemon and Lime laughing as Grape's dick spilled his milky seeds onto the bed.

And then both Lemon and Lime shuddered, watching each other dump a load into their new recruit.

An hour later, they were back at it. Lemon and Lime switched positions, with Lime using Grape's mouth and Lemon pounding the boy's ass.

Always bareback. Always contrary to the message that the people they called "elite" were trying to send about having safer sex.

And just before they went to sleep, Lime told Grape, "You know, the walls in this apartment are really thin. That means all the neighbors heard you when we were spanking you like a bad little boy, and when we were screwing you and fucking you and everything else. Just want you to know. Everybody here knows you belong to us now."

The next day, Grape went to his apartment, packed up his few belongings and moved into the frat house with his new brothers. He didn't own much, but he made sure to bring his growing collection of Care Bears. Yes, he knew they were especially popular with young girls, but he liked them. He wanted to display them around the frat house, if Lemon and Lime would allow it. No one knew that Grape liked to cuddle with Bedtime Bear while he slept. Tonight, his secret would be exposed, because he was determined that no one would deny him his source of comfort.

FIVE

All four members of the Board of Directors of The Sanctuary Society of South Philadelphia lived in Center City Philadelphia. Personally, it was rare for me to venture outside those boundaries, set by the two rivers on the east and west sides and Spring Garden Street to the north, and South Street on the southern border of the area. I had that small-town mentality that considered a small area to be my "turf", my hangout, the area where I felt most secure. I spent almost all of my time in the eastern portion of Center City, meaning I rarely crossed Broad Street. I jokingly called that West Philly, though, in reality, it was still Center City.

So, when it was suggested that our next Board meeting should be held in Manayunk, in the northwest part of the city, well, Henry had to use all his persuasive powers, including the lure of his delicious dick, to get me to agree to that proposal.

Today, you might know Manayunk for the very popular Manayunk Arts Festival, which draws hundreds of thousands of people to its hilly terrain. And when I say hilly, I mean those hills are steep as fuck. It was embarrassing to be as out of breath as I was climbing those hills to reach our destination, all the while sucking on cigarettes. I still wasn't ready to take those warnings seriously.

It was Thursday, September 2, 1982, the day before the start of the long Labor Day weekend. At that time, Manayunk was a mostly-industrial area, but a few members of the LGBTQ community were beginning to move there, the first wave in what would later become a tsunami of queer artisans who would inhabit the area.

66

Our friend Leonardo was one of those pioneers, and he had invited us out to his restaurant to sample his new menu items.

It was cool to see his name in pink neon outside the restaurant he had named after himself. Leonardo's was quickly becoming a neighborhood favorite with his signature Northern Italian dishes.

Henry and I joined Alejandro and Georgina at the table, since they had arrived a bit before us.

"How's everybody doing today?" Jando asked. We all replied that we were all fine, in the customary way.

"Really? Everybody's fine? Just fine?" Jando asked.

I wondered what he was up to. He was always up to something.

"Everybody reach inside and take one," Jando told us, placing a brown paper bag on the table.

I looked at him with suspicion. "I know I'm not going first," I said, turning the bag in Henry's direction.

"Don't be silly," Henry chided. "There's probably some skinned grapes in there like they do for fake eyeballs at a Halloween party," he continued, reaching into the bag without hesitation.

"Oh cool, it's a mood ring!"

"Now we're gonna see how everybody really is today," Alejandro said, taking the bag and spilling the rest of the rings out on the table. Each of us grabbed one.

Georgie's ring turned bright green. Calm. Her look matched her mood. No problems there.

Henry's ring was blue. Relaxed, having fun. He was in a good place.

My ring turned black. "Oh no," I told the group. "I'm not stressed. I think it was the walk up that mountain they call a hill," I continued, shaking my hand as if to get the ring to change color again. But no, it stayed black.

Jando was the last to place a mood ring on his finger. His ring immediately changed from white to a fiery red color. Romantic passion, high energy.

"Somebody's horny," I said, as we all laughed.

Unable to contain his excitement, not even able to wait until we ordered some pre-meal drinks, Jando was jumping up and down in his seat.

"I met a man!" he blurted out. "Not like the usual. This is a real man."

"Whaaaaat?" I shrieked, a little too loudly for our surroundings.

Henry was laughing. "You're telling me the Whore of The Hole got himself a steady man?"

Jando had earned that nickname, the Whore of The Hole, as he had recently been spending almost every night at The Hole, the leather/levi/bdsm bar located in the basement of the club. And never with the same guy. Always someone new, someone different. And usually with more than one as he played in the section called The Blackout Room, where casual, anonymous sex was the norm.

"This was so different, guys. I saw him for the first time at the party. And I couldn't take my eyes off him. He was…he *is* the most gorgeous man I've ever seen."

That was quite a statement coming from the Whore of The Hole, I thought.

"You mean you didn't do your usual and drag him into the bathroom, bend him over the sink and dry fuck him right there for all to see?" Georgie said, laughing.

We were all laughing, including Jando. The four of us had become the very best of friends. We knew everything about one another, and we were used to teasing each other about some of our sexual exploits. Especially Jando, who was so openly kinky and promiscuous.

Three of us leaned forward in anticipation of the news about to be spilled by Jando. I, for one, had been hoping that he'd find one special guy. I was starting to have doubts about the promiscuity that was so common in our community.

Jando took a deep breath, his beautiful brown eyes opening wide, and he started.

"Her name is…"

I almost fell over. Her? Her? Jando was as gay as they come. And didn't he just say that he met *him* at the White Party?

Taking a sip of his drink, Jando almost spat it out as he started to laugh.

"Just kidding, you guys. You know I like dick way too much to start lusting after a female."

With that, he gave Georgie a wink, who smiled back and started laughing that throaty laugh that I found so appealing.

"His name is Kirk. He's so cool, so wonderful. Yes, he's a little older than me but I can't wait till you meet him."

I started thinking. Kirk…Kirk. There are probably a hundred gay guys in Philly named Kirk. Could Jando have fallen for the guy I first saw at the VA Center? The one who told the story about buying gay magazines and books when he was 13 years old? The guy with…with only one leg?

I didn't want to ask directly. "Tell us more," I encouraged my friend.

Jando started describing Kirk's facial features: gorgeous eyes, perfect nose, clean-shaven with a strong jawline, etc.

"And his body?" I asked.

Jando grinned, licked his lips, and told us all about Kirk's huge uncut dick that was able to shoot cum like a cannon. We heard about his perfect balls…the taste, the smell…and how his ass was like a gift from the gods. Firm, fleshy mounds of man-meat that were just meant for Jando to eat with gusto.

I was losing patience. Neither Henry nor Georgie had any suspicions about this guy Kirk, so they were hanging on every word about Jando's new love interest. I was the only one stupid enough to ask this question.

"Is he a good dancer?"

Jando stopped abruptly, looking at me in a way that let me know that he wanted to tell the story his way. In other words, I should just back off and shut the fuck up. I sat back in my chair, drink in my hand, took a big sip, and decided to give Jando the space he deserved in telling us about his new man.

Alejandro paused while the waiter took our orders and refreshed our drinks. After the waiter left, we sat in silence for what seemed like forever.

"Will Miss Joey X-Drag-a-Vaaaahnza please allow me to continue?"

I recognized shade when I heard it. "Please, go on. Don't let my fabulousness stop you," was my somewhat snide reply.

"Before you start, I want to apologize. I don't want to act that way with you. You're my friend, one of my best friends. Sorry if I got out of line."

Jando smiled at that, a warm, genuine smile.

"I already told you I met Kirk at the White Party. And you know my regular style. Quick, anonymous sucks and fucks in a dark place, usually at The Hole."

We were all nodding.

"I felt like he was different. In a good way. So, after Miss Joey here finished fucking up her song, I went over and introduced myself to him."

I winced at the memory of my performance, especially now, because it was the sight of a guy named Kirk, standing on one leg and crying as he clapped for my performance who had thrown off my lip-syncing.

Alejandro continued. "I've never seen you here before, were the first words I said to him."

"That's when Kirk looked me right in the eyes and I felt my heart melting and my dick turning to wood at the same time," he said. I never heard Jando speak about anyone with such sincerity.

"I had to help clear a way for us to get over to the bar so we could talk," Jando continued, "because some of those assholes at the club wouldn't make way for a guy in a chair."

"In a chair?" Georgie asked.

Jando looked over at Georgie, then at Henry, finally gazing at me with a steely look.

"A wheelchair," he said firmly, as if he had practiced exactly how he wanted to tell us this part of the story.

Alejandro captivated us as he related the story about that first time he met Kirk.

How he had ordered two queens off their bar stools at the end of the bar so he and Kirk could sit together. How he had helped Kirk out of his chair and onto the stool, then folding the chair carefully and placing it in a corner. How they made plans, not for sex that night, but for an actual, real date…dinner and a movie, and a walk in the park…for the very next night.

Always a little too quick to show my emotions, I felt my eyes watering, but I didn't want to cry. Not here. Not now. Not under these circumstances.

Instead, I clenched my fists under the table, feeling my face turn red, as I tried not to show how I felt. The way Jando told it, it was so romantic, so beautiful, so incredibly different than any story I heard Alejandro tell about anyone else.

He described part of their conversation at the bar that night. How Kirk described the difficulty of just getting into the club. How he hated it when people stared at him, but hated it even more when people ignored him, staring into space as if he didn't exist.

"I think that hurts the most," Kirk had confided to him. "That feeling like I'm not even there, that people don't or won't even see me."

Henry was taking in every part of the story, having a mind more analytical than mine. I heard the same story, but I didn't realize the implications of what Jando was saying.

"We fucked up, didn't we?" Henry said to me.

I hate to admit this, but I didn't know what he meant. "How so?" I stupidly asked.

"We never made any accommodations for someone who might not be able to walk into the club."

Henry stated that as an obvious fact, but clearly, it wasn't that obvious to any of us before now.

Jando slowly shook his head side-to-side. "We're not the only ones. But we are guilty."

"We can't fix the entire world, but we sure as hell can fix our club." That was it. Decision made.

But of course, the devil is always in the details.

"I have a proposition," Jando said. "I asked Kirk if he would meet all four of us at the club tomorrow afternoon. I want him to meet you guys. And I want you to meet him. And he has a few things he'd like to say to our group."

We all agreed to be at Sanctuary at 2 PM the next day.

***

Henry and I decided to walk to the club that Friday afternoon. We left early, giving us time to wander around the Gayborhood for a bit. The streets in the area were always filled with young, queer men. Sometimes solo, some in pairs, and lots of groups of young, obviously queer men. A few women. And it took me a few years to realize that I never saw any children in the area.

Since it was rare for me to leave the Gayborhood, that meant that I never saw kids at play, or doing anything else for that matter. One time, I remember saying to a friend of mine who was a teacher in Philly, "But where do the kids come from?"

Clearly, they lived in other neighborhoods, and there were plenty of them. But my point is, our neighborhood was segregated, consisting almost entirely of queer males.

I considered that a good thing. I felt safer that way. But is it ever good for a community to be that isolated?

As we passed by the many queer shops and restaurants, where Henry and I knew practically every entrepreneur, every owner, every waiter, every cashier, and probably half of all the customers, I had an idea.

Grabbing Henry's hand, I steered him into the first bookstore we saw.

"Patrick, do you have a vintage section? You know, those old magazines and books from maybe 15 or 20 years ago? Maybe even older than that?" I asked.

Patrick had owned this bookstore for years, and he prided himself on having a good collection of queer literature.

"Not too many guys are interested in stuff that old," he told me, giving me an odd look. "But go upstairs and hang a right. You might find what you're looking for there."

Taking two steps at a time, I was on the second floor before Henry even had time to climb two steps. "What the hell has gotten into you?" he asked when he joined me in the vintage queer porn section.

I didn't answer. I was too busy scanning the titles. It seemed like 15 minutes before I spotted the prize, though in reality, it had only taken me a minute or two.

I reached into the stack and pulled out three different editions of exactly what I wanted. A magazine I knew would make the perfect gift for our new-to-be friend. Three copies of *The Bicep Boys*!!

I had to take a minute to look through those magazines, with Henry peering over my shoulder, breathing deeply into my ear and against my neck. I think it started with him making fun of me and faking those sounds of male desire, but between the hot horny guys in the photos and Henry's heavy breathing and sounds of desire, my dick was getting hard as fuck.

Henry always knew when I was getting turned on. He could see it in my face, hear it in my voice and I'm pretty sure I just gave off a scent that he would immediately recognize as a male bitch in heat.

Placing the magazines back on the rack, right in front where they could easily be found, Henry turned me around to face him, grabbed the hardness in my jeans with his hands, and smiled.

"Didn't Patrick say that hardly anyone ever comes up here?"

I knew Henry well enough to know what he was thinking. He liked adventure and public sex, with the possibility of being seen, was just the kind of adventure he was looking for today.

He pulled me by my cock to the back of the store.

"You got five minutes to work on me and I wanna be creaming your mouth before those five minutes are up." His voice was a low growl. He knew how to be sexy, bossy, dominant, and demanding all at the same time.

Pushing me down to my knees, pulling his rapidly growing dick out, and pointing the tip at my mouth, he pulled the back of my hair so I'd open my mouth and swallow him whole.

"And no, you ain't allowed to touch yourself, not this time," he commanded when he saw me reaching to open my jeans for some stroking.

Three minutes later, Henry grunted loudly as he released himself into my slobbering mouth. I was licking him clean when I heard Patrick call upstairs, "You boys need any help?"

"Nah, Patrick, we're all good up here," Henry called out. "Even better than he thinks," Henry whispered so only I could hear.

A minute later, we were at the cash register paying for the magazines, leaving for our meeting at the club, while my cock was still hard and dripping in my briefs from that quick encounter that left me almost crazy with desire for release. That's how Henry liked it. He liked to keep me hungry and horny so that when I was finally allowed to cum, the feeling of pleasure was almost indescribably beautiful.

As I handed the money to Patrick, Henry took hold of my chin, saying, "Honey, it looks like you got a little juice there on your chin. Let me get that for you."

Oh, he was sly. One of the many traits I loved about him.

He took his finger, wiping what I thought was an imaginary bit of his cum, then placing his finger against my lips, pushing, making me open my mouth right there in the store. I sucked his finger as Henry winked at Patrick, saying, "This one here's been a bad boy this morning. A very good bad boy."

I was surprised when I tasted the sweet saltiness of Henry's cum when I licked his finger. Damn, there really had been cum on my chin. I was laughing when we walked out the door, back onto the streets of the Gayborhood. I felt at home here. And Henry always added that extra layer of protection. I knew I could count on him for love and support. Always. Unconditionally.

SIX

As we were leaving the bookstore, Henry unexpectedly grabbed my arm and held me back.

"We've got a few minutes to spare, babe. Let's go back in for a quick look and see if *our book* is in stock."

Of course, I knew what he was talking about.

It happened the first year that we opened Sanctuary. I was just 19, and Henry was 3 years older. We were out on the dance floor of the club, doing a popular dance that was called The Bump. If you've never heard of that dance, well, the name pretty much says it all. The two dancers would bump their hips together to the beat of the song.

It's no exaggeration that Henry and I made a cute couple on the dance floor, two hot guys with beautiful, big butts, bumping our hips together like two gay guys in heat. Which is pretty much what we were. Being the more dominant one, Henry would sometimes guide me so I was bumping my ass right up against his dick, and every time I bumped into it, I could feel it swelling in his pants.

After the song, we headed over to one of the bars for drinks. And that's when he approached us.

"I'm Wyatt," he said, in a voice so deep and strong that I could picture him as a star in a movie or TV show. His body matched his voice…strong, big, muscular, attractive. Later, I would describe him as a ruggedly handsome Black man with a heart of gold. Greeting us, his smile was so warm, so inviting, so…sexy…that I was immediately intrigued by him.

"Let me get right to the point," he said, his voice booming over the pounding music.

"You two boys have the hottest asses of anyone out there dancing!"

Henry grabbed my hand, then turned me around and placed my head under his arm, showing my ass to our new friend.

"You like this one, huh?" Henry asked.

"Oh yeah, I like that one. But I like yours too," Wyatt said to Henry, recognizing that he was the one he needed to talk to. No matter what was about to happen, both Henry and Wyatt knew that I had no say in the matter. It was really between the two men.

"Let's go to the back bar and have a little talk," Wyatt suggested, taking hold of my ass with his left hand and Henry's firm, muscular, round ass with his right hand.

Henry ordered bourbon on the rocks for himself and Wyatt, top-shelf, of course. He ordered a sloe gin fizz for me, laughing as he handed it to me. "Here you go, gurl. Try not to choke on it like you choke on my dick every night."

Henry did enjoy humiliating me in front of guys, especially super-masculine guys like Wyatt.

To be honest, it turned me on. I perched myself on a bar stool, crossing my legs like a proper lady, and sipped my pink drink while the men discussed the matter at hand.

"I'm a photographer," Wyatt explained, enjoying the bourbon. "My new project is a photo book featuring men's asses. Hot men with hot asses, of course."

Henry couldn't resist teasing me a little more. "Are girly men with big round asses gonna be in the book too?"

Wyatt's laughter could be heard all the way to the other end of the bar.

"Oh yeah. Tight, round, muscular asses on girly boys are definitely gonna be included!"

Henry agreed that we would meet in Wyatt's studio two days later for a photoshoot.

After signing the forms agreeing to be photographed, Wyatt got right to work. He wanted to showcase our butts in jockstraps. The old, classic jocks with the white pouch, the white leg straps, and the distinctive stripe in the center of the waistband. He gave one to Henry that had a blue stripe. I was told to wear one with a red stripe.

Wyatt's voice boomed as he gave directions.

"Both of you bend over, your butts against each other, then grind your asses together slowly. I wanna capture that passion of two butts seeking each other out!"

We both obeyed. It seemed unthinkable to do anything other than what we were being directed to do. Maybe, instead of starring in a movie or TV show, Wyatt would end up directing one day.

As we were posing differently, both of our butts aimed at the camera but slightly angled, Wyatt called out, "Henry, grab hold of that big jawn of yours and cover it up with your hand. This book is gonna feature your ass and your big cock is getting in the way of my shots!"

I don't know if you ever heard the term "jawn" before. I never heard of it before I moved to Philly. But here, anything could be a jawn. I'm not kidding.

Someone might say, "Did I see you at that jawn last night?"

Or, "Gimme that jawn over there."

If you were referring to anything, including people, places, things, even events, you could call it a "jawn" and everyone would understand exactly what you meant. So Henry knew that Wyatt wanted him to grab hold of his dick and keep it under control. Keep it out of sight. This book was all about men's asses. No ifs, ands, or "butts"!

"You want me to cover mine? Is it getting in the way too?" I asked in a high-pitched queeny voice. That almost brought the two men to tears, they were laughing so hard.

That's how Henry and I ended up appearing in Wyatt's first photo book, titled *Big Butts*. We were in a section called "Black and White Men's Butts Together," which of course featured interracial couples. Four of our photos were included in that first edition.

In one photo, Henry and I are lying on our stomachs, facing away from the camera, heads turned as we kissed. Wyatt captured us from head to toe, feet closest to the camera, but the main focus was on our asses. Another photo caught Henry from behind, standing over me with a leather paddle in his right hand, just about to strike my ass, which for purposes of realism, Wyatt had insisted had to really be spanked, to give it that perfect shade of red. I know I saw Wyatt's big boner bulging as Henry got my ass going from pink to red to swollen and hurting.

In my imagination, Wyatt pulled out his big fat bat and started swinging it as he moved towards me, aiming for my tight pink target, at the center of my very sweet cheeks. But that was only in my thoughts. Wyatt was perfectly professional during the entire shoot, even though he was hard and throbbing the entire time.

I still have a copy of *Big Butts* and I treasure it to this very day.

Wyatt went on to produce a series of photo books. *Black Butts; White Butts; Asian Butts* were new titles, each devoted to specific races. *Gay Butts; Young Butts; Buttery Butts; Butts 'n' Buns* and *Bent Over Butts* were additional titles in the series. All featured beautiful men, showing their faces and bodies of course, but always focusing on the part of the body that Wyatt loved the most. Their beautiful, fine asses.

The *Butts* series of books were reserved for those large, glossy, coffee-table style of books. Not one to miss an opportunity for a sale, Wyatt also produced a series of smaller, soft-cover books, aimed at the consumers who perhaps couldn't afford any of the books in the *Butts* series.

These were titled *Cakes*, as in *Pound Cakes*; *Cherry Cakes*; *Sweet Cakes*; *Candy Cakes*; *Ass Cakes*; *Cheeky Cakes*, *Taste My Cakes*, etc. You get the idea. Of course, each edition featured the finest men with the finest asses on the planet who would agree to be photographed by Wyatt.

That day, we couldn't find any copies of *Big Butts* in the store. Before we left, Henry asked Patrick at the counter if he could special-order a copy. Patrick winked and agreed. He knew all about that book and our part in it.

***

Luckily, we arrived at the club on time for the meeting. Going inside, we were greeted by Georgie and Alejandro, who introduced us to his new boyfriend, Kirk. No wheelchair was in sight. I wondered if it had been difficult for Kirk to get into the club.

I understood later that my wondering was part of the problem. I should have understood that our entrance presented unnecessary obstacles for Kirk and others, without having to be told about it. But, I was still learning. I'm not afraid to admit that.

After the introductions, I handed the package from the bookstore to Kirk. I could see why Jando liked this guy. He looked like someone out of a military recruitment photo shoot.

Starting with the short, buzzcut blonde hair, the blazing blue eyes and the killer smile just above a jaw so square I thought it must have been drawn by angels. For a brief moment, I thought about how excited Jando must have been to meet such a gorgeous guy, but I also wondered about their sexual activities. My thought was interrupted when Kirk opened the package and started laughing.

"Perfect!" he said. "I adore these old mags. And I already know that you know why!" He was looking directly at me, clearly pleased. His eyes gleamed with excitement as he went through the pages of all three magazines.

"The fuckin' *Bicep Boys*! One of my all-time favorites! I remember you from the meeting at the Veterans Service Center. You were there with Bobby."

"That was me," I agreed. "You told that story about wanting the gay porn books and magazines when you were a teenager. Great story!" I reminded him.

Kirk and Jando stood together for a minute, smiling and pointing at certain pages of *The Bicep Boys.* I heard Kirk tell Jando, "Yeah, boy, you're gonna be posing for me like that later on tonight. And yes, I'm gonna be taking pictures with my Polaroid camera. This is going to be fun!"

Since we were all standing at the club entrance, by the coat check room, Jando suggested we go inside and get comfortable at a table. That's when I finally noticed that Kirk was using crutches to help him walk.

Before joining us, Jando went behind the bar and got four bottles of Perrier. "No alcohol right now, sorry," he explained. "We want you to have full control of yourselves. We have a little something planned for later."

Kirk leaned heavily on the table as he went to sit down. The table started to tip in his direction, causing him to lose his balance just enough to cause Henry to grab hold of Kirk, preventing what could have been a disastrous fall.

"Thanks, man. Sorry about that," Kirk apologized.

"No, we're sorry. Sorry that our place isn't properly equipped," was Henry's reply.

After we were all seated, Kirk took hold of Jando's hand. "I already know what you're thinking," he began. "You're wondering what happened to my leg."

Even without knowing the story, I felt my eyes beginning to water. I glanced over at Henry and saw that his eyes were starting to redden. I didn't want to get too emotional, so I fought back the tears and listened closely.

"In 1970, I turned 18 years old. And yes, I can see Joey over there already counting on his fingers, so I'll just let you know that I'm 29 years old. I'll turn 30 in a few months," he said, laughing.

I quietly put my fingers away, feeling just a bit awkward.

"We had the draft back then. I hope you know what that means. But if not, it meant that I was forced to serve in the military, and I had the bad luck to be sent to fight in VietNam."

"Can I ask a question? I hate to interrupt, but…" Henry said.

"Sure, go ahead."

"Why didn't you get out of the draft for being gay?"

Kirk sighed slightly, glancing at Jando. "You remember this was 1970, right? And yes, I knew I was gay back then. But I wasn't ready to be open about it. I didn't know what might happen to me if I told those military officers that I was gay. I thought I might get arrested, or beat up, or even worse."

"Sorry, I wasn't thinking," Henry admitted.

"I understand. It was different back then. But even today, you know lots of guys are afraid to come out. Even in these modern times."

We all knew just how true that statement was.

"Anyway, to make a long story short, I got sent to VietNam. Scared to death. No real training for what I was about to experience. Running around with a rifle in a god-forsaken jungle filled with insects and wild creatures. And besides all that, we were fighting an enemy who wasn't easily identified. Calling the experience horrible doesn't do it justice. It was complete holy hell."

Kirk was interrupted by the sound of Georgie sobbing. Then I started crying. I couldn't help myself. Even Henry, the strongest of all of us, was rubbing his eyes and nose with a tissue.

Kirk waited patiently while we calmed ourselves down.

"We had to serve for two fuckin' years. And I'll say it again, I was scared shitless every day I was there. You never knew when your unit might get attacked, so you could never let your guard down."

I tried to imagine that level of stress in my life, but I truly couldn't grasp what it must have been like for Kirk.

"One night, we were on patrol. Me and my buddy were responsible for a small area, and we were trying to be careful while watching for any signs of the enemy. And that's when it happened. A huge explosion right in front of my eyes. All I saw was a bright orange and yellow hot flash of light that hit me immediately. And through the flash, I saw that my buddy, André, had his whole body torn to shreds."

Georgie was starting to cry again. I took a deep breath and held it. But on the inside, I felt like I was dying.

"I didn't feel anything except the heat from the blast," Kirk continued, with no sign of emotion. It was like he had somehow taught himself to hide the emotional pain as he related what had happened to him.

"I started to run to try and help Andre, and that's when I stumbled and fell. I didn't realize until later, when I woke up in the hospital, that the bottom of my leg had been torn off in the blast."

Even Jando, who had already heard the story, was crying along with the rest of us now.

Kirk took several sips from his bottle of Perrier, again waiting for us to process what we had just heard.

Slowly, we calmed down. But this was a conversation that I knew I'd never forget. And once again, I was reminded of just how lucky I'd been in my life experiences.

Jando spoke next. "We want to ask you guys to do something."

"Anything," I croaked.

"It's one thing to hear about the obstacles that people in wheelchairs face, but it's entirely different to experience it."

Then Kirk added, "I don't always use a chair. Sometimes I use crutches, even a walker. I tried to get a prosthetic leg, but they haven't been able to get me one that fits right. They always hurt like fuckin' hell when I try to wear one."

Jando then told us a little about the night he and Kirk went on their first date. How Kirk didn't want Jando to push him in his chair. That he wanted them to walk side-by-side. And how hard it was for them to do that. Most of the time, the sidewalks were crooked, or broken, or uneven, or steep, and sometimes, they were just too narrow.

"Come on," Kirk finally said. "Let's head outside."

It hurt me to see how difficult it was for Kirk to go down the outside stairs of the club. There were only a few steps, but they were steep, and I noticed that the railing made the steps too narrow for a wheelchair to fit.

A van was parked outside. Jando opened it and asked Henry to help him unload. Inside were five wheelchairs.

We were asked to spend one hour experiencing what it was like to try to get around Center City Philly in a chair.

Let me tell you, it was mission impossible. While walking, we might notice a problem with the sidewalk, but trying to get around in that chair made us realize just how huge the problem was. And recently, the city had begun to install curb cuts, which were meant to help, but didn't always accomplish their purpose. As we traveled down 13th Street, I came to a cut that if I used it would have caused me to crash right into a streetlight pole.

What brilliant urban planner designed this? I thought.

I wasn't at all emotional during our one-hour tour in our chairs. To be honest, I was too busy trying to successfully navigate the streets and sidewalks to think about anything else.

I noticed three things. First, as I said, the sidewalks were in horrendous condition. I got stuck a few times, and it wasn't easy to free myself so I could continue the journey.

Second, I noticed the reaction of other people. A few stared at the sight of five queer-looking people making a wheelchair parade down 13th Street. But to most people, we were invisible. Let me say that again. INVISIBLE.

It was amazing the lengths to which people would go to ignore us. At one point, I accidentally bumped into a middle-aged woman at a corner, waiting for the traffic to pass. She stared straight ahead. She didn't look to see who had bumped her. She already knew. But her refusal to acknowledge my very existence cut through me like a hot knife through butter.

Third, I was very aware of how physically demanding it was to propel oneself through space in a wheelchair. My arms were burning, my hands had blisters and my lungs were wheezing from the constant output of energy.

When we reached The Parker Hotel on Spruce Street, which had originally been called The Spruce Hotel, offering rooms for "bachelors" and currently a seedy, run-down "welfare hotel", we turned around.

The trip north on 13th Street, which was inclined upwards, was even more of a challenge. But eventually, we made it back to Club Sanctuary.

I guess I was holding in all my emotions during our field trip. Because as soon as we reached the club, and I got up out of the chair, I started crying hysterically. I can't explain what I was feeling. Part of it was relief, with the trip being finished. Part of it was empathy for those who wouldn't just be able to get up out of a wheelchair after a one-hour excursion. And part of it was the feeling of exasperation as I at least partly understood the feeling of losing my independence.

During the entire time, except when we were spotted by friends in the Gayborhood, no one offered to help any of us. Even when I was stuck in a broken piece of sidewalk, rocking back and forth to try to free myself, at least 4 or 5 passers-by did just that – they passed me by. I was horrified that in the past, I might very well have done the exact same thing.

Since all of the Sanctuary Board members were present, Alejandro offered a proposal to spend whatever funds were necessary to make our club more accessible for anyone with a disability. I barely heard him as I was still quietly sobbing, but of course, I voted with everyone else to make a unanimous decision to improve the club.

Once those changes were made, including a ramp, wider doors, spaces inside that could be reached by anyone in a chair and improvements in the bathrooms, was there a sudden influx of wheelchair-bound attendees at the club? Well, no. But, there were times when people who needed those accommodations did come out to the club, for whatever reason. And those few times made all the time, money and effort well worth it. We were not going to be another obstacle in the path of anyone who wanted to come out and party with us.

SEVEN

The White Party at Club Sanctuary was held on July 25. It was Labor Day weekend, the beginning of September, when we had our lesson in the wheelchairs.

Alejandro had first met Kirk at the White Party. Jando was interested, intrigued even, but a little cautious. He was glad that he spent some time talking to Kirk during the party, getting to know him as a person instead of one of his usual anonymous fucks.

They went on their first date the night after the party. Jando was nervous. It had been a long time since he had gone out on a real date. And he'd never dated a man in a wheelchair or on crutches. Still, he was looking forward to the experience, because he liked Kirk. He liked him a lot.

Jando wasn't sure what to wear. His club outfits usually consisted of extremely tight black jeans or leather pants, a tee shirt with a sexy, suggestive graphic or logo, black Timbs, maybe a pair of suspenders or a leather armband. You know, some accessories just to attract attention from the type of guys he liked.

He stood naked in front of his full-length mirror, trying to decide what to wear, but also admiring what he saw reflected back at him. Alejandro is a blonde Puerto Rican, with large brown eyes, a perfect nose and a mouth that looked like it was ready to invite any part of a male body to enter it. His lush lips were the perfect size and shape.

His smooth body was practically hairless. He trimmed his bush so there was just a hint of hair at the very top of his cock. Arms, legs, ass…all perfectly smooth.

He smiled at his tan complexion and admired his abs, slowly rubbing his hand along his abdomen, feeling the taut muscles there. He was tempted to pinch his nipples, one of his most sensitive zones, but instead, he cupped his balls, pulling them up to squeeze his dick and balls together. He loved the way his dick, much darker than the rest of his skin, almost black, looked like a fat snake, if a snake could be long, black and uncut. He pulled back the foreskin, thinking, *No, not a snake. A horsecock. Or a bull. Yes, a huge uncut bull cock. That's what he had. He called it El Toro, the Bull.*

Although Jando liked his sex on the kinky side, he wasn't sure about Kirk. They hadn't discussed sex at the party. Not even information about being a top or a bottom.

He was tempted to dress conservatively, but he wasn't sure if that was a good idea. He didn't want to scare off Kirk, but he also wanted to be his true self.

Hell, if he doesn't like me the way I am, then it just isn't meant to be, he thought.

He pulled on a bright red jockstrap and found matching red and white socks. He already liked the look, hoping that Kirk would get turned on if Jando got the chance to strip for him tonight. He turned to admire how his fat, muscular ass cheeks jutted out from the leg straps of the jock, then turned again to admire how his bull cock stretched the fabric of the pouch.

He decided on the black jeans rather than leather pants, stretching them over his long, lean legs and up over his butt, pulling the jeans on tightly. His tee shirt collection was huge compared to most people. Hundreds were hanging in his closet, with more neatly folded and placed in dresser drawers. Scanning his collection, he went for one of his favorites. On the front was a graphic of a muscular leatherman, somewhat akin to a Tom of Finland work of art, with the man bulging in all the right places. Behind him sat a lion – with a massive mane and a passive look on his face, sitting directly behind the man, so close that it seemed like they were touching. Or something. Just above that graphic were the words "The Lion's Den." Jando had gotten the tee shirt on a visit to some club, named The Lion's Den of course, but he didn't remember where the club was. Not in Philly. But other than that, he couldn't remember.

Fully dressed for the date, Jando again checked himself in the mirror. He liked the black and white outfit, but, being Puerto Rican, he wanted just a little more color. So he carefully tied a red bandanna over his left bicep and a blue bandanna over the right.

They planned to see a movie at the Ritz Theatres near Head House Square. That would be in the Society Hill area of Center City. Alejandro was to meet Kirk outside of Kirk's apartment building at 7th and Walnut Streets. Then they would walk/ride to the theatre from there.

When Jando arrived, Kirk was already waiting outside. The sidewalks are fairly wide in this part of the city, so they were able to travel side-by-side, as Kirk wanted. He felt it was easier to talk to someone walking next to him, as opposed to someone behind him, pushing him along.

When they got to 6th Street, Kirk said "Damn! Will you look at that!"

He was pointing at a lone figure in Washington Square Park, who seemed to be shadowboxing. Rather vigorously.

"That's Danny. He's in the same counseling group as me at the Veterans Service Center. He was in Nam too. That boy has some real problems."

"Like what? Jando asked.

"Nothing physical. He never got wounded. But it's his head. Whatever he saw over there, or whatever he did, well it fucked him up big time."

They both watched as Danny got into a crouch, still boxing with his imaginary demons.

"He thinks he's fighting right now. I only know because he described these episodes to me. He thinks the Cong are attacking him and he's using martial arts and boxing to fight them off."

"Do you think we should go over there and do something? Try to help him?" Jando asked.

"No, when he's like that, it's just best to leave him alone. That's a battle he has to fight by himself."

Kirk and Alejandro continued walking, talking, and getting to know each other better. By the time they got to the theatre, Jando found himself impressed with Kirk's intelligence, compassion and sense of humor. He was hoping that Kirk was finding him equally interesting.

They had a choice of three movies that night. *E.T. the Extra-Terrestrial,* which they both had already seen, *Poltergeist*, or *Victor/Victoria*.

They chose Victor/Victoria, thinking the premise sounded interesting. They had no problems getting into the theatre, as there were no steps. They sat in the back row of the center section, after stopping for a huge bucket of buttery popcorn and a couple of packs of Twizzlers. They settled into their seats at the end of the row, after folding Kirk's wheelchair and leaning it against the back wall.

It didn't take long for them to become bored with the gender-bending premise of the movie. A woman playing a man playing a woman. Ho-hum.

About 30 minutes into the movie, Kirk leaned close to Jando and whispered, "I see better acting every day with queer guys pretending to be straight." Jando agreed, laughing quietly, and settled back into his seat, stifling a yawn.

Kirk reached across Jando's lap, placing the popcorn and Twizzlers on the empty seat next to Jando. Then he took hold of Jando's hand and placed it in his lap.

Don't tell me this guy wants a handjob right here in the theatre, Jando thought.

But that wasn't Kirk's intention at all. Instead, he turned Jando's hand so it was palm-up, cradling it in Kirk's strong right hand. Then, using just the tip of the middle finger of his left hand, Kirk began tracing very small imaginary circles on Jando's palm.

The electricity was shocking and immediate. Jando had never felt anything like that before. He didn't realize just how sensitive fingers and palms could be. After the initial shock, the pleasure kept growing in intensity.

Jando let out a deep sigh. No, it was more of a moan. He leaned back, closing his eyes, completely forgetting the movie. His dick was growing rapidly, pushing and straining against the small pouch of his red jockstrap. He reached down between his legs, moving the position of his cock so it was pointing upwards, allowing it to have more room to grow to its full length.

"Holy fuck!" Jando whispered, as Kirk circled his palm incessantly. Never using much pressure, because the trick of this technique was to use a very light touch. Jando felt the wetness in his jock, getting sticky as he oozed pre-cum.

Kirk leaned closely into Jando again, his hot breath against Jando's ear. "Let's get the fuck outta here, babe."

Jando didn't care that he was sporting a gigantic hard-on that would be apparent to anyone looking his way as they left the theatre long before the movie ended. He was ready to follow Kirk anywhere and everywhere. He wanted more of what Kirk had to offer. Much, much more.

On the way back, Jando walked behind Kirk's chair, pushing. Why? Because the sidewalks in this direction were inclined upwards, making it more difficult, though not impossible, for Kirk to manage on his own.

When they got to Washington Square, they were surprised to see that Danny was still there, still beating the air with his fists, but now he was grunting and screaming, in the midst of hand-to-hand combat with the unseen enemy.

"Are you sure we shouldn't do anything?"

"I'm positive," Kirk replied. "He'll tire himself out soon and go to sleep on one of the benches. He'll be fine."

Getting to the end of the block, Kirk added, "Danny lives in the same building as me. It's a rooming house for vets. A bunch of us gay vets kinda took over the entire house. So when he's ready, it'll just take a minute for Danny to come back home."

They were still walking on Walnut Street, along the northern edge of the square. There was a pizza and sub shop down on the southern side and Kirk asked if Jando was hungry.

"Starving," Jando said, "But not like you think."

"Okay babe, I got you," Kirk said, laughing.

Jando took a second to think before replying. He wasn't sure if he should take a chance, to open himself up this soon after meeting a guy. Then, he took the leap.

"Do you know what Rican guys call their girlfriends?"

"No, what?" Kirk asked.

"They call them Bae. You just called me 'babe'. Now, I'm not sayin' I wanna be your *girlfriend,* but I wouldn't mind it too much if you called me Bae."

For Jando, the few seconds that went by before Kirk replied seemed like an eternity. He started to curse himself for moving too fast. But Kirk only paused because he was smiling so much that his face hurt, although Jando, walking behind him, couldn't see that.

Finally, Kirk said, "Okay, Bae. Okay, Bae." He considered it. "Yeah, dammit, I like the sound of that, Bae!"

Without thinking, Jando did a little jump in the air. Just enough to slightly throw Kirk backward in his chair. Not enough to cause a spill, but enough for Kirk to notice.

"Calm down, Bae!" he laughed. Jando leaned forward and kissed Kirk on the top of his head.

When they reached Kirk's apartment building, Kirk turned and looked at Alejandro. "I know you're hungry for some man-meat, but I'm hungry for real food. See that pizza shop down there?" Kirk asked, pointing down 7th Street.

"I want you to go down there and bring back a large. On my half, I want pepperoni, green peppers, onions and mushrooms. Get whatever you want on your half," he said as he handed a twenty-dollar bill to Jando.

"Oh, and get a cold six-pack. I'm almost out of beer. And here, take these." Jando caught the set of keys that Kirk tossed his way.

"Just let yourself in with the big key and the smaller key is for Room 9, straight down the first floor and on the left when you get to the end of the hall. I'll be waiting for you in my room."

In the pizza shop, Jando grew impatient, but the workers were in no hurry. They didn't know he had a hot date set up for as soon as he could get out of there. But while he had time to think, Alejandro wondered why Kirk didn't come down to the shop with him. Was he planning to be undressed, maybe hiding under the covers, maybe ashamed of his body, his missing leg? He also wondered if he'd be uncomfortable seeing Kirk without clothes for the first time. He wasn't quite sure what to expect, but he was extremely horny and he knew he wanted to pounce on Kirk as soon as he could.

When he let himself into Kirk's room, he found Kirk sitting on a small sofa in front of a 13-inch black and white TV with no cable. The picture was fuzzy and the volume was low while a rerun of *Happy Days* was on.

"Just put the box on the coffee table and we can eat here. And keep out two beers and put the rest in the fridge."

Kirk proceeded to eat, with no hint that anything sexual was about to take place between them. This felt awkward to Jando who didn't really know how to act on a date. He was used to quick fuck-n-sucks, usually in a public place like The Hole at the club. So, he copied what Kirk did. He figured Kirk knew how to act better than he did.

After a few minutes, there was only one slice of pizza left. Kirk looked at the young Puerto Rican guy sitting next to him with a mischievous grin.

"Hey Bae, you know what I always wanted to do?"

"Please don't tell me you always wanted to smash a guy in the mouth with a slice," Jando joked.

"No, not that. But you know how in the movies, a couple will share something they're eating, until they end up mouth-to-mouth. And then they have to decide whether to kiss or what they're gonna do next?"

"Yeah," Jando said. And not just people do that. Remember in that cartoon where Lady and the Tramp were eating spaghetti?"

Kirk laughed, actually snorting a little as he thought about that famous scene.

"If you're the Lady, I guess that makes me the Tramp," Kirk said, still laughing.

"You wanna try it?" Kirk asked, reaching for the final slice, trimming it into a very slim slice and pointing the uncrusted end towards Jando's mouth.

Kirk closed his eyes and started to eat the crust on his side of the slice. He felt the pull as Jando joined him, taking small bites of the other side.

Kirk started laughing again. "Damn! I didn't think about that we actually have to stop to chew."

Now both of them were laughing, as Kirk continued to hold the slice in mid-air between their two mouths.

"Keep going, Bae. Keep going."

With gooey cheese dripping down and various pieces of pepperoni, green peppers, onions and mushrooms falling, and while they tried to keep from laughing, their mouths continued to inch closer.

Finishing the slice, they were both chewing as their lips finally brushed up against each other's.

Swallowing hard, Kirk took the lead and kissed Alejandro forcefully. He pushed Jando back so he was prone on the sofa as he slid his tongue into Jando's mouth, tasting the pizza but also the sweetness of Jando's lips and tongue. Jando returned the favor, kissing with a passion that he'd been holding back for a few hours, needing some release soon.

"I wanna do this right. Let's go in the bedroom," Kirk whispered, lifting himself off Jando's writhing body. "And bring the beers with you," Kirk reminded him as he took hold of a walking cane that was next to the sofa, unnoticed by his Bae.

Before climbing onto the bed, Kirk popped a mixtape he had made into the boombox he kept on the top of the dresser. The first song to play was an oldie, "Lovin' You is Easy 'Cause You're Beautiful" by Minnie Riperton.

The slow jams continued playing as Kirk and Alejandro explored each other's bodies with their hands, lips, tongues. Little by little, they were shedding their clothes, as they continued to grasp, clutch and squeeze nipples, asses, cocks, balls, and everything else.

After Jando was naked, his long, hard dick oozing with wetness, Kirk picked up one of the bandannas Jando had removed from his biceps. Looking deeply into Jando's eyes, Kirk slowly wound the bandanna tightly, then wrapped it around Bae's dick and balls, squeezing them so tightly that Jando winced just a bit.

"It's time, Bae," Kirk announced in a whisper so quiet he could barely be heard over the music that filled the room.

With that, Jando watched as Kirk opened his pants, telling Jando to pull them off. The huge bulge in Kirk's military-style white boxers was throbbing through the thin fabric. And then Jando saw what he was wondering about.

The part of the leg where it ended, just below Kirk's knee.

"I want you to kiss my feet, Bae. I want you to kiss and lick and slurp everything. Everything!"

And that's exactly what Jando did, with no hesitation, no fear, lustfully enjoying the feel, the taste, the smell of every inch of Kirk's magnificent body.

When Kirk's feet, both of them, were being licked and sniffed, he was writhing in pleasure, moaning and grunting loudly and sweating profusely. He was so close to the point of climax that he had to bring Jando's face up to his own, allowing himself to relax enough to stop the orgasm from happening so soon.

A minute later, Jando was on his back, legs spread wide open so Kirk could see his ultimate goal, the hot hairless little hole of intimacy. Just before plunging inside, Kirk reached for a small package, tore it open with his teeth, took a minute to adjust something and then fucked the Whore of The Hole harder and longer than that boy had ever taken dick.

Jando's dick exploded first, as the feeling of his balls tied tightly with the bandanna, combined with the pounding flesh inside his ass, forced jets of man milk out onto his chest, some even landing on his own face.

Two minutes later, it was Kirk's turn, forcing his version of "El Toro" into his Bae's hole of happiness, climaxing and then collapsing onto the boy.

Jando spent the night, sleeping peacefully in Kirk's strong, protective embrace.

When he awoke the following morning, he could smell the coffee, eggs and bacon inviting him into the next room.

As they ate, Kirk said he wanted to explain a few things.

"First, different amputees have different ways to describe their bodies," he told Jando. "Some people call what I have a 'stump'. Others call it a 'residual limb' which is a little too clinical for my taste. So I just refer to it as my leg or my foot. To me, it still feels like my foot is there somehow. I don't know how or why, but I still feel it."

"Okay, I understand."

"And that word 'stump', well, it sounds like something dead to me. Like a tree stump. And my leg isn't dead. Not to me, anyway. But if someone calls it a 'stump', I don't get offended. I just don't think of my leg like that."

Alejandro was impressed with this man, who had clearly given this matter a lot of thought and had come to terms with his situation in a way that made him feel comfortable, even being in a tough situation.

"And one more thing. Most gay guys aren't even aware of something called a condom. Some guys call it a rubber. But every guy in my unit used a rubber when they were fuckin' with the prostitutes in Nam. That's what I used last night when I was pounding you."

The thought of last night made Jando's dick begin to stir back to life.

"Now I don't really have any idea what's going on with this new disease that seems to be affecting us gays, but if it is spread by sex, maybe using a rubber will help prevent it. I'm not sure, but I hope you're okay with that."

Jando was just starting to get concerned by the rapidly spreading disease. He doubted that using a condom would be the answer, but he also liked Kirk, so he agreed that if they had sex again, it was okay for Kirk, or even Jando, to wear a rubber.

A little later, Jando was ready to go back home. "I left your keys on the table. Remember you let me use them after I got the pizza last night."

Kirk placed the keys back into Bae's hands. "No, I want you to keep those. I want you to come back anytime you want. Maybe even later tonight. Maybe this afternoon. Maybe you won't leave at all today."

And that's how the relationship between Kirk and Alejandro started.

EIGHT

Back in 1981, BJ, one of the most popular and beautiful bartenders at Club Sanctuary, developed the lesions identified with Kaposi's Sarcoma, a rare cancer normally only seen in the elderly. After a few months, his disease went into remission and his lesions disappeared, leaving no sign of his infection.

BJ had earned his nickname by being ready, willing, and able to give a blowjob to anyone with a dick who wanted one. He loved having a dick in his mouth so much that he had no qualms about swallowing any dick, anytime, anywhere. He was famous for giving blowjobs in the bathroom at Sanctuary, whenever there was a pause in the demand for drinks from his customers.

When Sanctuary first opened, BJ, a young Italian guy from South Philly, worked at the back bar along with Lonnie, an Asian-American who later moved to San Francisco with his naval officer boyfriend, Stephen.

When I think of BJ, I remember him as a fun-loving, happy, proud gay man, often dressed in various costumes for work. But for a regular shift, he was usually found wearing a pair of bright red short shorts, that clung tightly to his round butt, and a white athletic shirt, showcasing his tight torso, desired by so many of the men that crowded around his station at the club.

I was thinking about that while Henry and I walked into the church. Five years had passed in the blink of an eye. It was a beautiful spring morning in 1986 and we were here to honor our friend and co-worker, who had just experienced a horrible and painful death.

Just two years ago, in 1984, scientists had discovered that it was a virus, now named HIV, as the cause for this

101

terrible disease. And one year ago, in 1985, a blood test was developed, allowing men to find out whether they too had been infected. It was a terrible time for many. Not sure if they wanted to know. Fear of the knowledge. Fear of the consequences, including discrimination, loss of employment, insurance cancellation, as well as facing the loss of friends as people were beginning to live in fear of one another.

There was no treatment. No cure. A positive diagnosis was a death sentence. That's why so many people in our community refused to get tested or gave a fake name when they went. Justin Case was a favorite alias used by many. Just In Case.

Adding insult to injury, many of the institutions that were provided by society to help grieving members of the straight community were now being denied to gays. BJ's family, a tight-knit Italian-American Roman Catholic family, were now experiencing the ugly face of discrimination.

They had worshipped for years at Saint Barnabas Roman Catholic Church, known locally as Saint Barney's. When they went to the pastor to make funeral arrangements, the reverend was nosy and obnoxious.

"No, we will not allow a sinner to be buried in a holy Catholic cemetery. Your son was an abomination to the Lord," the priest told BJ's mother.

They went to the next parish and were met with opposition, but not a complete refusal. Father McDonald told the family that they could have a funeral Mass for BJ, whose real name was Antonio, but the body wouldn't be allowed into the church. In other words, the priest would say a Mass for an empty coffin rather than allow a gay man who had just died of AIDS to be given a proper final farewell.

That's how Henry and I found ourselves walking into The Church of the Resurrection, to attend a sham funeral for a man who deserved better treatment than that.

The day before the fake funeral, we had gone to the real service, where hundreds of friends had gathered at the banks of the Delaware River, at Penn Treaty Park, located along the river near the Fishtown neighborhood of Philly. Several people spoke, remembering and mourning our dear friend.

I kept my remarks very brief, as I wasn't good at hiding my emotions.

"BJ, Antonio, you were one of the brightest lights among the many stars in our community. The world seems darker to me now. I wish I could see you again. Order one more drink from you. Watch you take care of your customers. And I want everyone here to know that BJ will never be replaced. Someone else might work at BJ's position, but that person could never, will never replace BJ. I love you so much," I said, before my voice trailed off and I just couldn't say any more.

Henry was the next to speak. "BJ was one of the best of us. He showed us how to enjoy life. He was never ashamed of who he was. He was the proudest gay man that I ever met. He didn't tell us how to live. He showed us. I'm so proud to have known him as a friend. In BJ's memory, Club Sanctuary is establishing a fund – a scholarship really, as a way to memorialize BJ's contribution to our community. The Antonio Roselli Scholarship Fund will be awarded annually to a deserving high school student to help with college expenses. To win the scholarship, high school seniors who identify as gay or lesbian will be asked to write an essay, describing positive contributions to society by gays and lesbians.

The Board of Directors at Sanctuary will be the judges and award a $5000 scholarship to the winner."

Henry's announcement was met with loud applause from those who had gathered for this somber occasion.

None of BJ's family members were present for this ceremony. They were grieving privately, but they didn't want to be associated with this particular display of honor and support for their son, their brother, their nephew, their brother-in-law.

There were even problems organizing the ceremony at the park. For the first few days after he died, several funeral homes refused to handle his remains. They were afraid, and that fear, combined with a general hostility towards gays, made them feel entitled to refuse their services. It took four days to find a crematorium that agreed to perform the service.

Right after Henry spoke, BJ's roommate, Lawrence, moved among the crowd, tears in his eyes, offering everyone the opportunity to grab a handful of ashes to be tossed into the river. My hands were shaking as I reached into the bag, understanding the enormity of what I was holding. Henry took a small bit, and we held hands as we approached the rushing waters of the Delaware River, scattering BJ's remains at one of his favorite spots to hang out in Philly.

"Rest in peace, buddy," I whispered as I let go.

***

Back at the church, after the service, small groups of people gathered outside, waiting for the coffin to be placed into the hearse for the drive to the cemetery. Hearing people speaking quietly, I was surprised to find that no one seemed to realize that BJ had already been laid to rest. They thought that BJ's body was inside that coffin and that BJ had died from an "unexpected" illness. Of course, I should have expected that, but it hadn't occurred to me that his family would go to such lengths to hide the truth.

Henry and I didn't go to the cemetery. What would be the point?

***

Five years later, 1991. I look back at events in the late 80s. So much had changed and yet somehow, certain things remained the same.

In 1987, Cleve Jones created the first panel of what would become the AIDS Memorial Quilt, in honor of his friend Marvin Feldman. Initially, panels were standardized at 3 feet wide by 6 feet long. Henry told me that was the typical size and shape of a cemetery plot.

That same year, Liberace, a flamboyant yet closeted gay man who earned fame and fortune as an Emmy-winning pianist, died of AIDS.

And also in 1987, Larry Kramer founded ACT UP – The AIDS Coalition to Unleash Power – to apply pressure to the government and to the pharma industry to research and find better treatments for those now known as PWAs (People With AIDS).

And AZT was approved as the first treatment for PWAs.

In October of 1987, Club Sanctuary sponsored a bus to travel to the National Mall in Washington, D.C. Henry and I were among half a million other visitors, who were shocked at the sight of 1,920 panels. Of course, that represented the lives and deaths of 1,920 individual people.

In 1988, people such as the young teenager Ryan White and Elizabeth Glaser helped to highlight the problems encountered by younger people affected by the disease. Transmission of the virus from mothers to their unborn children became a growing problem.

Elizabeth Glaser, the wife of actor Paul Michael Glaser (from the *Starsky and Hutch* TV show) had unknowingly contracted HIV during a blood transfusion she received while giving birth to her daughter. Her daughter was born with an HIV infection, and three years later, her son was also infected during his birth.

When her daughter developed advanced AIDS at the age of 3, Elizabeth fought with the FDA to allow her daughter to be treated with AZT, the only approved treatment at that time. The FDA refused, and her daughter died in 1988.

Elizabeth co-founded the Pediatric AIDS Foundation with several friends, to try to save her son and other children infected with HIV.

And Sylvester, who had performed at the very first White Party at Sanctuary, died of AIDS-related complications in 1988 at the age of 41.

And that's how it went. A seemingly endless series of events, with a few signs of progress against the virus while people just continued to die. Many famous people. Many more everyday, regular people. And of course, no one was to blame. No one deserved any of this. But that didn't stop some people from assigning blame. There was plenty of that to go around.

For me, all of this was mind-numbing. I couldn't comprehend the big picture, so I learned to just focus on the smaller events. It was the only coping mechanism that worked for me.

And that's how Henry and I found ourselves at yet another funeral, this 10th day of October 1991. Nothing had happened to change the shame, the fear, the stigma of having died of AIDS. Families still rejected their sons who were dying at an ever more alarming rate. Insurance companies still refused to cover PWAs and people were still afraid to get tested.

Berkley and his friends worried during the entire summer of 1990. That summer was hotter than normal, and if you've ever spent any time in Philly in August, you know that the air can be stiflingly hot. And of course, they knew that getting the night sweats was a warning sign not to be taken lightly.

Berkley's apartment had no air conditioning, and keeping windows open provided no relief from the sticky, hot air during the heatwave that we all suffered through during the second half of that month. Every morning, he questioned. *Am I sweating more than normal? Is it just the heat? Or is it something else?* He couldn't be sure.

He didn't want to get tested. Too afraid. He closed his mind and went on with his life, not wanting to know.

The summer heatwave ended. Berkley was no longer sweating during the night. Relief swept over him, as he considered himself to be virus-free.

He was at Sanctuary every Saturday night. One of the pretty boys, and a skillful, sexy dancer, he was popular and fashionable. He stood out for me because of his platinum blonde hair, which was unusual to see on a Black guy. I liked it. A lot.

Honestly, I don't know much, if anything about his sex life. Top? Bottom? Versatile? I don't know. Promiscuous? Kinky? Vanilla? Again, no idea.

But he did have a lot of friends, and he was very affectionate, always touching, kissing, petting whatever guy he was with on any particular Saturday night. I could see that much.

One day, while he was at work, processing insurance claims for one of those big firms located in an office tower in Center City, he felt a sudden change. He couldn't describe it. It just felt...different.

He walked quickly to the men's room, checking himself out in the mirror. But he didn't see anything suspicious. So he returned to his cubicle, trying to be inconspicuous, but feeling strange.

The feeling didn't go away. It was persistent, no matter how hard Berkley tried to ignore it. But he wasn't sweating at night, he didn't have any lesions, and so he was certain that it couldn't be THAT. It just couldn't be.

He started taking vitamins. He changed his diet. He stopped smoking. He went to the gym more often, working out harder than before. He still drank at the club, thinking that he didn't want to give up everything that was fun.

Weeks went by with no change. A trip to the doctor for a check-up didn't reveal anything. Of course, they never tested for THAT. Not without express permission. And Berkley wasn't about to give his permission for that test.

Hours, days, weeks, months of worry. Never telling his friends that he just didn't feel right. Afraid of their reaction. He already knew how PWAs were treated. They weren't always treated well; in case you've forgotten about the raging paranoia in both the gay and straight communities.

That's why, in the Spring of 1991, Berkley finally took the step he had avoided for so long. He took the test.

As the counselor explained his options, Berkley didn't hear a word of what was being said. All he could hear was an echo of the word "Positive." It rang in his ears, over and over and over.

Positive.

Positive.

Positive.

The word cut him, wounding him, almost strangling him. He couldn't breathe. Walking out of the clinic, dazed, he headed for Rittenhouse Square, one of his favorite places to just hang out, watching the people go by. *People with lives to lead. People with futures*, he thought, as he stared straight ahead.

Trying to decide what to do, he sat there for hours. A friend walked by, sitting beside Berkley, having a short conversation, never suspecting that Berkley's life had just changed dramatically. Later, Berkley would be unable to recall any of that conversation they had in the park. All he could recall was one word.

Positive.

Positive.

Positive.

He made a decision that day, right there in the park. He wasn't going to let a minute of his life go to waste. He was going to fight, not just for himself, but for others as well. And he was no longer going to be afraid. He wanted to leave a legacy, not of fear, not of sickness, but a legacy of hope, of determination and of love.

Berkley became one of the leading AIDS activists in Philly. As the vice-chair of the local ACT UP group, he organized marches and protests, hosted more fundraising parties, 5-K walks, 10-K runs, fashion shows, same-sex proms and many other events than anyone in Philly. He was a celebrity in his own right and he never shied away from sharing his experiences with racism, homophobia and AIDS phobia.

He tried to take his message into the schools, but he was always rejected. You might think that schools, charged with educating our young people, would understand the importance of Berkley's message. But they did not.

Just like BJ's church rejected him, Berkley's Baptist church would not allow a funeral for him on their premises. Today, we gathered at the local Metropolitan Community Church on Chestnut Street in West Philly for his final service.

While we were there, something happened to me that I can't explain, even to this day. Henry and I were seated together, as we always were. But as the pastor began to speak, eulogizing Berkley and all his many accomplishments, I felt the scene drift away into nothingness.

Instead of the church, I looked around and saw that I was in a theatre. The Academy of Music at Broad and Locust Streets, to be exact.

The theatre was completely empty, except for me. Many of the seats had a flickering candle in them. Some of the lights were very close and very bright. Others were at a greater distance, somewhat dimmer.

As I looked around, wondering what this meant or how this happened, some of the candles started to go out. Slowly at first, then faster and faster.

I turned to the seat next to me, where the candle was quite large and very bright and I was horrified to see the flame extinguish and the candle disappear into nothingness. The only sound was the gasp that escaped my lungs.

At that very moment, I felt Henry's hand touch mine, holding me as he cried thinking about our good friend Berkley, and then I was back in the church, at the funeral.

Later, I told Henry what had happened. I asked him if I had dozed off, thinking it had been a dream.

"No, you never fell asleep. You were right there next to me the entire time."

Those words filled me with dread. I was afraid that this vision, this premonition, or whatever it was, might be telling me that I had a bleak future ahead of me.

NINE

During most of the 1980s, there was a constant dull ache in my heart. Sometimes, the ache became sharp and acute, such as when a friend died. The grief never went away. We just had to learn ways to deal with it, finding ways to cope as the virus was unrelenting in its advance.

That doesn't mean we were always sad. Humans have this strange, wonderful ability to enjoy life even in the darkest of times. But we do cope in different ways. Some people were depressed and withdrawn, avoiding social interactions out of fear. Others worked in organizations that were dedicated to helping PWAs. Still others tried to ignore the problem, hoping that somehow it would all just go away.

Henry and I involved ourselves in several organizations, at the grassroots level. In other words, we were the worker bees. We cooked meals for PWAs and helped to deliver them. We attended demonstrations and protests. We even held fundraisers for AIDS-related organizations at our club.

But we also made sure to have other activities, mainly for the sake of our sanity. Henry, a natural athlete, joined the Master Batters, a gay softball league in Philly. They played their games at a small field at 5th and Lombard Streets, one block north of South Street. It was mostly for fun, and they tried to keep it non-competitive, but there were times when some of the guys forgot that the main idea was to have fun and to let everyone play, regardless of ability.

Henry was a star pitcher on his high school baseball team, so he was a natural at the game. I had been on the swim team and discovered when I played my first game of softball that I didn't have the vision required to be able to hit or catch the ball. Still, we played every Sunday during the season, which usually started in April and ended in June. Not too cold and not too hot.

Back in 1982, our friends Lonnie and Stephen, who had first moved to Los Angeles and then re-located to San Francisco, had met Dr. Tom Waddell, a former Olympic decathlete, who was organizing the first Gay Olympics. Lonnie had recovered from an initial bout with Kaposi's Sarcoma and Stephen seemed to be in excellent health. They called to invite us out to visit and to attend the Games, but we weren't able to travel that year.

In the world of sports, even today, discrimination against members of the LGBTQ community runs rampant. The US Olympic Committee in 1982 sued Dr. Waddell, claiming that using the word "Olympics" in association with gay activities would hurt their brand. The Supreme Court of the United States sided with the Olympic Committee, so Tom Waddell was forced to rename his event as the Gay Games.

In 1986, Philly's gay softball team, the Master Batters, was invited to send a team to the 2nd Gay Games, also to be held in San Francisco. Naturally, Henry was included on the team.

I understood why I wasn't invited to be on the team, though I didn't necessarily agree with the decision. I was a klutz on the field. But I did think my ass looked pretty damn good in my uniform, and I looked very cool wearing a baseball cap.

Henry laughed when I described my qualifications. "Don't worry, babe, we'll both make the trip. And you can wear your uniform when we're in bed in the hotel. I just love a cute boy in a uniform!" He knew that making a joke would make me feel better, and he was right.

I put together what I called a Philly care package for Lonnie and Stephen, thinking they might enjoy some food to remind them of back home. I filled a big bag with TastyKakes, including Butterscotch Krimpets, Jelly Krimpets, chocolate cupcakes and my personal favorites, Peanut Butter Tandy Takes (later re-named Kandy Kakes). A dozen gigantic soft pretzels, made in South Philly of course, were also included in the bag.

Luckily, at least a few of the items survived the plane trip, as both Henry and I both preferred our Philly snacks over the bags of tiny stale pretzels offered by the airline after they served our onboard meal.

Arriving in San Francisco and experiencing the Castro District for the first time opened my eyes. I was from the Gayborhood in Philly, with plenty of LGBTQ-friendly bars, coffeehouses, restaurants, bookstores and shops. But the Philly Gayborhood seemed subdued when compared to the Castro. (My apologies to my hometown folks, but this was my experience.)

From the male belly dancers at Hibernia Beach to the Twin Peaks Club with the plate glass windows, allowing the public to see inside the club, with patrons clearly visible, to the Meat Rack, where men would line the street after the bars had closed, I could see the possibilities of what was then called gay liberation. We weren't there during the Castro Street Fair, but Lonnie and Stephen did their best to describe just how freely people expressed their sexuality during that event.

I didn't know back then that the Castro District was known as "Little Scandinavia" in the early 1900s. Or that San Francisco saw a big increase in its gay population after the US military began to discharge large numbers of gay men in the area because of their sexuality.

When we arrived, the area was changing due to the ongoing AIDS pandemic. Though I could see so many signs of queer visibility, the scene was more subdued than it was in the 1970s and very early 80s. Bathhouses were being closed down by order of the city, and at least some of the residents were beginning to adopt safer sex practices.

Participating in the Gay Games in 1986 was an amazing experience. With 2,000 athletes participating, from all areas of the country, there were plenty of opportunities to make new friends and contacts.

The softball games, with Henry participating, were played at Moscone Field. On days he wasn't playing, we went to watch the swimming and diving events at Laney College in nearby Oakland. Being a former swimmer in high school, I enjoyed those events. And I could never get over the sight of beautiful young male bodies in skin-tight speedos.

One of the many highlights of the trip was when we met Tom Waddell, who was so gracious, knowledgeable and entertaining in person. He was clear in his objectives for the games: to promote inclusion and participation for gays in a segment of society where we often faced obstacles – in the world of sports. He viewed sports as a means of personal growth and wanted as many people as possible to have a positive experience with whatever sport they liked.

He didn't share with us that he had already been diagnosed with AIDS. But that was his personal choice, of course. He won a gold medal in the javelin event that year, but like so many AIDS patients, he went into a deep decline the following year and died on July 11, 1987.

Another highlight was when we met Aaron and Isaiah, two members of a swim team from New Orleans. Not only did they have the cutest swimmer bodies that you can imagine, but they also had those charming accents from that part of the country. I could melt every time I heard one of them speak.

They were staying at the same hotel as our delegation from Philly. Their room was four doors down from us. But we saw them for the first time at the breakfast buffet in the hotel restaurant.

"I'd like a piece of that for dessert," I joked to Henry, when Isaiah walked by our table, his muscular swimmer's ass just inches from my face.

It turned out that I'd get my opportunity that night, when the two swimmers joined us at our table for dinner.

The discussion was all about the games. At least, at first, it was about the games. But when I felt Isaiah's foot brushing against mine under the table, well, I know an opportunity when I see one. Or in this case, when I feel one.

By the time dessert was served, it was already decided that the four of us were all interested in some "after-dinner coffee" upstairs.

We invited the two guys to our room. Of course, Henry and I were married, and Aaron and Isaiah had been lovers for two years already. We weren't sure what arrangements they had made with one another, but Henry and I had agreed a few years before that if we were going to play with others, it would always be together. That way, we could remind each other to be careful, to not engage in what was now known as risky behavior.

When we got up to the room, Henry started mixing drinks. No one really expected any coffee. I sat on one bed and the two swimmers stood in front of the other bed, already taking off their team tracksuits.

They both had brown hair, in buzz cuts that would be expected of swimmers during a meet. I also knew that if they had any body hair, it would be shaved for the same reason – to limit any resistance in the pool while they were competing. Aaron had hazel eyes in a round face with a perky nose and kissable lips. Isaiah had the same brown hair with brown eyes, an angular face with a square jaw and equally kissable lips. Two very cute, very athletic, and very willing young men for us to play with that night.

"We have one basic rule," Aaron was telling us as he was stripping, bending down to remove his pants, showing those gloriously round buns just above legs so muscular they were popping. "You can cum on us, but not in us. If we can agree on that, then it's all cool."

I was practically drooling at the sight of them. I loved Henry and I loved our sex life together, but there was also a hunger in me for other men. Henry and I both readily agreed to the terms.

It took about two seconds for all four of us to be naked, four hard cocks swinging, oozing, already throbbing.

"Hold on for a sec. Watch this," Isaiah told us. We watched as Aaron laid on his back, threw his legs over his head, and goddammit, he started sucking his own dick. Hearing him slurp on his own meat, watching as he took half of his shaft down his throat, and seeing his tiny little pink hole seeming to open and close on its own, I was ready to shoot that fast, without a touch from anyone.

But I didn't want it to end that quickly, so I looked away for a few seconds, just long enough to bring me back from the brink of manly ecstasy.

Isaiah was crouching at the top of the bed, where Aaron's feet were behind his head. He started sucking on Aaron's toes, then licking his feet. Aaron was still busy sucking his own cock, while his balls were already tightening as if he were ready to blow a load into his own mouth.

Isaiah looked at Henry. "Go on, man, play with his hole. I like to watch a man finger fuck my boy," he whispered, then going back to worship his boy's feet.

Henry jumped into the action, playfully inserting a wet finger into that pink manhole, then two, and then stretching it wide with three of his fingers.

I was watching this scene, totally fascinated by the spectacle, when Isaiah turned his attention to me. "Boy, get behind me and start licking. Lick my ass you little bitch!"

Henry chimed in after Isaiah. "Yeah, bitch do as your goddammed told and suck that boy's asshole."

I was an expert in that department and I eagerly dove into Isaiah's cheeks, spreading them open with my hands while my tongue darted in and out of that delicious point at the center of his round, hairless, muscular ass.

Aaron's body began to tremble. The feeling of sucking his dick, and having three guys watch him do it, raised the level of his excitement to just below unbearable. His balls were so tight against his body that they were practically invisible.

There's something about watching another man shoot his jizz that fascinates other men. Well, other gay men, I should say. I truly have no idea what a straight man would think about any of this.

Back in the time when gay porn was widely available on DVDs, many of them let you go right to the money shots, you know, those juicy jizzy shots where you can just watch the actors cum and cum and cum and cum.

That's sort of what happened in our hotel room that night. When we heard Aaron panting and grunting and saw him move his legs farther back so the tip of his dick just brushed his lips, we all instinctively knew that it was time to watch the man show.

Isaiah stopped worshipping his boy's feet; Henry took hold of his own dick with one hand while continuing to finger that young boy ass, but watching Aaron's manhood closely. I stood next to Henry, pinching my nipples hard and starting to stroke myself, hoping to join with Aaron in making a milky mess, when Henry reminded me, "Not till I say it's okay, boy."

That's when Aaron just couldn't wait any longer. His hand was a blur, jacking his hardness as fast and hard as he could, till he arched his back and shot jets of creamy cum all over his own face.

Henry was next, his mega Black dick growing even larger as he roughly pushed and pulled, till that little hole opened up and streams of milky manly male juices covered Aaron's cock, running down his balls wetting the sheets under him.

I looked at Henry for permission but he ignored me, enjoying his own moment of ecstasy. Then Isaiah stood over his boy, aiming his dick at his partner's face, rising onto his toes as his cock shuddered, releasing gobs of gooey jism, hitting Aaron's face, with webs of cum getting into his hair.

"Your turn, boy," Henry finally said to me. "Show us what you got."

The sight of Aaron covered in cum, his own, and the offerings from the two other men in the room were all I needed to bring myself to a quick climax. Just before I shot, Henry reached behind me, inserting two wet sticky fingers into my rear, forcing me to release every drop of cum, spurting and sputtering all over the beautiful body of this young swimmer boy.

It always takes a moment for men to calm down after shooting. But just a moment. The intense feeling has been released, but the pleasure can last for a surprisingly long time.

That's what I was thinking as I watched Aaron smearing all of our cum together onto his body. His dick was still hard, enjoying the attention he had been given and knowing the pleasure he had given to us.

Isaiah laid down on top of him, grinding into him, enjoying the sensation of sliding along his partner's slippery, steaming body.

All too soon, the two men got up from the bed and asked to use our shower, inviting us to join them as well. It was a tight squeeze, but we were laughing and carrying on like kids in a locker room shower, as we soaped each other's bodies, rinsing, soaping, rubbing, and generally having fun in the steamy warmth of the water.

Henry and I both felt an intimacy with these two guys from New Orleans. They seemed special, so we invited them to sleep in our room. They accepted the invitation and all four of us slept in the same king-sized bed, spending the night cuddling, caressing and sometimes inserting a finger into a place where maybe it didn't really belong.

And for us, that was safer sex. We didn't know what was safe and what wasn't. There was a debate raging within the gay community on that topic. We did the best we could. We wanted to be safe. We wanted to live. And we also still wanted to have fun. Was it possible to have fun and stay safe?

***

We attended the closing ceremony of the 1986 Gay Games with Aaron and Isaiah. They were fun and we enjoyed their company. The ceremony was spectacular, with none other than author Armistead Maupin as the Master of Ceremonies and a hot performance by singer Jennifer Holliday. After the torch was extinguished, we joined thousands of others rushing down to the field for the biggest Tea Dance I ever attended.

We said our goodbyes to Aaron and Isaiah at the Tea Dance. Promising to stay in contact, they invited us to visit them in New Orleans at any time. But they hoped we could join them for Mardi Gras the following year.

Before we headed to the airport for our flight back to Philly that night, we had one more stop to make. We had to see Lonnie and Stephen one more time.

The truth is, we had seen them every day of our visit to San Francisco, but I've been putting off telling you about it.

I had first met Lonnie when he came to work at Club Sanctuary, shortly after he was outed by a Philly newspaper when he was caught on camera wearing a plastic rhinestone-studded tiara while attending the visit by Queen Elizabeth II during the Bicentennial. The paper made fun of him, in public, causing Lonnie to be kicked out of his home and disowned.

Later, he met Stephen, an officer in the US Navy, at the club. They moved out to California together when Stephen was transferred to a new station.

It hurt me to my core to see how Lonnie had changed. He had contracted HIV at least four years before, when he developed the lesions associated with Kaposi's Sarcoma. For a while, he went into remission, and he hoped that somehow, he might be a survivor.

But it was now clear that wasn't going to happen. Lonnie, who had been beautiful, sexy, athletic and energetic, had turned into a shell of his former self. I don't think he weighed 100 pounds when we saw him. His face was so gaunt, his body shrunken, his facial features distorted by the extreme weight loss. And worst of all, a feeding tube had recently been inserted, since he could no longer handle solid food. And by inserted, I mean that the feeding tube was now a permanent part of Lonnie. He could no longer live without it.

That first day when we arrived and went to see Lonnie and Stephen with our Philly care package, I felt so stupid when I saw the longing in Lonnie's eyes, wishing that he could eat real food. I never would have brought along those food goodies if I had any idea how badly things had gone for him.

I tried so hard not to cry when I saw him. He always smiled at us weakly, trying to act like things were the same. But they weren't the same. Not even close.

I hugged him so tightly the last time I saw him, I think I actually might have hurt him. But I had to hold him. I couldn't just let go and walk away.

Finally, Stephen took hold of my shoulder, guiding me away from beautiful, young, dying Lonnie. When Henry and I got into the cab for the trip to the airport, I was sobbing, trying to choke back the tears but failing, wailing, unable to control my grief.

I don't know how we survive the loss of the ones we love. I don't know how Stephen found the strength to go on after he lost his partner. But somehow, we do it.

Eight days after I saw Lonnie for the last time, he died a quiet death at home, in the arms of his lover.

TEN

When I first realized I wasn't like the other boys, I didn't know why or how I was different. I didn't have the vocabulary. I didn't know it was even possible for two people of the same gender to have sex, let alone fall in love and develop a life together. I never heard of anything like that. There was nothing about gay people on TV, in movies, books or magazines. At least, not any that I had seen.

That was back in the early 1970s. Once I realized that I wasn't the only person in the world who felt an attraction for people with the same equipment I had, I was okay with it. I accepted it. I enjoyed it. I never felt ashamed or embarrassed.

Now, as the mid-80s transitioned to the late-80s, there were some portrayals of gay and lesbian characters in both movies and TV shows, though many were shown in a negative light. It was also unfortunate that so many of the characters were written as victims of the AIDS pandemic. Not exactly something that would encourage a young person questioning his or her sexuality to come out. Still, that's what was available. At least queer people were shown as existing, while during my youth, we were completely invisible.

Everyone should be able to choose how and when to come out. It doesn't always happen that way. And it can still be a very difficult decision. It changes your life in so very many ways.

Some organizations were beginning to realize that queer youth needed some safe spaces. It wasn't that unusual to see young kids living on the streets, right here in Philly. And I'm talking about young kids, sometimes 10, 11, 12 years old. They weren't all gay, of course. But some of them were.

Yandi had started using drugs at an early age. It was part of his upbringing. Everybody in his family used something. His mom, his big sister, his older brother. Yandi never questioned this. He didn't know any better. But though he liked the feeling that drugs provided to him, he also knew that he was different. You know, *that way*. The queer way.

He was 14 years old when he told his mom. He thought he could trust her. He thought she loved him. And maybe she did but she didn't show it. Once she knew that her son was gay, her attitude changed completely. Ignoring him, then hitting him, then beating him. Feeling betrayed, Yandi slipped out of the house one night, planning to never return.

Kids on the street talk to one another. They go into survival mode, looking for any resources for food, clothing, shelter. Some end up with predators. There are too many of them out there to completely avoid them. The trick was to get what you want without giving up too much of yourself in the process.

There are all types of predators. You may have immediately thought of sexual predators, but there are other types. The drug dealer using young kids to sell on the corners. The factory owners who would hire kids to work for impossibly long hours for very little pay. How hard are you willing to work to earn 25 cents an hour? But if you need a buck to buy a sandwich, are you willing to put in 4 hours of labor? Decisions had to be made.

I was watching a movie called *An Early Frost*, a movie that had been released a few years earlier, about a lawyer from Chicago who tells his parents that he's not only gay, but he has AIDS. I was uncomfortable watching the movie, even though I was snuggling on the sofa with Henry, due to the subject matter, which hit me hard. At the same time, I was glad that people in America could see at least a glimpse of what was happening in the gay world.

While my eyes were filling with tears at the plight of the movie character, I wasn't aware that a 14-year-old gay boy named Yandi was wandering through the alleys of the Gayborhood, looking for scraps of food and a safe place to rest.

A man approached Yandi, who immediately went into "fight or flight" mode. Depending on what happened, Yandi was prepared to either run like hell or defend himself using the switchblade he carried for protection.

Luckily, this time, the man wasn't a predator. He was an outreach worker, looking for kids just like Yandi. He sat down on a stoop several feet from the boy, providing a safe distance, and told him about a place called Haven House.

Yandi listened as the man explained that this was a place of refuge for kids up to the age of 18, totally free, providing food and shelter to anyone in need, adding that it was welcoming to gay kids too. Just in case Yandi needed to hear that.

The only requirement was that kids staying there had to attend school, or take classes that were taught at the Center, if school wasn't a comfortable place for someone.

Yandi wasn't sure about this offer. He hesitated.

"They let gay kids in there? They won't hurt me or tease me or beat me? They won't rape me?"

"Come and see for yourself. If you don't like it, you can always turn around and walk right out," the man said softly. Yandi got up and walked with the man. It was just two blocks away. But Yandi kept a safe distance, worried that he'd be grabbed and end up in a hostage situation.

When they arrived at Haven House, which had no sign outside, nothing to indicate that it was a place of protection, Yandi liked what he saw. Young kids his age, seated in a great room, watching TV, playing board games, reading. You know, usual activities for kids. Not like at home, sitting with his family in a darkened room, often without electricity, smoking, snorting, or even shooting up some kinda shit.

And even though he was practically starving and exhausted, his mind was aware enough to notice a beautiful young boy, who looked Puerto Rican like him, or at least some sort of Latino, off to the side by himself, flipping through the pages of a teen magazine. Yandi had hopes about that boy. But he also knew that he could be wrong about him.

Settling into the routine of the house wasn't easy for Yandi, but he tried his best. He refused to attend regular school, so he was taking classes in English and Math at the house. He liked to read, and he liked to write, but he hated Math.

There was a constant change in the population of the house. Some kids came in off the streets, stayed a few days, and left as suddenly as they arrived. A few were referred by social service agencies, though not many. Most of those places were either run by religious organizations or the government, neither of which wanted to be viewed as encouraging gays in any way and would never refer a young queer kid to a place like Haven House.

Yandi found out that the boy he saw that first night was named Eloy, and he was indeed from Puerto Rico. But

Eloy kept to himself, making Yandi unsure whether or how to approach him.

They were both 14 years old, in the same classes at the home. In English class, they were given an assignment to write a poem.

The teacher only told them to write about what they were feeling. He provided a few examples of poems to get them started, then challenged them to write. The assignment would be due in two days.

On the day the assignment was due, the teacher asked for volunteers to recite their poetry. No one volunteered. This wasn't an easy group to teach. The instructor wasn't even sure that anyone had completed the assignment.

He called Yandi to the front of the class. Yandi stood there, shuffling his feet, his palms clammy with sweat as he held his notebook in unsteady hands.

Eloy was surprised at the sound of Yandi's voice, which was much deeper than most 14-year-old boys. And this is what Yandi read to the class:

Hit The Streets
By Yandi

Gettin ready to hit the streets
Me n my boyz feelin them beats
We young n strong n run with the gang
Heard out the window
Just bang bang bang

I'm lookin round
Seein my boyz
Talkin that shit
Makin some noise

I wanna join
Gotta fit in
They got rules
Committin them sins

But if I ain't make it
Be alone on them streetz
I become their victim
Feelin their beatz

Fists poundin
Feet kickin
Just another dude
Takin his lickin

But I got a secret
No one can know
If they found out
Toss me out in the snow

I'm so scared to be caught
Holdin my bag
Can't nobody know
I'm really a fag

Joinin the gang
That's my true goal
Pressured to be
Someone who ain't me

Can't stand the pain
Deep in my brain
My blood leaves a stain
Washed away in the rain

Listen to me
This ain't no gag
They gonna kill me
If they know I'm a fag

Avoidin his gaze
Cause he'll never be mine
He like the bitches
I think they witches
Castin a spell
To make him forget
I could be his
You wanna bet

He think I don't like him
That ain't the truth
Better he think that
Cause…

This ain't no gag
I think he gon' kill me
If he know I'm a fag

Then Yandi quickly closed his notebook, went and sat in his seat, staring blankly ahead.

The silence in the classroom roared in Yandi's ears. No one seemed to have any reaction to what he had just read. If Yandi had looked around, he would have seen that none of the other students were even looking in his direction. Except for Eloy, who had suddenly developed an interest in the newcomer.

The teacher started to say, "Ok class, what do you think..."

"I thought it sucked," one kid called out.

"Yeah, it sounded like a second grader wrote it," said another student.

Eloy remained silent.

The teacher was stunned. He took a minute to consider what to do. While he did expect the poetry to be raw, written in street language, he wasn't sure whether he should first talk about the lack of any poetic structure, or talk about the content. So, he decided to dismiss the class early, asking Yandi to stay, in case he wanted to talk.

Yandi didn't speak to anyone the rest of the day. At dinner, he ate quietly, head down, silently telling everyone to leave him alone.

He went to bed early, hiding his head under the pillow, arguing with himself whether he should have told everyone in the class what he was really thinking, what he really was.

Eloy slept in the same room, in a twin bed, placed a few feet away from where Yandi was sleeping. Eloy decided to go to bed early too. When he went into the room, he got undressed down to his boxer briefs and climbed into his bed.

But Eloy couldn't sleep. He was also torn about what to do. So he decided to do what felt right. He got up, walked quietly over to Yandi's bed, and climbed in with this other boy. He placed his arms around Yandi, who was facing away from him and hugged him. Then he pushed his body closer to Yandi's, feeling happy and surprised when Yandi pushed back.

That's all they did that first night. More would come later, but not yet, not right now. To be comforted was everything in the world that Yandi needed at that moment. And that's what Eloy gave to his new friend.

In class the next day, it was Eloy's turn to recite. He started with an introduction about his poem, in a voice not nearly as deep as Yandi's.

"Some of you know that I moved here from Puerto Rico about two years ago. I wish I was still there. I wish I never came to Philly. But here I am."

Just like Yandi did yesterday, Eloy started shuffling his feet, getting nervous as he spoke.

"I don't wanna stay here. I wanna go back home. I was thinkin' about what it'll be like when I'm really old, like 40 years old, and I'm back on my island. And this poem is what I think I might be thinkin' about in the future, when I'm back where I belong."

"Oh, and if you don't know what a coqui is, they're these beautiful tiny little tree frogs that sing every night all over Puerto Rico. It's the most beautiful sound in the world to me."

Coqui
By Eloy

Nearing the end of my long journey
Accepting the reality of no more me
Looking for comfort, longing to be free
Finding the song of my beautiful coqui.

A stranger in this land
Not accepted by my people
Do I find the answer
In a church, under the steeple?

No, not there

131

Not really belonging anywhere
Arrived here just looking for some fun
Searching for my special place in the sun.

Solo me, solo me
Just like the little, lonely coqui
He wants to be found, by making his sound
Just like me.

So many lost, living in dread
Friends and lovers gone, in prison or dead
When I'm feeling low key
I listen for the sounds of my friends, the coqui

No peace under the Knowledge Tree
No, that wasn't meant to be
Where did they go?
Why can't I ever know?

Solo me, solo me
Just like the little, lonely coqui
He wants to be found, by making his sound
Just like me.

Loneliness brings my tears
Solitude my greatest fear
Waiting for peace
Not afraid, not in the least

At my final hour, at the end of me
With no lover's voice to soothe me
I hope to hear just one sound
The music of the coqui.

Solo me, solo me
Just like the little, lonely coqui
He wants to be found, by making his sound
Just like me.

Coqui! Coqui! Coqui!

When he finished, Eloy stood in place at the front of the class, frozen. He was ready to storm out of the room, furiously fearing a cold reception from his classmates, just like the negative reaction to Yandi's poem the prior day. But then Yandi, who rarely displayed any emotion at the house, jumped out of his seat, clapping loudly, running up to Eloy and hugging him right there in front of everyone. He grabbed Eloy by the hand, and pulled him out of the classroom, out of the building, and they went running through the streets of the Gayborhood.

After running two blocks, with the open joy best expressed by the youngest among us, they stopped and sat on the pavement in one of the many small alleys in this part of town.

"That was fuckin' awesome, man!" Yandi was saying, as he pulled a pack of cigarettes from his rolled-up shirt sleeve, offering one to Eloy, who gladly accepted.

"I've never been to Puerto Rico, but my mom told me about the coqui. Man, I hope I get to hear them sing someday."

When they did return to the house, after spending the afternoon just wasting time and getting to know each other better, they sat together at dinner and later played video games together.

When the teacher approached them and reprimanded them about leaving class without permission, they tried to act like they cared. But in reality, that talk was meaningless to them.

And when it was time for bed, they already knew that they'd be holding onto each other all night.

If anyone thinks that there's anything wrong with two 14-year-old boys sleeping in the same bed, holding each other, and quickly learning how to explore each other, well, I beg to differ. I think it's one of the most natural, most beautiful things that could possibly happen.

Yandi and Eloy enjoyed each other that night, and for many more nights after that.

Young love. Fast, furious, fleeting. But not wrong. No, not wrong at all.

ELEVEN

May 27, 1987, was rapidly approaching. That date would fall on a Wednesday this year. And three very important events would be occurring.

You may have forgotten that Henry and I shared the same birthday. Yes, on May 27, I would be turning 29. *The final year of my youth*, I thought foolishly. Henry was already over 30. The year he passed into that new decade, I started calling him "old man" until he got tired of it. Okay, maybe I kept calling him that even after he got tired of it, until he let me know that he was *really* tired of it. So eventually, I let it go.

But even more important than our birthdays, this would be the *tenth anniversary* of Club Sanctuary. What an amazing accomplishment. Gay people can be notoriously fickle about where they choose to party, but our members remained loyal and I was so grateful for that.

Not every club in Philly lasted long. As one example, a lucky guy who won the PA lottery decided to open a gay bar, right on the outskirts of the Gayborhood. He named it "Bucks." Cool name, right? Multiple meanings, referring to men and money. Perfect location. But closed after less than a year. The place just never caught on with the crowd.

As we discussed plans for our birthday party, Henry gave me one of his looks before asking me, "Do you ever think about the old queers? You know, the ones who were around long before us."

By this point in our relationship, I knew better than to just blurt out the first thing that came to my head when talking with Henry. Because my first reaction would have been to say, "No, why would I think about them? Didn't they already have their time to shine?"

Instead, I paused to consider the question. Henry had a way about him, constantly teaching me new things, encouraging me to consider different perspectives. He was the best teacher I ever had.

"I admit, I don't usually give them much thought. They always seem to be on the outside of the crowd, if you know what I mean," I finally answered.

"Exactly!" Henry agreed. "We see them everywhere really, but they get ignored. All the time. Think about how that must feel. I think the last time we went to Cafe Coco, quite a few older guys were sitting at tables by themselves. You know they were queer guys. A few were sitting at tables together, but others just sat by themselves, eating, or sipping on a coffee or whatever."

"I hope we don't end up like that," I replied hopefully.

Once again, Henry looked at me, clearly pondering how our futures might look.

"We have a long, long time before we'd be in their shoes. But I have to wonder, are we missing an opportunity by not including queer seniors in our lives? They must know a lot of things that we don't know."

"I wonder if anyone will want to listen to our stories, when we're sitting in our rocking chairs, probably still listening to the same music we listen to right now, stuck in our ways, trying to vogue in the gay senior housing development," Henry continued, laughing.

It was funny to think about that, but I also knew that Henry had a point. He always did. But in reality, with the current pandemic killing our people in alarming numbers, I wondered if it was worth worrying about the future very much. Would we ever see our 40s? Our 50s? Our 60s? I had serious doubts about that.

Speaking of age, Henry told me that he wanted to invite Old Man Joe to our birthday party. Joe was probably the oldest guy who had ever come to our club. How old? Sixty, at least. Maybe even Seventy. Truthfully, I was afraid to ask him.

But Joe was an entertainer, unlike any gay entertainer I had ever seen before. Joe would put on little shows with characters that he called ThumbThings.

His catchphrase, when asked what his creations were called, was: "It's a ThumbThing...they're really thumthing!"

That line was always followed by his raspy laughter, as he did his best imitation of that stereotypical gay lisp.

Let me explain. This was at the start of the age of the personal computer. The Apple Macintosh had just been launched a few years before. There was no Internet. No email. No chat.

Business was mostly done on paper. Clerks were processing millions, if not billions of pieces of paper every year. And someone had to look through those papers.

So someone, somewhere, invented the rubber finger. Clerks would wear them on their fingertips, allowing them to quickly thumb through large quantities of papers, searching for whatever.

Old Man Joe used to be one of those clerks. But in his spare time, he started playing with the rubber fingers, first drawing funny faces on them, then adding small bits of cloth or other material, creating little characters. And those characters he lovingly referred to as ThumbThings, because he'd wear them on his thumbs and act out little skits.

Eventually, he started taking them to bars and he'd decorate them to look like customers, who'd buy one for a buck or two and have a fun little reminder of their night out. Tourists visiting Philly and exploring the Gayborhood were among his best customers.

Henry thought it would be fun to have Old Man Joe at the party, to make little characters as party favors for the guests. I agreed, since it seemed to be a fun idea.

We decided to have our birthday party a few days before the actual date. We didn't want our birthday celebrations to interfere with a more-important event. The 10th Anniversary at Club Sanctuary would also be an AIDS fundraising event.

By the end of 1986, there were 28,712 cases of AIDS reported in the United States. And an astounding 24,559 of those people had already died from the disease. That's a death rate of 86%. Think about that. 86% of the people who had been diagnosed were already dead.

And the deaths came quickly. To be diagnosed as positive was to be given a death sentence.

The Board of Directors meeting in April was predominantly about planning for the party/fund-raiser. We met at the Crystal Tea Room, on the 9th Floor of the John Wanamaker Department Store, at 13th and Market Streets in Center City. The setting was a bit more elegant than our usual diner or deli, but we had a reason for meeting there. We wanted to bring attention to what was happening in the LGBTQ community, which was being largely ignored by the government, politicians and other movers and shakers in Philly. And if they weren't at the Union League across the street, many of them would gather for lunch at the Crystal Tea Room. Or at least, their wives did.

ACT UP, the AIDS Coalition To Unleash Power, had just been officially started in New York City a few months before. Our friend, Darryl, who lived in NYC, was part of that organizing group, and he wanted to meet with us in Philly to discuss the goals of the group, with the possibility of opening a Philly chapter. He asked to meet with us before going to the meeting and that's when he presented each of us with a black tee shirt, sporting a bright pink triangle on the front along with the words "Silence = Death."

We made quite a scene when we appeared at the entrance of the grand showcase called the Crystal Tea Room.

We were met with resistance almost immediately. They didn't want to seat us, but finally relented when Henry insisted that we had a reservation and we would not be denied service.

Instead of talking about our upcoming fundraiser, the conversation centered around ACT UP and its tactics. Darryl explained that the idea was to be disruptive. To not allow society to ignore us. To demand that the government and pharmaceutical companies stop ignoring the deaths of gay people and start to do something for us. To demand equal treatment.

We were getting riled up. At one point, Darryl stood up, raised his fist high in the air and began shouting:

SILENCE EQUALS DEATH

SILENCE EQUALS DEATH

SILENCE EQUALS DEATH

We all stood up and joined him.

The police were there in 10 seconds flat. Apparently, the management of the Crystal Tea Room had already called them, as soon as we were seated. Once we became disruptive, the cops took hold of all 5 of us, the 4 Board members and Darryl, and forced us out of the venue, down the elevators and out onto the street.

I was shocked, but not surprised, at our treatment. Today, you might hear a slogan like "Silence Equals Death" and think, well, that's a nice slogan. But it was more, so much more than that. To remain silent, to hide, to allow our lives to be ignored by those in power, would be the death of us. I was determined to do my part to be sure we were not forgotten, not ignored, not discriminated against.

A few days later, the Board met again, and we did make plans for the upcoming fundraiser. At Jando's suggestion, the plan was to hold what would be called The Black and White Ball. He also came up with the advertising slogan: "Wear Black and White or Get Read!" Of course, getting read was when a queer would get called out for some sort of flaw. In this case, wearing something other than Black and White to the party.

Georgie came up with a cool idea. She suggested changing the text to say, "Wear Black and White or Get Read (Red)". That would essentially permit people to wear outfits with black, white, and red components. All of us loved the idea and the double meaning of read/red.

The poster was designed to show a gay male couple dancing, dressed in black and white outfits, with each wearing a bright red crown of thorns.

We unanimously decided that 100% of the proceeds would be divided equally among three AIDS organizations: The Philly chapter of ACT UP, which was just now being organized, the Sons of Oko, still dedicated to the care and feeding of mostly Black gay PWAs in North Philly, and Project Casa, a new organization that began working to assist with paying rent and other housing issues encountered by Latino PWAs, concentrating their efforts in the mostly-Latino neighborhood called Kensington.

Henry and I held our birthday party at our home on Sunday, May 24. We kept it small, subdued. Of course, all the Board members of Sanctuary were there. Jando brought his new boyfriend, Kirk. I never saw Jando so happy. It looked like he was ready to settle down and had finally found the right man for him

I had invited Carl and Karl, the two guys I had met at Sanctuary a while back. They were the ones who called things Karlicious and Carliffic. I saw them at the club lots of times, and I thought they were funny. And weird. And sometimes, I needed a little weirdness, if only for some comic relief. It was a coping mechanism for me.

***

As more and more members of the community were becoming infected, getting sick, and dying off quickly, people adopted strategies to not only cope with the misery, but also to try to avoid becoming infected.

Some people, probably more than I ever suspected, just dropped out of the gay social scene completely. Some of them stayed in isolation. Others tried to somehow "forget" that they were gay, thinking that they could turn themselves straight. Still others continued to have gay sex, but changed their approach to sexuality.

Chazz had a lover, Kendall, known to all simply as Ken. They were both Black, having met at Sharkey's, the mostly Black gay club in North Philly. About the time that HIV started to affect the gay community, Chazz and Kendall had already been together for three years.

Kendall was faithful to Chazz, and he thought Chazz was also faithful. But no.

Every two weeks or so, Chazz would take the subway from North Philly to South Philly, where he'd secretly meet up with Robbie, a white guy that Chazz had met shortly after he met Kendall. Chazz enjoyed his secret meetings with Robbie, and he didn't want to stop seeing him.

When Chazz first learned about the mysterious new disease, no one knew if or how it was passed from one person to another. There were so many rumors. Who knew what to believe?

But some people were saying it was best to not touch anyone. When Chazz showed up at Robbie's place, he told Robbie he wanted to be careful. Climbing into bed, instead of their usual bareback sucking and fucking, Chazz placed himself in the opposite direction as Robbie, so Chazz's feet were near Robbie's head and vice versa. Chazz started sucking on Robbie's toes and kissing, licking, sucking his feet. Robbie discovered that he liked that, and he was now doing the same thing to Chazz. As they worked on the feet of their partner, they played with themselves, slowly stroking, while still sucking, licking, sniffing feet. Robbie climaxed quickly. Chazz, well, even though this was his idea, he didn't enjoy it all that much. He wanted his fat throbbing cock to be buried deep in Robbie's pink asshole because Chazz just loved to fuck whiteboy ass. But now, he was afraid to.

Chazz went home frustrated that time.

Two weeks later, Chazz called Robbie to set up a date, telling Robbie he'd be there in an hour. Of course, Chazz never gave much notice. He had to sneak away when he had the opportunity.

This time, he had a different plan. He stopped at a drugstore on his way to meet Robbie, on his way to fuck Robbie's whiteboy ass.

Robbie was ready to suck on Chazz's feet again. He found it stimulating to be worshipping the feet of a strong, young, handsome, sexy Black man.

But Chazz told him, "No. That didn't do anything for me last time. I wanna go back like before and fuck you."

Robbie watched as Chazz took a box of latex gloves that he had purchased at the drugstore, pulling a glove onto each hand. Then he pulled out a pack of Magnums and told Robbie that he was gonna wrap Chazz's dick in the rubber condom, so Robbie would know it was in place. And then Robbie was going to lie face-down on the bed, lift his ass in the air, just like he used to do, and Chazz was going to fuck Robbie's hole, as if nothing had changed.

And that's what happened. Chazz got what he wanted. After he thrust his hardness into Robbie, who was on all fours on the bed, Chazz reached around Robbie and grabbed his nipples, pulling and tugging on them as he rode his whiteboy. Then he was slapping Robbie's milky-white ass, as Chazz watched his Black rod moving quickly in and out, in and out, in and out. Chazz loved to watch his cock like that, seeing it slide into a willing white guy's throbbing, sweaty hole. Chazz erupted inside Robbie, filling the tip of the condom with his streams of sperm.

This time, Robbie had no climax. He was horrified at what had just happened. He didn't know if it was safe to have anyone's cum shot into him, whether with a condom or not. And while he did like the way Chazz took a dominant attitude with him, he didn't like the feeling of being touched by someone wearing latex gloves. This was all too new for him. He hoped that this wasn't the future of gay sex. But he didn't tell any of this to Chazz.

Instead, when Chazz called him again two weeks later, Robbie just didn't answer the phone. Two weeks after that, the same thing. Robbie wasn't sure how he was going to cope with this new reality of having to think about being safe while having sex. He needed more time to figure out just what he was going to do.

A few days after his last sex session with Chazz, Robbie found himself wandering the aisles of the Adam and Eve adult bookstore on Arch Street, looking for a small vibrating dildo. He liked the feeling of getting fucked, preferably by a dick, but he thought it might be a while before that would ever happen again.

***

Likewise, many of us struggled to adapt to our new realities.

That's one of the reasons I invited Carl and Karl to our birthday party. They were always good for a laugh.

About a week before the party, Carl and Karl had been arguing. They had agreed on a mutual goal. They wanted to add some new words to the English language. And they wanted all of the new words to somehow include the name Carl. Or Karl. And that's where the friction started.

Although they weren't boyfriends, they quite often had sex together. One night, after spending hours drinking at Sanctuary, they stumbled back to Carl's apartment. They were both horny, starting to make out as they lay sprawled on Carl's sofa. Kissing passionately, tongues flickering in mouths, on necks, onto nipples, and heading downward, sniffing along that treasure trail that led to the promise of a creamy delight.

Stripped down to their underwear, Carl took Karl's hand and led him into the bathroom, into the shower, turning on the warm water as they continued grinding into each other under the rush of the spray. Karl stood directly under the showerhead, enjoying the warmth of the water as his soaking wet briefs clung to his asscheeks and his cock stiffened in the tight cotton manpouch.

Carl was oozing into his bikinis, pushing hard against Karl's gyrating ass, ready to penetrate the meaty mounds of flesh under his grasp.

He didn't pull Karl's briefs down. Instead, he reached under the leg band, pulling the briefs up and over to the right, so he could feel Karl's little pleasure hole with his finger.

Just like Karl's briefs were pulled to the side in the back, Carl pulled his briefs open, freeing his hot throbbing dick from its prison, positioning the wet tip at Karl's back entrance. And then he started fucking Karl, bareback. He liked watching his dick, wet and soapy, plunging into Karl, whose black briefs were soaking wet.

Carl erupted quickly, spilling his sperms into his buddy. Karl never even got the opportunity to pull his dick out, grunting with the animal heat of passion as his jizz filled the front of his briefs, oozing through the material before being washed away by the shower.

Carl leaned heavily against Karl, breathing hard, almost gasping from the ecstasy of the moment. He pressed his lips against Karl's neck and hoarsely whispered, "You just got Carled."

"Fuck yeah," Karl replied. You can Karl me anytime if you make my ass feel like that!"

Relaxing on the bed after they fucked, they talked about it. They decided they didn't know any word in the English language to describe the act of fucking or getting fucked in the shower while still wearing underwear. They agreed that it should be called Carling/getting Karl'd.

And of course, that's also when the disagreement began.

Carl thought that the act of fucking like that in the shower should be called Carling.

Karl disagreed, claiming that the correct spelling should be Karling.

Even worse, they couldn't agree on the naming convention for the passive part, the part where the guy got fucked.

Carl thought it should be spelled "Carled", adding an "ed", just like you add "ed" to get the word "fucked."

But Karl said that people might mispronounce the term if they saw it written that way, and say that someone got "Car-led." As in the car lead the parade.

Instead, Karl thought it should be spelled "Karl'd", so that it would be clear that Karl'd rhymed with snarled.

They argued about this for days, continuing the discussion at our birthday party.

While they argued, Old Man Joe jumped into the conversation.

"You two fight over the dumbest, craziest shit I ever heard," he admonished them, as he handed each of them a ThumbThing that sort of resembled each one of them.

"Ain't nobody gonna call getting fucked in the shower with your panties on getting Carled or Karl'd or nothing even close. They're just gonna call it wet fuckin', because that's what it is."

"We'll see about that," Carl said, slipping his ThumbThing on his thumb and play-fighting with Karl. "This could really take off and then we'll both be famous."

The conversation continued, with all of us joining in, tossing out terms that could be added to the dictionary. We zeroed in on changing words to "gay words."

Thunder brought up the subject, asking us what we thought language might be like if the world was completely gay. "I think we'd be living in the United Gaytes of America," he said, getting laughs from all of us.

"And of course, we'd be parking our cars in the gay-rage," (gay-raj) Bolt replied.

Jando jumped in, literally standing in front of Bolt, gyrating his hips, his dick just inches from Bolt's lips, saying, "Do me a gay-vor and suck my cock!"

"Eat my gay-nana," Bolt laughed, rubbing his crotch suggestively.

Henry, never one to be left out of a funny conversation, added, "Let's go to the park not today, but gay-day. As a matter of fact, every day would be Gayday. No more Sunday, Monday. It'd be Sungay, Mongay, Tuesgay…and on down to the gayest day of the week, Saturgay!"

"Instead of daycare, in our world, it's gaycare!" I called out. "And daytime is gaytime, obvo!

Carl and Karl, of course, were still stuck on Karlifying the world. "Let's light up the karlecue!" Karl told me.

"And I'll be making the carly fries!" was Carl's reply.

About a month after that party, I saw Carl and Karl at Sanctuary. Carl wore a tee shirt that said, "I got Carled in the shower" on the front.

Karl's tee shirt said, "I Karl'd him in the shower."

They had both gone to a store in the Bourse Building, located at 5th and Market Streets in Old City Philly, a very popular spot for tourists in the historic area, which had a store that made custom tees.

Wearing custom-made tee shirts became sort of a signature for Carl and Karl, who thought it was a cool way to get their ideas across to more people. Maybe they could change the English language.

***

The same night that Henry and I had our birthday party, there was another party going on in the Gayborhood. A completely different type of party. They called it "Gifting."

It's hard to explain something that you don't really understand yourself. Did you ever have a teacher who seemed to be confused by the material that he or she was supposed to be teaching to others? That's how I feel right now. Because I just don't understand how anyone could consider this to be a Gift.

The party was being held at the House of NEG. You remember the "No Elite Gays" group, who refused to wear white to the White Party. Original group members Lemon and Lime had been joined by new member Green Gay Grape at the White Party. Later, Agent Orange and Big Apple had joined, moving into the apartment, which was already crowded. Five gay guys living together, trying to build a movement based on rejecting the beliefs of those they considered to be the "elite" leaders of the gay community.

There was no real consensus in the community on what approach to take, especially at the time the pandemic began. The advice we would hear would be confusing and contradictory.

Abstain from sex. No touching. No kissing. No cock-sucking. No fucking. Fuck with condoms. No

148

swallowing. No deep kissing. No hugging. No kinky sex. No anonymous sex. Contact tracing. Anonymous testing.

While all that advice was enough to confuse anyone, there was one thing I thought everyone agreed on. That the virus was to be avoided. The methods might differ, but that was always the goal. Or so I thought.

Somehow, the NEGs, along with a few others, had decided that in order to be truly "gay", one had to have the virus. Now I understand that the word "gay" can mean very different things to different people. But I always associated the word with positive images. Fun. Dancing. Singing. Fashion. Make-up. Partying. Being Different. Being Queer. Community. Belonging. Chosen Families.

Never did I imagine that anyone would associate being gay with death and disease. Now, that's what the straight world was doing to us. But for it to happen from within our own community?

And yet, that's exactly what Lemon and Lime told me when they invited me to the Gifting Party. They explained that every guy at the party would fuck every other guy, or as many as he could before the well ran dry. No protections allowed. No condoms. No safer sex. Lots of cum, spit, even piss. If it was a liquid, they'd be taking it in the mouth, in the ass, anywhere and everywhere.

That idea horrified me. Scared me. Repulsed me. For any queer to knowingly try to give HIV to anyone else was beyond my ability to comprehend. Why would anyone want to do that to another person? But even more difficult to understand is why anyone would want to get infected and put themselves in a position where it was almost certain to happen to them. To this day, I have no answers to these questions.

I'm sorry to report that the NEGs were successful in their efforts. They "gifted" the virus to one another. They saw it as a badge of honor. I'm sorry, but I can't agree with that.

Everyone has some responsibility to keep himself safe. I think we also have a responsibility to keep others safe. To knowingly allow yourself to be infected with a disease, and to knowingly infect others, well, I consider that behavior to be disgusting and disrespectful.

All of them died. Lemon, Lime, the Green Gay Grape, Agent Orange and Big Apple.

I have a terrible time dealing with my feelings about that. They were young, gay men, with what should have been a long future ahead of them. Instead, their lives were cut short and I can't understand why. It was like watching a suicide in slow-motion. With no way to stop it or prevent it.

And part of me wanted them to stop spreading their dangerous message. I would have preferred that they just changed their minds and attitudes. But they chose a different path. I could only hope that no one else would follow their example.

TWELVE

"Business at the club is down about 25% from last year," Henry was telling me.

"That sounds like a lot. Are we gonna be all right?" I asked.

"We're okay for now. But we should cut back on some of our personal expenses."

"Okay," I agreed. "Right after we make a quick shopping trip to New York, to get our outfits for the Black and White (and Red) Ball. Right after that, we'll start trimming our expenses."

Henry sighed, knowing that it wasn't a good sign that I still wanted to shop in New York.

"Too bad Fiorucci's is closed," Henry said, knowing how much I adored shopping there in the past. "Remember that time we saw Andy Warhol in there and you screamed, 'Yo, Andy!' like you were best friends.

"I didn't scream his name," I countered, though we both knew it was true. What, I'm not supposed to get excited seeing Andy Warhol right there in front of me?

"That was a cool store," Henry continued, remembering fun times spent in New York City before we started making good money. We'd take the train up and spend a weekend, sometimes not able to afford a hotel room, but instead staying at the Y or even just getting a room at Saint Marks Baths. Or, if we did have a little extra, we'd splurge and get a room at the Holiday Inn not far from Times Square.

We spent the afternoon strolling along Seventh Avenue, also known as Fashion Avenue. I never got tired of looking up at the skyscrapers, almost getting dizzy, with huge crowds of people everywhere. So different than what I was used to in Philly. It was just in 1986 that the city began to allow buildings taller than Billy Penn's hat, which was located at the top of City Hall. Before that, buildings in Philly were relatively small in height.

We were lucky and found some fabulous outfits for the Black and White Ball without spending too much time shopping. That gave us some time for sightseeing, so we headed down to Christopher Street, in the heart of the Village, one of my favorite queer neighborhoods.

We stocked up on some cool tee shirts, a couple of books and magazines, and Henry couldn't resist getting some new leather gear for himself.

Our plan was to spend the night in the Meatpacking District, bar-hopping among the clubs catering to the leather crowd. Henry enjoyed the atmosphere in those places, and so did I. But I mainly enjoyed going wherever Henry went. Even after being married for more than a few years, I still liked to follow him around like a little puppy dog.

"I wonder what it's going to be like in these bars tonight," Henry said, as he was trying on a pair of leather chaps that he thought might be the perfect outfit for a night out at places like The Anvil and The Mineshaft, known for drawing crowds of men who were into kinky, anonymous, public sex.

Later that night, we were surprised to find that those bars had been ordered shut by the city. That was one tactic being used to try to stop the spread of HIV.

As we walked along the area, looking for a place to hang out, Henry told me, "You know, I don't like the idea of a place being shut down. But I have to wonder about the way guys act in those spots. I'm thinking we should close The Blackout Room in The Hole."

For those who don't know, The Hole is the leather/levi/bdsm bar located in Club Sanctuary and The Blackout Room was an area set off for men to do whatever they wanted. And what they wanted in there was to have open, anonymous sex with any dick or ass within reach.

I told Henry I'd think about it, but I already knew he was right. We couldn't call our club a resource for the gay community if we were in some way contributing to the daily horrors going on all around us.

I don't know how we ended up there, but somehow we were drinking in a pretty cool place called Uncle Charlie's North. They had a good crowd and we were having fun. Henry never had a problem starting up a conversation and we were chatting with two of the bartenders. I think their names were Colby and Jesse.[8] But I'm not 100% sure about that.

They acted like they were a couple. As in, lovers. You know that look that lovers have when they're together. Sometimes, you can just tell these things.

At one point, Henry was telling them about our club, Sanctuary, and he asked the two boyfriends if they would ever consider moving to Philly to work at our club. "Lots of good tips!" Henry said, smiling.

I don't remember Jesse's reaction, but a look of absolute horror was apparent on Colby's face.

"Philly?" he said, with such obvious disgust that I was a little embarrassed. "You couldn't pay me to live in Filthydelphia!"

---

[8] You can read more about the adventures of Colby and Jesse in *Dancing Before the Crash,* by C. C. Everill, Copyright 2021, available from Amazon.

Back in those days, that was a fairly common perception of our city. It was dirty. I can admit that. But back then, so was New York. So, I really didn't think he had that much room to talk.

Jesse quickly moved to ease the tension, explaining that Colby was in New York for acting and singing opportunities, and assured us that they really didn't have anything personal against Philly.

But that was okay. I understood. Coming from a small town, I loved Philly and considered it a big city, as well as a safe place to be openly gay. At least, it was safer than the white-bread suburban area that I came from.

And to be honest, Philly residents always had an inferiority complex when it came to New York. We really couldn't compare with the Big Apple's size, scope, and glamour.

We chatted with those two handsome young men, wishing them well when we decided to head out and look for somewhere else to continue our night of drinking.

Before we left, Colby, the more handsome of the two, again apologized for calling Philly "Filthy."

"I actually visited Philly once, and it wasn't all that bad," he said as I laughed.

"That's okay, sweetie, it's already forgotten," I said, while air-kissing both of them. Then Henry and I were on our way, enjoying the never-ending sights and sounds of the largest city either of us had ever visited.

If I could meet Jesse or Colby today, I'm sure that neither one of them would remember that conversation. I only remember it because of that complete look of disgust and horror on Colby's face at the thought of living in a city that I loved. Those kinds of things stick with you, I guess.

***

The night of the Black and White Ball. May 27, 1987. My 29th birthday. Henry's 32nd birthday. And the 10th Anniversary of Club Sanctuary.

But before we went to the club, Henry had a surprise for me. I always loved his surprises. I had grown accustomed to receiving lavish gifts, and I was sure that Henry wouldn't disappoint.

As he handed me a very long box, he said, "Happy 10th Anniversary, sweetcheeks," a name he sometimes used when he was penetrating me, calling me nasty names that got him all hot and sweaty along with the rather nice term of "sweetcheeks."

The box was very long and had the logo of Bruno's Florists, which I knew to be the most glamorous and expensive floral shop in Philly. I just knew that roses were in that box, and maybe some diamonds as well.

I tore the box open, and I admit, I probably looked greedy while doing so. I should have known better. Henry didn't like that side of me, and he tried to get me to change, but we all know that roses and diamonds are a girl's best friend, right?

"What the hell is this? You're joking right?"

Inside the box, there were no roses. No diamonds. No jewels of any kind.

I pulled out another box, almost as long as the first one, and waved it in Henry's face.

"Reynolds Wrap aluminum foil? That's my gift? What the fuck?"

"Tenth-anniversary gifts are tin or aluminum. It symbolizes the strength of the marriage. In this case, it symbolizes the strength of our work for the community at the club," Henry explained.

155

I wasn't happy. Not with this crappy gift. I didn't care what it meant.

"But there's more," Henry said, smiling that devilish grin of his that always made me want to kiss him, to taste him, to serve him.

"Look inside."

"Holy shit, you go all out for a girl, dontcha?" I said, as I pulled a small figure out of the box. Yes, it was a ThumbThing, a tiny rubber finger. Actually, there were a few of the rubber fingers attached together, dressed in tin foil, my very own little Tin Man from *The Wizard of Oz*.

I had to laugh. Henry could be funny and I knew a good joke when I saw one.

And while I enjoyed laughing with Henry at his jokey present for me, I couldn't help but think that he better do a helluva lot better when it was our real wedding anniversary.

Finally, it was time to get dressed for The Black and White or be Read (Red) Ball, as in what happens when one queen reads another. As we all know, those scenes can get pretty ugly, very quickly.

I was going dressed as Billy Idol in his "White Wedding" video. Spiky, platinum blonde hair. Red lipstick. Black eye shadow and mascara. Black leather pants. Black boots. Black leather vest with a red stripe on the back, just for fun. And to top it all off, I was carrying a white electric guitar slung over my shoulder. I did my best Billy Idol sneer and Henry nodded his approval.

As Henry dressed, he asked me for the thousandth time, "Are you sure people understand that the acceptable colors for tonight are black, white and red?"

"Yes, darling," I told him, "that's why we put the word 'red' in the slogan and added some red to the fashions on the poster. Remember?"

156

Henry looked sexy while he wore probably the most iconic outfit of the 1980s. His outfit was an exact replica of Michael Jackson's look in the "Thriller" video. Although he refused to wear a wig to match Michael's style, he did have the same make-up. That gorgeous red and black jacket, with the padded shoulders and the striped accents. Tighter than tight red leather pants. Black shoes. And the only white in the entire outfit were those white socks. I thought he looked fabulous.

Although business had been suffering at the club for the last few months, the turnout for the Black and White (and Red) Ball was more fabulous than I could have imagined. Lots of folks who had been hiding away, trying to avoid any possibility of being infected, were ready to venture out for a good cause. And when we ran a fundraiser, it was 100%. Every dollar earned that night went straight to help AIDS organizations. The only exceptions were the tips made by the bartenders. Some of them opted to contribute some or all of their tip money, but it wasn't required. They needed that money for their living expenses.

As soon as we got there, Henry and I climbed up to the DJ booth. I felt my emotions rising as I watched the crowd partying below. First, it reminded me of old times. Times that were more carefree than today. Second, a sea of gays, lesbians, their friends and allies all dressed in some combination of black, white and red, made an impressive sight. And to see all of those people united for a good and worthy cause. That took my breath away.

"Look at Kirk and Jando over there," I said, motioning in their direction for Henry to see. They were dressed all in black, looking like Ninja warriors.

"That's Javier there with them! It's good to see him finally out of jail!" Henry called out, waving to try to get their attention.

Kirk had invited everyone from the Gay Veterans Support Group, and a few of them, five if I remember correctly, were in wheelchairs. I was glad that we had learned about the importance of providing accommodations.

Many of the party-goers had opted to dress in formal wear. Black tie. White tie. *Was there an option in formal wear to dress in red tie?* I wondered, spotting one very handsome young man in a red tux with studded rhinestones. He sparkled as he walked through the crowd, looking very pleased with himself and drawing lots of attention.

Thunder and Bolt put on a magnificent show of music and lights. They played nothing but hits, from the present day to years past, when the disco era first started and I had this crazy idea to try to open a club.

There were no speeches that night. No trying to convince anyone of anything. We all knew why we were there. Brochures about resources and testing sites, free condoms and lube were all provided. But this was a party and we let it go on, feeding on its own energy as the crowd delighted in having the opportunity to just have fun.

Fun. It was like I had almost forgotten that it's fun to be gay. And while we do face adversity, and sometimes tragedy, I never wanted to forget that core concept, my basic belief that it's somehow a special privilege in life to be gay, lesbian, and all the other queer identities.

I went over to Henry, took his hand in mine, leading him down to the dance floor where we carried on like old times. It was one of the best nights of my life.

158

The chaos of the party reflected the chaos of the times. With thousands of people in attendance, even my practiced eye took some time to notice the finer details of what was happening that night.

The blonde boy in the white loincloth caught my attention. White loincloth, white bikini briefs, white sneaks. That was the outfit. On him, it was perfect. His sleek body was just made for showing off. He looked to be 18, maybe 19. Although not legally allowed inside our club according to the laws of the Commonwealth of Pennsylvania, I wasn't about to judge him or check his credentials. I understood his need to connect to the community, even at such a young age. Maybe especially because of his age.

No makeup. No jewelry. He was a vision of male beauty in its most simple form. Purely natural.

From what I could tell, he was there by himself. No group of friends. No older man preying on his youthful innocence. I wondered what he was looking for.

He found a seat at the bar. When he sat, facing the dance floor, he spread his legs open wide, allowing any interested guys to see what he was clearly displaying. I watched as he pulled the loincloth up, the better to expose more of those briefs, bulging at the pouch with the promise of a huge treasure inside.

His gaze at the sight of so many men, dancing, preening, cruising all around him, seemed passive, uninterested. It was almost as if he was looking above the crowd instead of at the crowd. Their displays were going unnoticed.

Three young, equally handsome Asian guys were dancing in a group, just off to the side of the blonde boy. They were dressed alike, and their looks were even somewhat similar to the blonde guy whom I had already

159

nicknamed Snake. Because I knew a big snake when I saw one curled tightly into the pouch of some white bikinis. After all, I was married to Henry.

Those three Asian dudes each wore angel wings, attached to their bodies with straps around their arms, cotton briefs, socks and sneakers. No shirts, of course, proudly displaying their tight, taut, lean, lithe bodies, now glistening with just enough sweat to make them even sexier.

One wore an all-white outfit. The other, all-black. The third, all-red. I started to think of them as *Charlie's Angels*, but when I couldn't remember all the names of the characters or actors on that TV show, I had to select different names for them. Naturally, I gave them names that would be easy for me to remember. One was Charlie; one was Angel. The third was Farrah, because I did remember the name of one star, Farrah Fawcett. I mean, who could ever forget her gorgeous hair?

Those three boys danced their asses off as DJ Thunder made the transition from the Whitney Houston hit "I Wanna Dance With Somebody" to "It's Raining Men", sung by The Weather Girls. Incidentally, did you know that The Weather Girls were originally called Two Tons O' Fun, and sang back-up for disco legend Sylvester?

I watched as the angel dressed in red, the one I called Angel, made his move on the boy in the loincloth, Snake. He jumped from the dance floor, which was a few inches above the ground, onto the floor, making a beeline for Snake. Not shy, Angel leaned against the bar, looking to order a drink, while placing his bare leg firmly between Snake's bare legs, grinding against Snake's package, which I could see was growing in size, even from where I was perched, high above the floor in the DJ booth.

160

Just minutes later, Snake and Angel were dancing, grinding rhythmically, in perfect harmony with the beat of the song. It looked like they had been dance partners for years, instead of two guys who had just met five minutes before.

Watching these two young men do that oh-so-familiar gay mating ritual on the dance floor, you know…meet, dance, makeout, dance a little more and head out for some type of sexual adventure, did my heart good. In those two boys, I saw hope for the future of the gay lifestyle. Because if we ever became too afraid to meet, to mingle, to *have sex*, well, how would gay culture survive?

They didn't stay at the party for too long. Snake wanted to spend some "alone-time" with this young specimen, whom he found attractive, sexy, alluring. And Angel was in a slight hurry to explore the packaged meat that Snake had so readily put on display inside the club.

Two young, attractive gay men, walking through the Warehouse District, clad in their undies, one wearing angel wings. But in this area, on this particular night, there were many gay men out in costume, so these two didn't really draw any particular attention to themselves.

Until they stopped for slices of pizza. There was a window where they could order take-out, but instead, they went inside and found a table.

"You can read, right?"

"What?"

"Look at the sign, dude," yelled the kid behind the counter. "No shirt, no service."

"Really, Andy? You're gonna throw me outta here for not wearin' a shirt after that blowjob I gave you last week?" Snake shouted, making sure everyone could hear.

Although no one in the shop would actually be *offended*, they did take notice that maybe a bitch slap fight was about to begin, something that many of them would enjoy watching.

"Oh, so that was you gaggin' on my thick piece of meat, your eyes waterin' so bad you damn near choked to death?" came the reply from Andy. "I almost didn't recognize you without seeing the back of your head between my legs, slurpin' on me like a pig."

At that point, both Andy and Snake were laughing, as Snake walked over to place his order, giving Andy a quick kiss on his cheek. Those two already knew each other and all that was just for fun.

"We'll take those to go," Snake told him. "Wouldn't want you to get into trouble with the management and block your career path!"

Arm-in-arm, laughing, stuffing pizza into their mouths as they headed for the exit, Snake and Angel were just having a good time.

Of course, Snake and Angel were the nicknames that I had given them. One of my old habits, naming people whom I didn't really know.

The blonde boy in the loincloth was named Byron, but everybody called him By. The angelic Asian boy was named Tran, which is exactly what everybody called him.

Tran lived in a large building at 11th and Race Streets, one block south of Vine Street, very close to the club. It was too large to accurately be called a rooming house, though it offered rooms for rent. Not even full rooms, though. They were more like sleeping cubicles, with enough space to store a few items of clothing and some personal items such as soap, toothpaste, a hairbrush. The bare essentials.

The first 6 floors were reserved for females, with floors 7 through 12 occupied by males. Mostly Asian, though not all. The common thread was that everyone here was

162

poor, most struggling to make ends meet. Everyone coming in here hoped it would be for a short time, temporary, but there were some long-term residents.

Tran took By up to his cubicle on the 12th Floor. He could have had a beautiful view of the city if he had any windows. But no. There were no windows.

They stayed just long enough for Tran to pull on a pair of pants and grab a shirt. The next stop was By's building, at the corner of 10th and Pine Streets, located in a courtyard. The only view from By's room was the courtyard. Not much of a view to brag about.

Once By and Tran left the party at Sanctuary, my attention turned towards others. But after I noticed they were no longer at the party, I fondly remembered the joy of being gay that I felt while watching them. The recent events, with so much disease, sadness, suffering and death, couldn't be forgotten nor ignored. But my chest swelled up a little as I watched those two, clearly attracted to one another, unafraid to meet, to be together, to have fun.

And it was a night of fun for both of them. After dressing in more appropriate attire than walking around Center City in their briefs, they headed down South Street in the direction of Penn's Landing. They found a comfortable spot right there along the Delaware River, a little surprised to see boat traffic at that time of night, but it did make for a beautiful, relaxing sight.

Removing their shirts, using them like blankets as they lay on the grass, they enjoyed the feel of the cool, river breeze brushing against their bodies.

Tran was resting against By, leaning into his chest, as they both gazed towards Camden, New Jersey, the city just across the river from Philly. He reached for a long weed, sprouting seeds at the top, pulling the stem from its roots and using the silky part of the plant to brush lightly against Byron's sensitive body. First, lightly playing against By's cheeks, his nose, his lips. Moving farther down and tickling By's nipples, watching them tighten as By laughed and moaned ever so slightly.

Tran watched as Byron opened his pants, allowing his new friend to gently tickle his hardening dick with the tip of the plant, producing new and exciting sensations for By to enjoy.

Tran saw and then felt the hardness, as he rubbed his body suggestively against his new friend. Tran was excited too, wanting to feel that hardness inside him. His mouth, his ass, either or both would make Tran a happy guy.

By didn't disappoint. Right there on the lawn at Penn's Landing, above the hard concrete of the main walkway, Tran reached down and into By's trousers, seeing and feeling the thick meat, pulsing with veins, getting harder with each passing second, opening his mouth to swallow that monster whole.

"Take your time, babe. I like getting' my balls licked first," By said, guiding Tran's actions so hopefully they'd both have maximum fun.

Before long, both of the boys had pants open, sucking, licking, sniffing each other without a care in the world.

"Do you swallow?" Tran managed to ask when he took a quick break from the oral action.

"I will if you will," was the reply.

And so they continued, grunting, groaning, panting, whispering to each other, fondling balls and fingering asses, till each one exploded in orgasmic ecstasy into the other's mouth.

Not at all sure if what they had just done was safe or not, they held onto each other for another hour, enjoying the male companionship, the beautiful night, and the sweet, salty taste that each of them had left in the other.

Just before dawn, they headed back to the Gayborhood, where they reluctantly went their separate ways, promising to keep in touch.

***

I didn't notice him at the time, because the club had been packed and I couldn't possibly notice everyone, but a young guy named Mark was at the Black and White Ball. He was a college student, attending Temple University, taking classes in the College of Education. It was the end of May, 1987, and he had just finished up his freshman year.

Living in the dorms at Temple, and studying to be a teacher, Mark thought it best to keep his gay lifestyle quiet. He made many friends during that first year, spending most weekend nights attending house parties, getting drunk, dancing, you know, the kinds of things college kids do for fun.

The one problem was that all of his classmates were straight, and Mark was trying to fit in with them. Despite that, Mark knew he was gay, and he knew about the clubs, about the Gayborhood, about the gay cruising areas in the parks. He knew all about that. He was going to participate in that. And somehow, he was determined to keep all that from his straight friends.

On the night of the Black and White Ball at Sanctuary, Mark strutted out of his dorm in the gayest fashions he could afford. Hair gel kept his streaked-blonde hair in the spiky fashion of the time. For extra effect, he had sprinkled glitter in his hair and was wearing mascara to enhance his eyes. Black slacks with flared legs contrasted with his white silk blouse, the one that was so far out of his price range that he had to empty his bank account to purchase it. A long string of white pearls hung casually around his neck, matching the clip-on pearl earrings. His black dress shoes with the square toes had heels just a bit higher than most straight men would wear.

His roommate tried to ignore Mark as he got dressed and put on his make-up and jewelry. His roommate had been trying to ignore Mark for the last 4 weeks.

"You can call me *Pearl*," Mark snapped to his roomie when he was about to leave. His roommate never even bothered to look, to know why Mark said that.

Mark went out to Sanctuary that night and had a fabulous time. He loved being gay. He loved going out to the club. He loved to dress up, dance, have fun, particularly if he was having fun with some adorable young queer guy. Another one just like Mark.

I guess you're thinking that I'm confused because I'm telling you that a young closeted college student just got dressed to go to a gay ball, walking out of the dorm without trying to hide his queerness.

Well, no, I'm not confused at all. That's exactly what happened. How? Why?

Four weeks ago, Mark and two friends were talking about housing arrangements for the following year. Their sophomore year. They didn't want to keep living in the dorms. They thought of dorms as freshman territory. They wanted to share an apartment, giving them more freedom, without having to deal with what they considered to be stupid, ridiculous University rules about what they could and couldn't do in their own rooms.

Mark thought about this for a long time. He did want to live in an apartment. Maybe that would mean he could bring guys home with him. You know, for sex. To fuck.

166

But he'd have to have his own bedroom. And he didn't want to have to sneak guys in and out of the apartment.

So, he decided to tell these two friends his secret. Just those two. No one else had to know. But he thought it would be impossible for him to share an apartment with two good friends and still try to hide his identity.

Four weeks before the ball, Mark asked his two friends to join him for lunch downtown. *In the Gayborhood*. His two friends agreed. They just thought of it as a trip to Center City. They had no idea that this part of the city was queer-friendly.

They went to Hasty Tasty, a local queer-friendly deli. A favorite hangout for queers of all ages, sizes, shapes, genders and colors. Mark had no intention of being coy. He had to be sure his straight friends, with whom he had spent most of the past year, their freshman year at Temple, would be cool with this.

The three young men sat at a booth. Lunch was ordered and quickly brought to the table, as the discussion centered around the new apartment they would share the following year.

"What do you think about this area?" Mark asked. "For an apartment, I mean."

His two friends didn't say anything at first.

Finally, one of them suggested that they think about it, but that they might also consider moving to South Philly, which would be cheaper.

"Before we make any final decisions, I just wanna tell you guys something," Mark said, suddenly getting nervous. He had thought about this moment for weeks. *It was now or never*, he thought.

It occurred to him that after he told his secret, maybe one, or even both of his friends, might also reveal that they were gay, too. Mark thought he noticed that one of them would look at him a little too intently when they were deep in conversation. Did he sense some sexual attraction, some sexual tension, between them? He thought that he was about to find out in just about a minute.

"I'm…"

His friends were giving him the oddest look. But it was too late to back down. He had to do this. He knew that he was going to take that huge step for any gay person. The moment when they first come out to someone they know.

He blurted it out. "I'm gay."

Continuing quickly, he said, "I have to let you know. I can't be roomies with you if you don't know. And it has to be okay with you."

He relaxed when his friends told him it was okay. He remembered one of them saying, "It'll be all right."

When he would tell the story later, he couldn't remember any other details. He was so relieved. He could be gay, just in front of these two friends, and he could live in an apartment and his secret would be safe. He wondered why he had been so worried. Coming out could be easy!

The next day in class, he immediately knew that something was wrong. The classmates who normally sat next to him during lectures took different seats. Friends who would usually say hello, or pat him on the back, or who would just treat him like another human being, were suddenly cold and silent.

He was confused, but just for a moment.

His two friends had spread the word. It had never occurred to Mark that he would have to tell them that he only meant for them to know that he was gay. He wasn't ready for everyone to know. He assumed that his secret would be kept confidential.

168

His friends didn't see it that way. They couldn't wait to get back to campus, telling everyone they knew.

"Mark is gay."

"Did you know? Mark's a queer."

"Yes, Mark. He's a faggot. He told me, that's how I know."

And as the news spread, more and more people told even more people.

To put it simply, Mark was shunned for the rest of the semester. Not just by classmates. But by people who were supposed to be his *friends*. Including the two he had told originally.

He was never sure if they were lying to him when they said that everything would be all right. Maybe they were okay with the news and thought that everyone else would be too. And then when they got a negative reaction from their other friends, they simply jumped on the bandwagon against Mark.

Or maybe they knew all along what they were doing. Pretending everything was okay while right there in front of "the faggot," only to go back to campus to spread what they thought of as the ugly news. One of them, one of their group, was a queer. A homo. A fag.

It took a little time for Mark to adjust to his new reality. At school, he became a loner. That first day when he came out to his "friends", he went to dinner at the dining hall. He sat at the same table where he had sat, chatted with, joked with and generally just enjoyed sharing a meal with his friends for an entire school year. But that day, he sat alone. The people he thought of as friends were suddenly sitting together at a *different* table. The message was loud and clear, though no words were spoken.

No queers allowed.

169

Although Mark was aware that some people hated queer people, this time that hate was aimed directly at him. He struggled to understand why. He had never done anything to any of them that might be considered offensive. So it was clear to him that he wasn't being hated for anything he did. He was being hated for whom he was.

If any other student in the College of Education was gay, they didn't share that information with Mark. It would have been nice if someone would have come along to help him deal with and process the feelings of betrayal and isolation. But no one did.

That's why Mark flaunted his queerness when he left the dorm for the party at Sanctuary the night. It was partly a defense mechanism, partly defiance, and partly pride in himself.

By the night of the ball, Mark knew that his time at Temple University would have to end soon. He didn't want to be known as "the queer teacher." He didn't think that would be safe for his career. He decided that he would try to live a double life. Queer when not at work. Straight, or at least straight-acting, while at work, teaching.

He wouldn't be able to do that in Philly. All those future teachers already knew about him. He knew that some of them would go on to become principals, supervisors, teacher-mentors, maybe even faculty members at Temple. Not only did they know about him, but he also realized they would never forget. He might be denied advancement in his chosen field. He might get fired from his position. And all of that would be perfectly legal.

By the night of the ball, Mark had already decided. He had applied to Boston University. He had already been accepted. He would move to Boston, and he knew that he would never reveal his secret to anyone working in the

170

field of Education. He already knew what could happen. He refused to take that chance. He would be silent about his social life while at work.

On the day he left Philly for good, he took the train, leaving Philly's 30th Street Station, heading through New York City and on to Boston. Departing Philly, the train slowly made its way past the Museum of Art, past Boat House Row, and through some of the neighborhoods, possibly neighborhoods where Mark might have found a career teaching.

The thought that ran through his mind, over and over and over again, was:

Fuck Y'All! Why the fuck did you have to tell? What the fuck did I ever do to you to deserve that treatment from you? I FUCKIN' HATE YOU!

***

Another party, another huge success for Club Sanctuary. More importantly, a lot of money was raised that would be distributed to organizations devoted to the care and treatment of PWAs.

When Henry and I got home after the ball, I was still feeling playful. As in, you know…horny. Feeling that itch, just like a bitch. Hahaha!

While Henry gathered up some snacks and drinks for us to enjoy as we settled in for a movie, I headed for the bathroom to prepare myself. No, not like you're thinking.

I took my anniversary present with me. Remember the roll of aluminum foil? So, after removing my Billy Idol costume, I put on a new thong, color bright red, that I had purchased and saved for a special occasion. Like this one. Then I took a large piece of the aluminum foil and carefully wrapped it around my head, like a turban. Think

171

Marlene Dietrich or Greta Garbo and you'll understand the look I was going for. But instead of glamorous fabrics, my turban was aluminum foil! I was laughing, looking at myself in the mirror, thinking I looked more like some crazy guy trying to repel laser rays from an alien rather than a glorious queen from a bygone era.

So, that gave me another idea. I took some more of the foil and fashioned two pieces into something resembling antennae. You know, like on the head of an insect…or an alien from another planet. Quickly, I found some tape and attached the antennae to my headpiece.

I checked myself out in the mirror, front and back, thinking I was looking both fine, with the thong accentuating my hot ass, and ridiculous, with my little alien headgear.

Henry was on the sofa, munching on some chips, when I emerged from the bathroom.

"Beep…beep…beep! Danger Will Robinson, Danger! Danger!!" I said in my deepest monotone, while swinging my arms wildly, just like the robot on that TV show, *Lost in Space*.[9]

Henry almost spit out his chips, laughing at my silly antics. I tried to keep a straight face.

"Danger, Will Robinson!" I said again, turning and bending over, showing a view of the "full moon."

At that, Henry was right behind me in an instant. Still dressed in his "Thriller" outfit, I could feel him getting hard as he was grinding his hips into me, pushing me down, bending me into a position where my ass was high and my head was low.

---

[9] Lost in Space was a TV show that aired on CBS from 1965 to 1968.

He started pushing against my tight hole with his fingers, as I heard him start to breathe more heavily. "Searching for Area 51!" he whispered, as he continued to probe into me. "Coming in for a landing!" he said, pushing the head of his big beautiful uncut cock right at the landing strip for Area 51.

That's how we liked it. Fun. Yes, sex could be fun. It should be fun. Even now, in the midst of turmoil, we are determined to have fun.

Later that night, Henry was in bed, when I crawled in and snuggled next to him. And we performed what had become a ritual, a routine, for us.

"Good night, Henry. I love you!"

"I love you too, babe!"

And then we both drifted off to sleep.

THIRTEEN

Edward felt that it was important for him to understand the concept of beauty. That was one of the first things he told me about himself when we met.

In 1990, I decided to take a class at the Community College of Philadelphia. The campus was located near Broad and Spring Garden Streets, not far from Club Sanctuary, which was just a few blocks east in the Warehouse District. Since it was so close to work, I figured I could take a class in the early afternoon, then head over to the club.

The course was titled Personal Growth and Development. My interest in the topic came from a few friends who had attended weekend seminars called est – Erhard Seminars Training, which combined elements of Buddhist philosophy with the techniques of Dale Carnegie about winning friends and influencing people.

I wasn't quite sure what effect est was supposed to have on people. My friends, after returning from the training, had developed the habit of carrying around daily journals, where they obsessively recorded every action they took and had somehow developed the odd habit of continually telling their friends that they were "fucked up." Without providing any details, of course. No suggestions for a course of action to take. Just tell your friends, "Dude, you're so fucked up," and then walk away. Weird.

Of course, there's nothing wrong with keeping a journal. I think it's healthy, and there have been times in my life when I had the self-discipline to maintain one regularly. However, that would usually end after a few months, much to my regret now, as I try to remember the details of my life.

It seemed to me that many people who attended the est seminars may have missed the point of the training. They didn't seem to be winning friends. And the extent of their influencing people seemed to be centered on recruiting other people to attend est seminars.

When I told Dane, a relatively new acquaintance, shortly after the White Party, that I wasn't interested in going to a seminar, he suddenly wanted to spend much less time with Henry and me. Instead, he decided to hang with all his new friends – graduates of the est program, of course. It all seemed just a little too cult-like to me.

The last time Dane spoke to me about attending a seminar, I asked him if it was true that attendees weren't allowed to go to the bathroom. For the *entire weekend.*

"Yes, that's part of the training." He said that so matter-of-factly, like it wasn't at all weird for grown adults to have their bathroom access restricted. For me, that was the end of any consideration about est. No one, and I mean no one, was going to tell me when I would be allowed to use the bathroom facilities.

That's how I found myself seated in a folding chair, in a classroom at CCP, awaiting the instructor. Edward came and sat next to me, immediately introducing himself.

The course ended up being mostly a waste of time and money. I wanted to develop some perspectives and techniques for self-improvement, but I didn't learn anything that I didn't already know. At least I was one credit closer to whatever it was I wanted to attain by taking these college classes.

After every session, Edward invited me to the school cafeteria for a light snack before he went on with his day and I went to the club to prepare for the evening. And that's how I learned so much about what Edward wanted because he never got tired of talking about the subject of beauty. Or of talking about himself.

I'm not sure Edward ever got to know much about me. I was the passive listener, which wasn't my normal role, but I was fascinated by what Edward was sharing with me.

He started by telling me about a class he had taken recently called "The Philosophy of Beauty." There, he had learned that the heart of the issue was whether beauty was subjective or objective.

If you believed that beauty was subjective, then the adage that "beauty is in the eye of the beholder" would apply. It was all a matter of opinion.

On the other hand, if you felt that beauty was objective, then it could be measured, and beauty could be achieved by reproducing its objective proportions. For example, a certain ratio of eyes to nose to mouth could be reproduced to achieve a state of beauty.

It was during our second or third after-class meeting when Edward confided to me that he believed that he was ugly.

Yes, that's the exact word he used. "Ugly." And he explained to me that he wanted to confront his condition head-on, so he didn't want to use euphemisms such as "unattractive" or "plain" or the ridiculous word "unlovely."

I didn't know how to respond. I didn't want to agree with him and I didn't want to disagree, either. So, I silently nodded and tried to maintain a look of neutrality. But I did take a careful look at his face, wondering how to judge this person.

He didn't have any obvious feature that made his face disfigured. No huge scar or cleft lip or anything of that nature.

As I was thinking about his face, he started to share some of his experiences.

"I went to a family reunion, years ago. I guess I was 5 or 6 years old. I heard my aunts talking to my mother about me. First, they teased my mother about not feeding me enough, since I was very skinny as a young boy. Then I heard my Aunt Kathleen say, 'He has such beautiful eyelashes.' At the time, I was quite pleased with that remark. To the point where I still remember it to this day. But it was years later when I realized that if the only compliment my aunt could give was about my eyelashes, well, what did that say about the rest of my face?"

I stared down at my plate, hoping that was a rhetorical question. Indeed, Edward answered his own question.

"It meant that she couldn't even bring herself to say that I had a nice smile, or cute dimples, or pretty eyes, or anything. Just my eyelashes."

I cleared my throat, as if I had something to say, but in reality, I was drawing a blank. The entire conversation was getting awkward.

Luckily, he stopped talking about his personal experiences to talk about beauty in general.

"I can't figure out what beauty is," he said. "I know it when I see it, but I can't define it. For example, I'll see a guy who, in my opinion, is gorgeous and he'll have big, wide, expressive eyes. Then I think that being beautiful involves having eyes like that. But maybe later I'll see another guy, also totally beautiful, who has eyes that are small and set quite close together. So I can't figure out what it is about eyes that make them beautiful. Do you know what I mean?"

To be honest, he had a point. To my eye, beauty came in all sizes, shapes and colors. I nodded and smiled.

"Look at your smile!" Edward almost shouted, seeing another opportunity to discuss this problem he was trying to solve. "You have beautiful straight white teeth. That seems to be a fairly common trait in beautiful people. But your lips are thin. And your mouth is beautiful. Then why do I see other guys with plump lips who are also beautiful?"

I had no answer. But I did take note of the fact that both of us were drinking coffee and smoking cigarettes at the table. It alarmed me that my beautiful white, straight teeth were being yellowed at that very moment.

When I got to the club that day, I used the office phone to call and make an appointment with my dentist for a cleaning and bleaching. Was I being vain, shallow? Or was this just good hygiene and proper dental care? I wasn't sure, but I wasn't taking any chances, either.

I don't remember every anecdote Edward shared with me during those sixteen weeks that we attended class together, but I can recall a few highlights.

One week, he was obsessed with the idea of fairy tales that focused on beauty…and its opposite. Ugliness. I have to get used to saying that word without feeling oddly uncomfortable.

"You know Beauty and the Beast, right? Sure, the Beauty fell in love with the Beast, but then he went back to being beautiful. What's the point that we're teaching children with that story? That ugliness is a temporary condition? What if it isn't? Why didn't the Beast stay ugly and still keep the Beauty? I'll tell you why. No one wants to hear a story where the ugly person is ugly forever and still manages to have a happy life. That's why!"

I was stunned. I never had an answer for Edward. He asked me so many questions and I just had never looked at the world through his eyes. I had never even considered such things.

"And how about that Ugly Duckling story? Sure, it was an ugly baby. But it grows up to be a beautiful swan. Again, we're teaching kids that ugliness is temporary; it can and will be outgrown. But that didn't happen to me. I was an ugly child and now I'm an ugly adult."

I felt an incredible sadness and I saw that Edward's eyes had gotten misty with tears.

He leaned in close to me.

"And I'm gay," he whispered. "Do you know what it's like to be ugly in the gay world?"

I couldn't ignore that statement. I reached over the table and took hold of his wrist.

"I'm gay, too," I assured him.

Edward had a funny look on his face as he freed his wrist from my grasp.

"Joey, I know you're gay. I know you own Club Sanctuary. Everybody knows that." He was looking at me directly in the eyes. "I just wanted to be sure you knew that *I'm gay*," he said, emphasizing those last two words. "But our gay experiences have been very different, don't you think?"

I felt like I was being accused of something, though that wasn't Edward's intention. And no doubt, our paths had been very different. I was married to Henry, a beautiful, young, strong Black man. I had sex pretty much whenever I wanted and with anyone I wanted. I didn't think Edward could make the same statement.

One night, I noticed Edward at Club Sanctuary. I was up in the DJ booth with Henry and DJ Thunder, casually watching the crowd below. I pointed Edward out to Henry. "That's the guy I was telling you about. The one

179

who only talks about beauty all the time. And he thinks he's ugly."

Henry gave him a quick look. "He looks like a beady-eyed beaver. He's right. He is ugly."

In my state of drunkenness, along with being high after smoking a blunt, I just laughed at Henry's statement. Later on, I would feel sorry about what I did. But that was my initial reaction. To laugh at a mean comment about a person who had opened up to me about his feelings. I'm not proud of my behavior. To be honest, I'm ashamed to even have to admit what I did. And I was really surprised at Henry, who was usually much kinder and more considerate of the feelings of others. But I guess he figured it was okay to tell me the truth. He would never say anything like that directly to Edward's face.

At a later date, Edward told me that was part of the problem. People would talk about him behind his back, but generally avoid the question of his looks when speaking to him.

Naturally, it was Edward who was consumed with thoughts about his appearance. Other people might not talk about it because it wasn't even in their thoughts. I suggested that to Edward.

He paused, considering my suggestion.

"Sometimes, that might be true. But let me give you a few examples of what I'm talking about."

He described being called into his boss's office one time to discuss his job performance rating. His supervisor went over the form, generally giving Edward a good evaluation. But then his boss said something.

"I have this theory that good-looking people have an easier time with everything, including this job. Think about Adam, the one in your department. Now there's a good-looking guy, you know what I mean? It always seems that Adam has an easier time making a sale than Ed…"

His boss stopped in mid-sentence, suddenly aware that he was talking to Edward, while using Edward as an example of an ugly man who had to work harder than a handsome man.

Edward was keenly aware of what had just happened. Apparently, his boss had told this story many times, maybe hundreds of times, always citing Edward as the example of the ugly guy.

His boss tried to cover it up, but the deed had been done. Although he had an excellent performance review, Edward's day had been ruined. He left the meeting feeling dejected, humiliated, and de-humanized.

Near the end of the semester, as our class was coming to a close, Edward shared his love for the Broadway musical, *The Phantom of the Opera*. He told me that he had gone to see it in Philly, at the Forrest Theatre on Walnut Street. He had been lucky enough to get front row center seats in the balcony, which he considered to be the best seats in the house.

He had two tickets, but the seat next to him remained empty throughout the show. Edward had the other ticket in his pocket. He didn't even ask anyone to go with him. He wanted a beautiful date, a piece of eye candy, but he didn't know anyone fitting that description who might accept an invitation from him.

"My date got sick," he told the gay couple who would be sitting in the next pair of seats, making his status as a solo attendee even more painfully obvious. The couple ignored him completely.

Edward's eyes lit up when he described the story of the Phantom, which of course I already knew. Henry and I had also seen the same show, but on a different night.

"You know, I feel like the Phantom, sometimes. He's deformed and is driven mad by his desires for the beautiful lady he adores. But he only has to wear a mask to cover part of his face. He isn't naturally ugly. He sings that there's an infection that caused part of his face to look ugly."

"But he wants to make the girl his prisoner," was all I could think to say.

"Yes, but what if he never got that infection? I think he could have been a wonderful vocal coach and lived a happy life. Although I love that show, I'm still looking for a story that tells about people like me. People who are born ugly, stay ugly their entire lives, and have to deal with it."

"You aren't really that ugly," was my weak reply. I regretted saying it immediately.

"You have no idea what it's like for me. You'll never understand," Edward said in a voice barely above a whisper. I saw that his hands were trembling with emotion and I was sorry that I had upset him.

"The Phantom wears a mask sometimes. I have to wear a mask *all the time*. Not a physical mask, of course. But an emotional one. I have to hide my feelings. I refuse to let people know how much they hurt me."

After our last class session, we again met for our usual meal. Though I sometimes tried to change the subject, Edward was determined to tell me everything about his obsession with beauty and his feelings about how he was perceived as being ugly.

"A few years ago, I decided to work out and improve my body," he told me.

I understood. Lots of men went to the gym. Lots of gay men seemed obsessed with trying to build the perfect male body.

182

"It actually worked and I had muscles for the first time in my life."

He saw that I was looking at his body somewhat skeptically, so he explained.

"I thought it would make a difference in how people treated me. But one day, I was walking on South Street, near Jim's Steaks. You know that area?"

I nodded. Of course, I knew the area.

"I was just walking along, doing some window-shopping, minding my own business. And do you remember when I told you how much it would hurt when people ignored me or made me feel invisible?"

I nodded again, wondering where he was going with this.

"I'm just walking along South Street," he repeated, "actually feeling pretty good about the way my body looked. That was the only time that working out had ever given me good results. And then a random guy, someone I had never seen before, walked up to me and said. 'You look just like that guy in *Beetlejuice*. You know, the one with the shrunken head.'"

"No one ever said that to you," I protested.

But Edward insisted it was true, telling me he felt like he was always in a lose-lose situation. He didn't want to be ignored, but he also didn't want to be noticed. Not like that, anyway.

That observation from a random stranger, that his head was too small for his toned body, caused Edward to give up on going to the gym.

Edward wasn't finished. "You want to know what the worst part is?"

He didn't stop to give me time to answer, because he was determined to tell me.

183

"The worst part is that I'm just like everybody else. I worship beauty. Especially gay male beauty."

"I do, too!" I offered.

Edward continued, saying "When I first realized I was gay, I was happy. I thought of gay people as young, beautiful, and cool. Somehow, I thought that by being gay, I would automatically be young, at least for a while, but surely I'd be beautiful and cool. But it just didn't turn out that way."

I understood his thinking, though it was illogical.

"And just like all the other gay guys who worship at the altar of the beautiful, I'm right there with them. You know I don't have a boyfriend, right?"

I didn't know that for a fact, though I had made that assumption.

"I could have a boyfriend if I'd settle for an ugly guy. But I can't do it. I only want pretty boys. So as much as I hate being rejected for my looks, I do the same thing to other guys. What's wrong with me?" he lamented.

"I spend hours in front of the mirror, trying to figure all this out." Edward was saying. "When I look at myself, I know I have some flaws. But I don't think I look all that bad. And then over and over and over, guys tell me, sometimes right to my face, that I'm ugly. And all the hotties pretty much ignore me. Or they hook up with me and then the next time I see them, they pretend that they don't know who I am."

I had no answers to give Edward. I tried to offer support by listening to him. I understood his problem and his pain, but I was at a loss for offering solutions.

"I'm so jealous of the beautiful people. I don't want to accept who I am…what I am. I want to be pretty too!"

I stood up from my chair and offered the only comfort I could. I gave Edward a hug. A long, warm, strong, friendly hug, meant to convey understanding and support.

"I won't be coming to any more classes here," he informed me, as our time together was drawing to a close. "I'm going to start spending all my extra money on my looks. I'm gonna start with braces for my teeth, which I should have done long ago, and then get plastic surgery, as much as I can afford, to fix as much as I can."

I didn't remain friends with Edward. He made no effort to reach out to me later, and I didn't seek him out either. Maybe he had shared too much of himself with me. Maybe I just couldn't take more of his conversation, which was always about himself. Yes, he had problems. We all do. Sometimes, you just have to let people go, to deal with things the best they could.

That's how I thought about Edward. I hoped he would find what he wanted. I hoped he would find happiness. Maybe he would even become beautiful after his surgeries. I would watch his progress, but from a distance. Somehow, I thought that was better for my own emotional health. At least, that's what I told myself.

FOURTEEN

Invisible.

That's what straight society wanted us queers to be.

When I was a kid, I think queers were invisible. The straights had won the battle. I never saw any type of LGBTQ person represented anywhere. Not in the movies. Not on TV. Not in books, magazines, or anywhere else. Of course, people in the various media were queer. They just weren't identified that way.

It was so bad that when I was reaching sexual maturity, I didn't even know what it meant to be gay. I knew I was different, but I didn't know how or why.

And I didn't have the vocabulary to describe what I was feeling. Or who I was. I also had no one to talk to about any of this.

But when I finally did find out that I was gay, and exactly what that meant, I was never ashamed. In fact, I was happy that I could finally identify myself, and I felt a real kinship with other gays.

From the beginning of my life as a gay person, I felt…special. I still do. Not that I think that gay people are superior. But we are different, and I think we're different in a good way. Maybe because we look at the world differently. I'm not sure.

But I can tell you one thing with certainty. If someone offered me a "cure", a way to change to be straight, I wouldn't want it. I like being different. I like feeling special. And I like being queer.

There are countries in the world, right now, in the present day, where I've heard some leader in that country proudly proclaim something to the effect that "We don't have any gay people here!"

I call bullshit on that. Whether the LGBTQ community in that part of the world is truly invisible, after being persecuted to the point of fearing for their lives, or if the government just controls the media to the extent that LGBTQ people are kept invisible from the public eye, I know that they are there.

We are everywhere. We always have been. We always will be.

And we may have to struggle, to fight, to bang on that closet door until we are finally heard, but I think that we will always find a way to let ourselves be known. When we are not known, invisible, hidden away, the world is less bright, less loud, less FUN.

Even during times of relative acceptance, not everyone gets to enjoy that visibility. Individuals experience things differently. We all know that, but sometimes, we have to be reminded.

***

April 8, 1990. A sunny, spring-like Sunday in Philly. Henry had been pushing me for months to go get tested. I made up excuses time and time again. He was getting impatient with me. I was running out of excuses. But I was still nervous, afraid, and couldn't be persuaded.

We found ourselves walking in the area of Broad and Race Streets. At the corner, on the east side of Broad, was a decrepit old building, with a pizza shop on the ground floor. We stopped in, sat at a booth, and Henry reached across the table, took hold of my hands, holding them tightly as he caressed my fingers.

He tapped on my wedding ring, a reminder of our illegal ceremony at the club, almost 10 years ago.

"Do you remember what it says in there?" he asked, "What I had inscribed on the inside of your ring?"

I looked at him with a mix of fear and wonder. I started to feel nervous, although there was no real reason to feel that way.

"Of course, I remember. It says 'Henry and Joey. We Are Family. Dec. 25, 1980.'"

"Family," Henry replied. "Does that word mean anything to you anymore? A family is supposed to be there for each other. Supposed to show love. Supposed to work through problems together."

"What are you trying to say?" I asked.

"You're being selfish," was the reply.

Those words hurt. Henry and I had been through a lot together. I couldn't remember ever hearing him call me "selfish" before.

The look on my face told Henry what I was thinking.

"Babe," he whispered across the table. "We can't go on forever not knowing. *I* can't go on forever not knowing."

I nodded slowly. I knew he was right. And letting my fear become an obstacle to knowing my status…our status…wasn't good for either one of us.

"There's an office on the third floor of this building," Henry told me, still rubbing my hands in his. "They do testing there. We can go up right now. Javi's waiting for us."

My eyes lit up. Javi! It had been a while since the last time I saw him.

Javier was our friend. He was also a nurse. Way back when Henry and I had first started dating, we met Javi at the hospital where Henry had been taken after catching a disease called anaplasmosis from a tick bite. A tick bite that occurred during a tubing trip down the Delaware River that I had talked Henry into.

Later, Javi had gotten into some trouble with the law, spending a few months in one of the city jails, and it was during that time that Javi thought he had become infected with HIV. And although he was poz, he wasn't showing any signs of his infection developing into full-blown AIDS.

The prison sentence ended his career at the hospital, but he was a good nurse and was now working at a clinic that catered to healthcare for gay men, including HIV testing and counseling services.

And we were seated in the ground-floor restaurant of the building that also housed the clinic where Javier worked.

"You're a sly one!" I said to Henry, who laughed.

"So, come on. Let's do this!" Henry said, tugging at my hands.

I could already feel my heart pounding. But I stood, and we headed for the stairs, where we could climb to the third-floor clinic.

Putting on a brave face, I stood before the door of the clinic, knowing my life could change in an instant, depending on what happened inside. Henry opened the door, wrapping his arm around me in a protective embrace as he ushered me inside.

We were the only people in the reception area. No receptionist, no line of people waiting to be helped, no one filling out forms as they tried to decide whether to provide their real name or not.

Of course, as he always did, Henry had already taken care of everything. He made a special appointment, just for the two of us. Total privacy. Completely discrete.

I heard a high-pitched squeal coming from the other room…

"Gurrrrrrl! C'mon over here and let me get a good look at you!"

I already knew that voice. Javier. My favorite nurse in the entire world.

But I wasn't quite ready for what I saw when he came out of the inner office to join us in the reception area. It looked like Miss Javier hadn't missed a meal since he got out of jail. He had gained at least 50 pounds. Maybe more.

I tried not to look surprised, but I'm not always good at things like that.

That didn't stop Javi from embracing me, then Henry, then me again.

Realizing what was going through my head, Javi explained. "I know what you're thinking. The gurl is fat. Right?"

Well, when he put it like that, a smile crept across my face, breaking into a laugh.

"Well…" I said.

"You don't hafta tell me. I got eyes, you know. But it's my sugar. It's been actin' up lately and that's when all this extra weight comes on," he explained, referring to his Type 1 diabetes.

"The doctor called me the O-word the last time I went in for a checkup."

I didn't have to be told what he meant. The O-word. Obese.

If anything, I had expected that he might be skinny as fuck, since I did know that he had HIV. We all suspected that occurred while he was in jail, seeking comfort with his cellie.

We spent a few minutes catching up, as Javier shared the good news that he had a new lover.

190

"And he's a doctor, sweetie! Can you believe I got me a doctor?" He was excited and rightly so. You're supposed to be excited and happy at the start of a new relationship. With luck, that feeling of excitement wouldn't go away any time soon.

Javier then turned to the matter at hand, suddenly becoming very business-like and serious.

"You're both sure you're ready to take the step? I know you've been puttin' it off, especially YOU," he said, jabbing me in the chest with his index finger.

"We are ready!" Henry assured him, pushing me in the direction of the examination room.

The actual test wasn't difficult at all. Just drawing a little blood. The next part was the problem. The wait.

"Come back next Sunday, same time. I'll be here, ready to give you the results."

Then the waiting began.

Back home, Henry was watching a rerun of Soul Train, which the local station in Philly played on both Saturdays and Sundays. We both liked watching the Black guys dance. If you never saw the show, well, they knew how to move! Especially during that famous Soul Train line dance. Sexy! I still remember when some of the dancers would carry these gigantic combs and picks, acting like they were fixing their hair as they danced down the line. Funny, but true!

After the show, the local news, followed by the national news. I didn't follow the news as closely as Henry, but he insisted it was important to know what was happening to understand the world around us.

***

I looked up to see if anyone was in the room with me. If anyone was listening to me. The blinds were pulled tight, blocking out any sunlight that may have been there. I heard a rustling sound, so I assumed that I wasn't alone.

"Did I ever tell you about Ryan White?" I asked.

"I think you mentioned him briefly a little while ago. But I don't really know that name. Tell me about him."

***

Ok. Henry and I were watching the news the same day we took our first HIV tests. And that's when we heard that Ryan White had died that day. April 8, 1990.

Ryan White was a hemophiliac. That means that he bled easily, sometimes uncontrollably because of a medical condition that kept his blood from clotting properly. And if he bled too much, he needed to get blood transfusions.

During one of those transfusions, he was infected with HIV. He was only 13 years old when that happened.

You might expect that his community would show some sympathy and support for a young teenager who was basically given a death sentence. Remember, there was no cure. No effective treatment. Instead, he was met with outright hostility from his community. The people of Kokomo, Indiana. I wonder how those people feel today. I wonder if they feel any shame or regret about their actions.

Ryan was denied entrance to his school. Court battles went back and forth. Parents argued and fought over this young boy, despite doctors' assurances that he posed no risk at all to other students. When he was re-admitted to school for one day, half the students in the school stayed home.

After Ryan was harassed unmercifully, including being called a "queer", and having a bullet shot into the family home, Ryan's family moved to another town, where the people were more educated about HIV transmission and he was able to resume his education.

For 5 years, Ryan served as a spokesperson for HIV educational and fundraising efforts. And today, April 8, 1990, we heard the sad news that he had died.

Fear and ignorance seem to be a constant presence in the lives and even the deaths of some people. On at least 4 different occasions, in the first year following his death, Ryan's grave was vandalized. Do people have no shame?

***

The following week seemed like the longest week of my life. In one way, I wanted to know the test results. I wanted to hope for the best. But there was another part of me that didn't want to know. If I was poz, how would my life change? How quickly would it all come to an end?

What about Henry? What if he was poz? What if we both were? Even worse, what would happen if we found out that one of us was poz and the other wasn't?

Of course, we weren't the only ones facing these questions. Every queer man who had any kind of sex with another man had to wonder. Did it happen to me? If it did, who gave it to me? Did I spread it to someone else? So many questions. Many of them unanswerable. But we were on the verge of answering two of the most pressing questions of our day. Positive? Or negative?

The night before we were set to return to the clinic, I kept thinking it might be my last Saturday night to really enjoy myself. I went all out, getting dressed in what I call "casual fabulousness," which that night meant black stovepipe pants with a belt that matched my Gucci loafers, a cream-colored silk chiffon blouse, with puffy sleeves and foulard collar, fabric tied casually at the neck and flowing freely with my every movement.

And then, looking casually fabulous, I proceeded to get as drunk and as high as I could. It had been a minute since I got so totally trashed, but I didn't know what tomorrow might bring, so I was going to have as much fun as possible, and for me, that meant getting drunk, getting stoned, and dancing the night away.

As tired as I was by the time Henry and I got home, I couldn't sleep. Tossing my clothes on the floor, I got into bed next to him, naked, hard, horny and scared. I clung tightly to him, my husband, my love, hoping against hope that somehow, through all our fucking around, all our orgies, all the cum both of us had taken, that somehow, by some miracle, we might be spared the death sentence.

In the meantime, Henry slept peacefully. I stirred him awake, just long enough to whisper in his ear, "I love you, Henry!"

And he whispered back, in a voice that made me wonder if he was talking in his sleep, but at least he said the right words, "I love you too, babe."

***

Nothing that happened the next morning mattered to me. All I could think of was *Today's the day that determines my fate. Our fate. I don't believe in you, Jesus, but if you're out there, it's okay if you help me out just this one time.*

I didn't want to turn to religion. I hadn't done that my entire life. I didn't want to do it now. But there I was, hoping for Jesus to save me, to save us.

Henry tried to calm me down, but I wasn't having it. This *thing* that scared me so much, frightened me to my core, could become my reality this afternoon. And in the back of my mind, I understood that I wasn't anyone special. No one deserved to be positive or negative. It wasn't something that was earned. This just so happened to be a virus that was transmitted through activities that gay men often engaged in. But even with that understanding, I couldn't help but hope that we'd receive some good news.

"Hey bitches!" was the greeting that we got as soon as we saw Javier at the clinic.

"Or, more exactly, hey my HIV NEGATIVE BITCHES!!"

I almost fainted. "Are you serious? Really? We're both negative?" I asked, with a sense of relief cooling my concerns.

"Yeah, babes. The test doesn't lie. We did the saliva and the blood test. Both tests negative for both of you queens."

Henry was smiling ear-to-ear. We hugged. We kissed. We jumped up and down. The three of us, encircling our arms together in joy.

That's when it occurred to me. We shouldn't show that kind of joy. Not in front of Javi, whom we all knew was poz.

"Don't even try to not be happy," he chided me, sensing what I was thinking. "This is a happy day. No question about it. Don't worry about me. I got this under control. And now that I got my new man, well, my life right now is pretty fuckin' good."

***

The next day, Henry asked me to go for a walk with him. We headed for South Street, stopped for a soft pretzel with extra mustard at The Pretzel Factory, and then he guided me down Third Street. Into the area called Queen Village. We turned left on Queen Street. The two-hundred block of Queen Street.

The first thing I noticed was how quiet it was. No street noise, like up in Center City. A large Catholic church was on the south side of the street, taking up a lot of space in the middle of the block. A neighborhood park, Mario Lanza Park, was directly across from the church. That meant that there were very few actual houses on the block.

"What do you think?" Henry asked me.

"It's pretty here," I replied. "Why?"

Just then, we were standing in front of a trinity, also known as a father-son-holy ghost house, because they had three floors. Henry pointed to the "For Sale" sign in the window, with the phone number of a well-known realtor hand-written on the sign.

"Whaddya think? You wanna make an appointment to see it? Maybe we can put in an offer?

I looked at him, not sure what to say We had never discussed buying a house before.

"Well, now that we have a bright future ahead of us, maybe we should think about really laying down some roots…since we're both negative, you know."

I thought about it for roughly two seconds. "Let's do it!"

196

FIFTEEN

Living in Queen Village was a new experience for me. In some ways, it was like my hometown. Quiet. Peaceful. There were even a few families living in the area, something you didn't find much of in Center City Philly. At least not in the 70s and 80s.

But it was also different than my old hometown. First, the area was integrated. Black and white people lived side-by-side in this area which covered just a few blocks. I never noticed any racial frictions. Henry was a member of QVNA, the Queen Village Neighborhood Association, so he would have known if any problems were being reported.

As we settled into the house, things seemed to be busier than ever for us. We invited the Sanctuary Board to visit the house, a sort-of small housewarming, before our regular monthly meeting in September 1990. There was a lot to discuss.

It seemed like our schedules were more packed with events than ever. And while the parties continued at Sanctuary, with business picking back up close to the levels we were at before all the death and misery, we were also involved in all sorts of AIDS-related activities.

Georgie, our lesbian member of the Board, had recently been named as the Director of WFA – Women Fighting AIDS, whose mission was to provide direct services to Persons With AIDS (PWAs). At that time, AIDS was primarily a disease striking the gay male community, so it was important and appreciated when our lesbian sisters got involved with us.

Alejandro, our main event planner, was in a state of constant motion, planning and coordinating many major events, both at Club Sanctuary and for various organizations throughout the city. He spent a lot of time in Kensington, a neighborhood with a large Latino population, which was being devastated by the pandemic.

Henry, my husband, had his hands full managing Sanctuary, but somehow he still found the time and energy to work with the Sons of Oko, which had the Black gay community as its focus.

Our team at Club Sanctuary was preparing to participate in AIDS Walk 1990, an annual 5K event that raised hundreds of thousands of dollars benefiting all types of organizations in Philly. Henry had designed the tee shirts for our team this year, which featured a drawing of a broken heart on the front, with a few drops of blood dripping down, with the names of our fallen co-workers written inside each drop. I cried when I saw the names BJ, Lonnie, and others who had been lost prematurely, and who could never be replaced.

The design on the back simply featured the words "Team Club Sanctuary."

Lots of organizations and clubs had teams of walkers banding together to raise money for a good cause. But not everyone at these events joined a group.

Jack spent his life, up to this point, living in the closet, afraid he might lose his job if he let anyone know he was gay. But at the same time, he wanted to help, feeling compelled to do something to help gay people in need. He signed up for the Walk, but he didn't ask anyone for donations. He sponsored himself, promising a $100 donation for completing the 5-kilometer walk starting at Eakins Oval, in front of the Art Museum, going up East River Drive and then turning back on West River Drive (later re-named Kelly Drive and MLK Drive) and ending right back at the Art Museum.

198

On the day of the event, he arrived by himself, signed in, and waited with the crowd for the walk to begin. As they started to walk, he could feel the energy of the crowd, as so many people had gathered together for the event. And though he felt like he was part of the group, he also felt alone. He didn't speak to anyone, and no one spoke to him. At the end of the walk, his legs feeling rubbery, he somehow found the strength to walk to the closest bus stop, and quietly rode the bus home.

The next day at work, he was surprised when one of his co-workers mentioned that he'd seen him at the AIDS Walk, and complimented him for his participation.

"Didn't you see yourself? Channel 6 showed you walking on the news last night. It looked like you were having fun, with all those people all around you. If you do it again next year, be sure to hit me up for a donation."

That brought a smile to Jack's face. Not only did he participate, helping people who badly needed it, but he had been recognized and complimented for his efforts. He couldn't help himself; his chest swelled just a bit with pride in himself. And if someone at work was willing to donate, maybe Jack would be able to form a team for the next year. That day, he felt a renewed sense of purpose and pride. Maybe he didn't need to hide as much as he thought.

***

To say that The Mural Arts Program is an important institution in Philly would be a major understatement. Founded in 1984, Mural Arts began as part of the Philadelphia Anti-Graffiti Network. Street artists were recruited to help the city change the landscape of the city by transforming bare walls of buildings into works of art.

There are thousands of murals throughout the city. Not all of them speak to me directly, but hopefully, each one has an appeal for some group of people. Many of them I love. Others I look at and wonder what was the thought process that went into that. Now I'm no art critic, but I know what I like.

During the Sanctuary Board meeting in September 1990, Henry informed us that the Mural Arts Project was interested in painting a mural on the outside of Club Sanctuary. We agreed in theory that it was a great idea, but we insisted on having input into the theme and the design of the mural.

I felt this was personal for me. After all, I owned the building. I had created the club there, of course, with the help of Henry and the other Board members. The last thing I wanted was a bland, meaningless mural greeting our customers.

"I want two things to be very clear in the design," I told the Board members. "First, it has to be gay-positive. Maybe a tribute to a gay pioneer. Maybe something more abstract, but I kinda like the idea of paying tribute to some individual."

"I'm with you 100% on that," Henry said, as everyone nodded their agreement.

"And a statement. A very clear statement about who we are."

Again, all the members indicated their agreement.

Not long before we were presented with this idea of having a mural on the face of the club, Henry had insisted that I read one of his favorite books. *Giovanni's Room* by James Baldwin was first published in 1956, but it had been new to me. And my reaction to reading the book was to be astonished at the artistry and the beauty of the prose, and the way the story touched me personally.

"Does anyone here know about James Baldwin? The author of *Giovanni's Room*?"

"Yes, yes, yes!" Georgie and Jando said in unison, as Henry sat there smiling at me with admiration.

We decided that the details of the design could be left to the artists, but that the main focus of attention would be a huge portrait of James Baldwin.

"What about a statement? Any ideas?" Henry asked.

I spoke up immediately. "I've had a mantra going through my head for two or three days now. I don't know where it came from, but I just started hearing it over and over in my head. And somehow, it's been a comfort to me during these rough times."

"What is it?" Henry asked, since I hadn't told him anything about it before.

"Every day is a good day to be gay," I replied. "For some reason, through all this shit we've been going through, that thought has helped pull me through. What do you guys think about it?"

For a few seconds, there was silence. *Was I the only one who thought it was a statement of joy, of positivity, of healing?*

Henry was the first to break the silence. "That's beautiful!" he said, and I thought I saw his eyes misting.

"Well look at Miss Poetry over there!" Jando said, laughing in a way that I knew meant that he loved it.

Georgie sat there, literally clapping her hands together.

"All together bitches, let's hear it, loud and clear for all to hear!"

"Every day is a good day to be gay!"

"Every day is a good day to be gay!"

"Every day is a good day to be gay!"

I felt more empowered in that moment than at any other time in my life. I could feel the love from my friends as we chanted those words that had become magical for me.

"Every day is a good day to be gay!"

It wasn't lost on us that we were taking a risk with the decision to feature James Baldwin on the mural. I have to remind myself that not everyone might be aware that James Baldwin, who died in 1987, was a Black man. A gay Black man. But part of our mission at Club Sanctuary was to be as inclusive as possible, trying to avoid the self-segregation that was still evident in so many gay clubs, even in 1990.

And as the author of one of my very favorite books, I couldn't think of anyone better to honor with a mural on our property.

The Mural Arts group worked quickly once we gave them the general idea. We were presented with several sketches and we selected one that featured a huge portrait of James Baldwin on the left, with the dates of his birth and death under the portrait, August 2, 1924 - December 1, 1987.

On the right side, there would be pictures of writing instruments, various types of pens and a typewriter, and books with covers painted in the colors shown on the Gay Pride flag. Some of his well-known titles would also be shown there: *Go Tell It on the Mountain*; *Nobody Knows My Name*; *The Fire Next Time*; *If Beale Street Could Talk*; and *Giovanni's Room*.

And of course, the phrase that had become my personal mantra would be written across the top of the mural: "Every Day is a Good Day to Be Gay."

Work on the mural began the day after the Sanctuary Board of Directors approved the design.

***

Henry and I spent many days walking around Center City, often spending hours within the small confines of the Gayborhood. We constantly ran into friends and would spend hours socializing, usually frequenting the LGBTQ establishments.

One day, as we walked along Lombard Street, on the block between 13th and Broad Streets, Henry stopped at a brown building, acting like he wanted to say something, but not quite finding the right words. I looked over his shoulder and saw the sign, Morris Animal Refuge.

"Are you thinking what I think you're thinking?" I teased.

"Let's check it out," he suggested.

I was willing to consider adopting a pet. We had space in the new house, a park a few steps from the house, and the time and energy needed to provide for a new member of the family.

"What kind of pet?" I asked. "Goldfish, maybe? A bird, like a parrot? A little parakeet? A hamster?"

We were laughing as we walked into the building. Heading towards the counter, I was stunned by the beautiful creature working there.

Beautiful creature. That was my exact thought. I wasn't sure he was human. It just seemed impossible for anyone to be that fucking beautiful and still be human.

Tall, taller than average. White, in a shade of pale that seemed like he was never touched by the sun. But not a sickly pale. His flawless skin seemed to almost sparkle. Blonde hair. Cobalt blue eyes. Perfect chin. Lucious lips.

Gleaming, straight teeth that I thought looked like an orthodontist's dream. And that was just above the neck.

The body, though hidden by the tightest of tee shirts and even tighter black jeans…well, anyone could tell he was perfect. And just before we approached him at the desk, he bent over to pick something up off the floor, showing the roundest, fattest, most perfectly masculine muscular ass cheeks that any god could have created.

At that sight, Henry squeezed my hand hard. I knew what he was thinking.

"What's your pleasure?" he asked us, grinning that evil type of grin that would let anyone know that this guy was all about sex.

Neither Henry nor I said anything for what must have been an uncomfortable amount of time.

"Like really, how can I help you guys?" he asked again, in a voice that dripped with masculinity.

I was watching his lips move, but his words seemed to drift away, completely meaningless. My head was in a state of lust that I was having trouble shaking off, trying to regain my focus.

Henry came out of his reverie first, managing to say, "We'd like to see your dog…your hot dog…your big dog…" His voice drifted away and then he suddenly came to his senses.

"Oh, please excuse us," he told the creature. "We're here to take a look at your dogs. We're thinking about adopting."

"You're in the right place, then," Mr. Man of Every Queer's Dream replied.

My mind was racing. You know how I like to assign nicknames to guys. He looked Scandinavian to me. *Dutch Boy? Sven? Thor?*

"Let me introduce myself," Mr. Scandinavian Hottie was saying, as he pushed open the door to where the animals were kept. "I'm Dagen. But my friends call me Dag."

Henry elbowed me as we walked behind Dagen, sticking out his tongue and making a licking motion as we both watched Dag walking slowly and sensually before us.

"And I'm Henry. We appreciate your help," Henry replied, reaching for and shaking Dagen's strong hand.

"This is my boy Joey," Henry said, introducing me. I already knew that if Henry introduced me as his "boy" instead of as his husband, that Henry was interested in inviting the dude back home for a threesome. It had been quite a while since I had been introduced to anyone as Henry's "boy."

"Take a look at these cuties," Dag said, pointing to an enclosure where a mama was feeding 4 tiny babies.

"Oh wow, they're so cute!" I exclaimed. "What kind are they?"

"Boston Terriers. They're so cute. I love their markings, with the black and white face and those white areas around the neck and on the top of the head," Dagen told us.

Opening the enclosure, Dag reached in to take hold of one of the tiny puppies. At just 4 weeks old, they were too young to be adopted yet, but Dagen explained that we could reserve one now and take him or her home in another 4 weeks.

As the gate opened, one of the pups turned from his mama, ran out of the enclosure and started running around the room as fast as his tiny, wobbly legs could carry him.

"He's high energy already, running around with the zoomies earlier than most do," Dagen said, laughing.

"Zoomies, huh? I didn't know dogs acted like that. Will he always run around wild like that?" Henry asked.

"No, he'll calm down. And of course, puppies have a lot of energy, but they also spend a lot of time sleeping," Dagen continued, telling us more about this Boston Terrier breed.

"I like him," I said. "And I think the zoomies sound cool. I think we should reserve him right now," I said to Henry. "And I want to name him Zoomie. But maybe spell it Z-u-m-i, Zumi. It seems more exotic that way."

Henry and Dagen both laughed at that, agreeing it was a cool name and fit this little guy perfectly.

"If you're serious about it, I need to get some information from you. We do a background check before anyone adopts from here, to be sure they can provide for the puppy properly," Dagen told us.

"Any problem with gay people adopting a puppy?" Henry asked, opening the door for an invitation a little later in the conversation.

"No problem at all," Dagen replied. "We usually find that guys like us make perfect pet parents."

That sealed the deal. Dag, the gorgeous Scandinavian, had just identified himself as one of us.

After filling out a short questionnaire, Dagen assured us that he would make sure that we could adopt Zumi in four weeks, as long as our application was approved. Then, arrangements were made for Dag to come over to our place at 7 PM that evening.

Shortly after the AIDS pandemic began, Henry and I had agreed that if we were going to play with others, we would only play together, never separately. There were a few reasons to do that. First, if one of us got too carried away in our passion and was tempted to do something "unsafe", then the other could put on the brakes.

We also thought that four eyes were better than two. It was known that some guys would promise to wear a condom while fucking ass, only to secretly remove it and cum in their partner's ass. We could avoid this despicable action if one of us was watching what the other guy did in the background, so to speak. Unfortunately, it was impossible to tell if someone was infected just by looking at them, and equally unfortunate was the fact that lots of guys would either lie about their status or refuse to get tested, so they honestly didn't know if they were poz or not.

As a couple, Henry and I agreed to take responsibility for keeping ourselves safe, at least as much as we could. We came to the conclusion it was best to just assume that anyone else we played with was HIV-positive. To assume anything else, well, that was like playing with fire.

Dagen arrived just on time. He even brought a gift, a little basket of goodies meant for new puppy parents. Sexy, gorgeous and thoughtful!

Henry and I were dressed casually. Very casually. No shirt, just a jockstrap under very short, very tight gym shorts and athletic socks. Hours at the gym spent working out for several years now, had turned our formerly skinny bodies into a nice set of muscles on both of us.

"Get some drinks for the men, bitch," Henry told me. "And you, you need to make yourself more comfortable. Let's see what you got under those clothes," he told Dagen.

I think Dag was a little overwhelmed when he saw our house. I didn't know anything about his background, whether he knew anything about art or literature, but I knew that we had decorated to impress. Henry especially loved African art, particularly art that celebrated the physiques of the Black male form. Busts, statues, masks, paintings and photos, all showing the glorious beauty of Black men, were tastefully placed throughout our home. A chess set with the pieces carved into African designs sat on a small gaming table.

Besides African and African-inspired art, we also had plenty of queer/homoerotic art on display. I loved the small replica of the Statue of David by Michelangelo that sat atop one bookcase. Several Keith Haring prints were hanging in our living room, beautiful reminders of a gifted artist, another victim of the AIDS pandemic, who died on February 16, 1990. Only 31 years old. An unspeakable tragedy to lose someone so talented at such a young age.

Dagen mentioned how much he admired our home, as he sat on the sofa to remove his shoes.

"Leave the socks on, babe," Henry told him. "Maybe we can find a pussyboy who might want to lick and sniff your socks before he pulls them off with his teeth."

Damn, did Henry have to give away my secrets like that? I thought.

Dagen laughed at that. The kind of laugh that let us know that he was open to having some fun.

Then Dagen reached for a coffee table book titled *Black Book* by Robert Mapplethorpe. Published in 1986, each page showed exquisitely photographed Black men, many of them naked, and some shown with full-frontal nudity.

"We don't have any Black men in Iceland, where I come from," Dagen explained, literally licking his lips as he flipped through the pages of the book.

"Iceland. Sounds cold," Henry said. "Snowy and icy and very Caucasian," he teased.

"Yes, all Caucasian. I never saw a Black man before I came here for school," Dagen explained.

"Ever have sex with a Black man before?" Henry asked.

"Oh yes! Yes, I like sex with Black men. I think they're sexy."

Henry was beaming. Although he didn't especially like if a guy had a fetish for Black men, feeling that meant being treated like an object, he had no objection if someone found Black men sexy in general. As a matter of fact, he viewed that as a good thing.

By now, Dagen had stripped down to his underwear and socks. He was wearing boxers with the name Joe Boxer on the waistband, decorated with cartoon characters against a black background.

"I wanna watch you two puppies play with each other first," Henry told us. It was no secret to me that Henry liked to control the action, sometimes directing the action like he was directing a porno.

"Right here on the floor, right in front of me. Show me what you boys can do."

Dagen took control of me at that point. He pushed me onto my back, leaned in very close and started kissing me. A minute later, he pushed himself forward, placing first his left nipple, then the right, against my mouth.

"Suck it, you pussy. Suck my titties," he whispered as I obeyed his commands.

Then he lifted himself into a sitting position, raising his arms over his head. "You know what to do. Lick me. You know where, then sniff me, you dirty dog."

I was sniffing and licking his armpits, while Henry watched closely, leaning forward with intense interest. I saw Henry's jock pouch being stretched wide as Henry's cock grew thicker and longer with each flick of my tongue on Dagen's body.

209

I reached for my dick, already at full staff in my jock, just needing to adjust the angle for comfort. "Nobody told you that you could touch your little clitty," Henry scolded, as Dagen laughed.

"She got a little clitty. That's what I thought. Figured she was a cumdump fuckboy the minute I saw her wiggling her ass in the shop," Dagen said, directing his comments about me to Henry.

That kind of talk always turned Henry on. He loved to make fun of my dick size, even though I wasn't really that small. Truth is, that talk turned me on too.

"She got a bird dick. I usually don't let that little bird out of its cage," Henry was saying as he rubbed his very stiff cock in his jock, and I could already see his pouch getting wet.

Suddenly, Dagen's feet were in my face. I already knew what was expected of me. I felt my cock straining hard in my jock as the scent of his socks and feet overpowered me. Licking the soles of his still-socked feet made me feel humiliated, especially because Henry was watching me perform like a submissive pussy.

The next thing I knew, Henry positioned himself so that his foot was next to Dagen's, waiting for me to switch from licking and sniffing and slurping one man's foot to the other's. I heard them laughing at me, in my prone position, clearly excited as I performed foot service for them.

One by one, I removed their socks with my teeth, as I had been ordered to do. That's when they put their feet close together, so Henry's right big toe was next to Dagen's left big toe, and I swallowed both of their big toes at once, enjoying the taste, the smell, and the knowledge that both of these men would never forget how they joined forces to place me in a position of extreme submission.

Wiggling their big toes in my mouth, Henry took hold of Dagen's rigid, throbbing cock, still in his boxers, and started rubbing it, massaging it, then bending close and sniffing Dagen's swollen cock and tightening balls.

Dagen started to reach for Henry's tight hole of pleasure, planning to insert a finger or two, but Henry pushed his hand away. "No part of you will ever penetrate any part of me," he growled and Dagen backed down, understanding there was only one bitch in the room that he was permitted to dominate.

Pulling their toes out of my mouth, Dagen picked me up and placed me on the floor, on all fours, pushing my legs open with his feet.

"I don't wanna hear one fuckin' sound outta you. I hope your man here trained you to keep quiet when you're told."

I squeezed my eyes tight, taking a deep breath, knowing that I was about to be invaded by Icelandic dick, but also knowing that Henry would make sure that the boy's rod was wrapped.

Keeping my eyes closed, I didn't know that Henry was handing his drink glass to Dagen. "You're from Iceland. Give that ass a taste of your homeland."

I didn't know what he meant until I felt a sudden jolt from the ice in Dagen's hand being rubbed against my hot ass cheeks, then he quickly reached around and held the melting cube of ice against my nipples, first the left, then the right. Water was dripping down onto the floor, water that I'd be slurping up later, just like a dog.

And then I felt it. Dagen was rubbing an ice cube right up against my asshole, bringing a mixture of pleasurable and painful sensations to my fuckhole. And then, he pushed it inside!

Involuntarily, I reared my head, but Dagen held my ass tightly in his grip, not allowing me to move. Without missing a beat, he slid another freezing cube into my ass and that time, without even being permitted to touch myself, I screamed, grunted, groaned and writhed in deep passion and my dick exploded all over the floor.

"Where I come from, the men like to fuck wet, cold holes. Just like the one you got there right now," Dagen told me as he pushed hard, penetrating me with 8 inches of rock-hard, uncut white meat.

"We fuck those tight wet cold holes until we see the steam coming out of your chimney!"

And just as Dagen started pounding my ass with Nordic passion, I heard him groan, and I looked back to see that Henry's 9 inches of rock-hard, uncut Black meat was now embedded deep inside Dagen's smooth pink hole.

Dagen shot off first, filling his condom with his sweet Icelandic nectar, shuddering and groaning as his slick body slid against mine.

Just two minutes later, Henry was overcome with the passion of fucking the fucker, and his heavy load of cream filled his condom. But even after finishing, Henry wasn't satisfied, pulling off one rubber, replacing it with a fresh one, and digging deep into Dagen's hot white ass for a second round of joy.

"You know where you belong, dontcha boy?" he commanded me, rather than asking.

I knew what to do, crawling behind Henry, reaching into his tightness with my tongue, watching his balls swinging in my face while he fucked that beautiful small hole in the middle of that gorgeous muscular, smooth, hairless Icelandic ass.

Finally, Henry collapsed against Mr. Iceland 1990, cumming for the second time in 10 minutes, gasping for breath, sweating, but feeling relieved as he had expressed his dominance over the two white boys.

Twenty minutes later, Dagen started getting ready to leave. "Not so fast, Ice Boy," Henry told him. "Let's get cleaned up. But first, put these on."

Henry tossed a pair of my red bikini briefs to our guest, tossing a pink pair in my direction.

"We're gonna show you a Philly tradition. You ever get Karl'd before?"

And with that, a heart-wrenchingly beautiful man from Iceland learned what it meant to get Karl'd. Having sex in the shower with your underwear on, dripping wet, slipping and sliding in the shower.

To be honest, Henry and Dagen both Karl'd me that night. And I gave a new meaning to the term when I Karl'd myself right into the pouch of my dripping wet pink briefs.

***

The next time we saw Dagen, it was at the unveiling of the mural on the wall of Club Sanctuary. A huge curtain was hung to keep the art from being seen as it was created. Of course, Henry and I were always sneaking peeks at their progress. And we both agreed that it made a powerful statement.

I think about 200 people gathered in front of the club on the afternoon of the unveiling. I quickly spotted Dagen in the crowd. That boy stood out everywhere he went. He was hanging onto a Black man, one I knew as a regular at the BDSM leather/levi section of the club, The Hole. Tall, bald, muscular, strong, and with a voice to match his menacing looks, those who didn't know him called him Black Adonis. I knew him simply as Jonathan. He was a club regular, and very active in the AIDS service organizations.

Henry stood before the crowd, after spending the previous night preparing some short remarks.

"Welcome, everybody," he began. "Today is a very special day for me and for Joey, my husband. You might know that we started this club about 15 years ago. We called it Sanctuary because we wanted to provide a safe space for us, for our kind, for the gay, lesbian, queer and trans communities to gather and celebrate our lifestyles. And from the start, we wanted to include all us queers, whether we're white, Black, Brown, Asian, Pacific Islander, Native American, or any race, creed or nationality."

I was standing next to Henry, so proud of him and all that he had accomplished. That *we* had accomplished.

"So many people have had an impact on our lives. In just a minute, you'll see a mural that was done in honor of one of my heroes. I never had the honor to meet him, but have no doubt, his impact on me has been profound. But before we show this beautiful art in honor of a truly great gay man, let me introduce Reverend Greene, another hero in the fight against this horror we now call AIDS."

There was a smattering of applause as Henry finished speaking and Reverend Greene arose to address the crowd.

This is the same Reverend Greene who held the memorial service at Club Sanctuary after the brutal beating deaths of Ruby and Rosetta, two transgender friends who lost their lives on Thanksgiving night, many years before.

"Thank you all my beautiful queer friends!" the Reverend began, to laughter and applause.

"It's a day of celebration today! I know how many of us have cried, screamed, sobbed, feeling that our hearts have been broken again and again and again by this killer virus, the hated and despised HIV. And I know, I understand, that the mourning, the grief, never really ends; it never leaves us; it is unbearable and unending.

But let's try to put that aside, just for a few minutes, and remember the joy that our lifestyle can bring to us. Remember joy? Remember celebration? Remember fun? Do you? Can you remember those feelings?"

Someone in the crowd screamed out, "Yes, Reverend, I remember! I want those days back!"

Acknowledging that statement, Reverend Greene continued, "Yes, we all remember. We all want those days back. But I'm here to tell you that we have enough room in our hearts for love and grief, both at the same time. Our fallen friends wouldn't want us to suffer all the time. No, they don't want to be forgotten. They don't deserve to disappear into the past. But I'm here to tell you that, dammit, our lost friends want us to LIVE! To celebrate that which makes us different. So yes, mourn those who have gone before us. But always remember to LIVE! To LOVE! To NEVER FORGET! And if you ever need a shoulder to cry on, or someone to just hold you and comfort you, know that I'm here for you. Your friends are here for you. Don't live in isolation. Don't hide. Don't be afraid to live your life, your beautiful, gay, queer life. Thank you very much!"

And with that, Reverend Greene stepped away as the curtain was dropped and the mural, that big beautiful bold mural, was finally on display for all to see.

215

The mural, in a word, was stunning! The artist had captured the image of James Baldwin perfectly. I had a sudden thought that the artist had captured the soul of the man, the artist, the author. The colors were vivid, bringing what was once a bare wall to a flaming brilliance.

As I looked at every detail, admiring the work and silently thanking the artists from Mural Arts, my eyes were drawn to the top. There, written in big, bold, beautiful lettering, the artist inscribed these words: Every day is a good day to be gay.

I read it over and over and over.

Every day is a good day to be gay.

***

Four weeks after Henry and I first walked into Morris Animal Refuge, and the first time we had seen the tiny Boston Terrier trying to zoom around the room, we returned to finally bring our little guy home with us. We were excited about adopting, but to be honest, we were both looking forward to seeing Dagen again. That night with him had been incredibly fun.

We were both disappointed to find that Dagen wasn't at the Refuge that day. We asked the attendant if he had the day off, but instead, we were told that Dagen no longer worked there.

"Yeah," the boy behind the counter told us, with a sly grin on his face. "Dag the Fag got caught with his pants down, and I mean he literally got caught with his pants down. Seems he was in the bathroom at his school, giving some Nordic dick to one of the professors, when one of the deans walked in on them. So goodbye scholarship, goodbye America, and they deported his ass right out of the USA."

"The funny thing is," the boy continued, "they labeled him as an undesirable alien. I figure it must've been a man who made that decision. No woman I know would ever call that guy 'undesirable.'"

We were both sorry to hear about what had happened, and we laughed at the naïveté of the new guy behind the counter. However, other matters demanded our immediate attention as the volunteer went and got our brand-new little puppy.

To say he looked adorable, with a tiny collar around his neck, his big, beautiful bulging eyes, and a tongue that seemed like he just couldn't keep it in his mouth, was an understatement to the nth degree. I felt a sense of joy and immense responsibility overwhelm me.

"Zumi!" I called. "Here boy, here boy!"

And dammit if Zumi didn't come running into my outstretched arms, bouncing from me to Henry and then back to me.

"You know he'll be super energetic at first. But don't let him think he's the boss. You gotta teach him who's in charge," the boy told us.

"No worries there," Henry assured him. "I've had lots of experience training puppies. Haven't I, pup?" he said, looking directly at me.

The boy snickered as we walked out the door with our little precious new member of the family. Zumi was on his way to a new adventure, a new life, and we couldn't possibly be more excited about it.

***

One of the benefits of living in Queen Village, a neighborhood just south of Center City, on the east side of Broad Street, was that cable TV had already been installed in the neighborhood. Yes, you heard me right. Cable TV was a luxury back then.

In Center City, most residents had to watch shows on TVs that had antennae. Maybe you've seen them in a museum somewhere, or in old pictures. They were these metal thingies that stuck out from the back of a TV set to catch the signals from the broadcasting stations. Some of the high-rise apartment buildings had something called "community antenna television", or CATV, with a large antenna on the roof that allowed access to more channels than most people could see.

But I'm talking about real cable. We were thrilled with it! We both enjoyed MTV the most, spending countless hours watching music videos.

Late one night, Henry was flipping through channels when he came across a public access station that was showing a program called "Living with AIDS." The show was hosted by a young man who openly admitted that he had HIV, which was still somewhat unusual at that time. People were still in danger of losing jobs, housing, and even insurance coverage, so most chose to keep their diagnosis a secret. I can still see the face of that young man. So hopeful. So lovely. Bright eyes. A young African-American man, with a round face and ears that stuck out, providing commentary and interviewing guests on the importance of living with AIDS, emphasis on the word *Living*. For a long time, most people thought of anyone infected as Dying from AIDS. His message was to convey hope.

Henry set up the VCR to record that show, in case we ever missed the broadcast. To us, the message was both welcome and necessary for our community.

As the show ended, I reached for the remote, ready to switch back to MTV, hoping to catch the latest Madonna video. Henry slapped my hand away. "Not so fast," he told me, wanting to see what show came on next on that station.

If I had switched the channel, we might have never known that a new program was being launched on this public access channel. But the moment we heard the introduction, we knew who it was.

"Listen up everybody, this is your host, the one and only Wyatt, here to bring you a brand-new show focusing on some important issues of the day. Each week, I'll have guests from our community...yes, I said...our community...on the air to talk about what's up!"

If you had ever heard Wyatt speak, you would never forget that voice. It commanded your attention. Deep, smooth, booming, and always upbeat. And of course, we recognized him as the photographer who had published photos of our butts more than a few years ago.

On the set of the new TV program, Wyatt had a few of his photo books on display in the background. And yes, there was the book where Henry and I had first exposed our backsides to the world, *Big Butts*. We were both laughing when we saw that.

Our laughter quickly died down when we heard Wyatt introduce his first guest and the topic for the show that night. The guest kept his identity hidden, appearing as a shadow behind a curtain, and his voice was altered to protect his identity.

Wyatt asked probing questions while at the same time, assuring his guest that he wasn't required to answer anything that made him uncomfortable. The topic was Intimate Partner Violence and Abuse, which is an affliction in the LGBTQ community, but often ignored and rarely discussed. Wyatt's guest was treated with dignity and respect as he told the audience about his experiences being in an abusive relationship.

Henry held me close as we watched the show, reassuringly rubbing my shoulders. As I listened, I wondered how many of the customers at Sanctuary went home after a night of clubbing to a place where they were treated with disrespect, or even had to deal with physical abuse. While at the club, it's so easy to pretend that all of us feel safe in our environment. So easy to forget the problems that awaited us on the outside.

Wyatt was doing a true service for the community by providing a forum for us to be reminded about issues that could hit any of us hard.

I leaned back into Henry's body. "Thank god I have you here to take care of me," I whispered.

***

Every once in a while, I just needed a break from all the intensity that seemed to surround me. Seeing Carl and Karl at the club always brought a sense of relief. Those two were so crazy, so much fun. I never knew what they were up to, but I always knew it would be funny and outrageous.

Tonight, I was watching them out on the dance floor at Sanctuary. Carrying on, like usual. But no throwing drink glasses to the floor. I had warned them about that sort of behavior long ago. Well actually, Henry had warned them. He was concerned that someone might get hurt on the broken glass. I depended on him to be reliable enough for the both of us.

From the DJ booth, I could see that they were once again wearing custom-made tee shirts, one of their trademarks. I couldn't read what was written on them, so I joined those two funny guys on the dance floor.

We were dancing to a string of hits, including songs by Wham!, Lionel Richie, Kool and the Gang, A-ha, ABBA, Cyndi Lauper, and others whom I can't recall right now. I kept looking at their tee shirts, but it looked like Math to me, so I decided to wait until we had a chance to talk before asking them about whatever was going on.

We finally took a break, and headed to the back bar, where Karl had a chance to explain those shirts to me.

About a week ago, they had gone to see a double-feature of *Back to the Future* movies. After the show, as they walked home (to enjoy some quick Carling/getting Karl'd) they were talking about how the characters in the movies traveled through time.

Karl had proclaimed that the method of time travel in the movie was ridiculous. However, he did think time travel was possible. Carl looked at him like he was some sort of alien space/time traveler, not believing what Karl had just proposed.

That's when Karl started to explain his theory, based loosely, very loosely, on Einstein's Theory of Relativity.

"You know Einstein's theory, right? $E=mc^2$. Energy equals mass times the speed of light squared."

"The cool thing is that no one can prove whether that theory is true or not," Karl explained. "So, I can have my own theory about time travel and no one can prove if it's right or wrong."

Carl laughed at the idea, not quite sure where Karl was headed with this.

That's when Karl proposed a new theory of time travel.

"I propose the Karl Theory of Time Travel," he told his friend. T=mc^3. Time equals mass times the speed of light cubed."

"Explaining further, Karl said that if something or someone could just move fast enough, say at the speed of light cubed, they would actually travel through time.

Of course, Carl wasn't about to accept Karl's theory without making one of his own.

"I think you're wrong, dude," he told his friend. "Maybe the real equation is T=m^{2}c. You know, you can travel through time if you square the mass times the speed of light."

"You're fuckin' crazy!" Karl argued. "How're you gonna square the mass of a person or a thing? Do you think you're gonna make some giant travel at the speed of light and send them through time? Think about it. If a 100-pound guy had his mass squared, that's 100 pounds times 100 pounds. That's at least 200 or 300 pounds right there! Or something like that," Karl said, as he tried to multiply in his head.

Side note: 100 times 100 equals 10,000, but does the real number even matter?

They were both laughing, but they each also thought they might have stumbled upon a good idea.

That's why, that night at Sanctuary, the back of Karl's tee shirt said:

Karl's Theory of Time Travel

T=Mc^3

And the back of Carl's tee shirt said:

Carl's Theory of Time Travel

$T=M^2c$

I couldn't stop laughing as they told me this story. Of course, I thought the whole idea was just crazy and ridiculous. But they argued about things with such passion, as if it were the most important thing in the world. Then, a week later, they would be on to a different subject, on a completely different topic.

That's why I liked these two guys. They always had something crazy going on. Some sort of scheme to get noticed. Change the world. Add the word Carl or Karl in a new way to the English language. Travel through time. Anything for a laugh.

Looking back now, I miss them even more. Neither one of them survived the pandemic. I could describe their deaths to you. I was there. They were horrifying, painful, gruesome deaths. But that isn't how I think about them.

I remember them as young, playful, fun-loving, proud gay men who died unnecessary deaths. When I think of them, I close my eyes and I see them on the dance floor of the club, having fun, enjoying life. And I miss them terribly.

Every once in a while, I give Henry a playful wink, stripping down to my underwear, pulling him towards the shower. "You wanna Karl me?" I tease. And every time, without fail, Henry will be stripped to his undies, already hard and stiff, ready to join me in a hot wet fuck in the shower, all the while wearing our briefs, bikinis, boxers, or whatever.

"You're gonna get Karl'd like you've never been Karl'd before," he'd growl, pushing himself against me and then into me.

When we would be in bed together later, I would lie there, listening to Henry's quiet breathing, feeling his body so close to me. And once I knew that he was sleeping, I would let myself go, sobbing quietly, not wanting to disturb Henry's sleep. But the pain was becoming unbearable. I could feel my world shrinking, day by day, death by death. And I wondered where all this was leading us.

And sometimes, I'd lie in bed, thinking about those two crazies. And I would think to myself, *I think Karl was right. I think the past tense of Karling should be K-A-R-L-apostrophe-d. Otherwise, someone might pronounce it Kar-led.* And that thought would make me laugh and cry at the same time.

And I wish I could figure out a way to make Karl's Theory of Time Travel work. $T = mc^3$.

Why? So I can go back in time, back to when Carl, Karl, and so many other young, innocent, beautiful gay guys would spend their weekends dancing and partying at Sanctuary and other clubs. I want that time back. I'd do anything to make that happen. Even travel at the speed of light cubed.

SIXTEEN

Though I no longer went to the club every night, I was still what you would call a "frequent flier." Sometimes, I'd hear people describe themselves as being "tired of the clubs" or "over that scene." I never felt that way. Even today, I like to go out to clubs. It invigorates me and I often have a desire just to be surrounded by queer people.

On this particular night, I noticed that the crowd seemed so young. But in 1991, I had turned 33 years old. Every time I thought about that, well, it freaked me out. Where did the time go? Why did it move so fast? And yet, if I was being really honest with myself, I had to admit that I was a little surprised that I was still alive. Too many weren't that lucky.

I was enjoying myself on the dance floor, with DJ Thunder playing a string of Madonna hits, including "Vogue," "Justify My Love," "Who's That Girl" and "La Isla Bonita." As I was doing my Vogue impression, which was laughable at best, a young guy came up and started dancing with me. Actually, dancing with us, as I was partying with a group of friends, but he kept positioning himself directly in front of me, clearly wanting my attention.

"You don't recognize me, do you?" he shouted above the music.

I looked at him intently, drawing blanks. Not a clue who this guy was.

"You haven't seen me in a long time. I was just a little kid when I met you. My parents bought your dad's house when you moved to Philly."

I finished up my last Vogue move of the night, waving my hands like a crazed person, and then took the boy by

225

his hand and led him over to one of the quieter areas of the club.

"Tell me that again. I'm not sure I heard you right."

"I'm from back home. My parents bought a house from you after you moved to Philly," he explained.

"I remember the people who bought the house. But I don't think I remember you. Of course, that was like 15 years ago. How old are you now?

"I'm 19 now. I hope you aren't gonna kick me out. I have ID to prove I'm 21 if anyone like the cops come in here to check," he said, suddenly getting a little nervous.

"No wonder I don't remember you. I guess you were about 4 years old when I left home. And I just turned 19 when I started this club. So, I'm not gonna worry about an underage guy being here. Especially not a cute one, like you."

"Thanks, man," he said to me, taking a final sip of his Cosmopolitan. I signaled to the bartender to bring us some fresh drinks.

"So how did you even recognize me?"

"Joey, you don't even know. Everyone back home knows about you. The guy that got out of town and made it in the big city. And us queer guys, well, I don't wanna sound dumb, but to us, you're a fuckin' hero."

A hero? I thought. I had never even thought about anything like that. I never went back home for any reason, except when my aunt died and I was there for her funeral.

While I was thinking about how I could probably take my place as the Grand Marshall of the Thanksgiving Day parade back home, three guys came over and joined us.

"Hey Joey, pleased to finally meet you," one of them told me.

"Y'all from back home?"

226

"Yes, we are. We're all here visiting Willie, who moved here about a month ago."

"I'm sorry, but I don't remember your name," I told the first guy, the one who was now living in my old house.

"I'm William," he said.

"And I'm Billy," another one said.

"I'm Bill," chimed in the next one.

"And I'm Willie. I live here now," the last one said.

"I know you guys are kidding me. You're trying to tell me that your names are William, Willie, Bill and Billy? So really, all 4 of you are named William?"

I was laughing at that thought.

One of them, I'm not sure which one, said, "Yep. We think our mothers did it on purpose. We all live close to each other and we think our mothers just wanted one of them to be able to holler, 'William, time for dinner. Come on home!' and all four of us would come running."

Laughing, I told all of them to order themselves drinks, then handed tickets that would be good for as many drinks as they might want later.

The one named Billy continued, "There's actually another William in our neighborhood, same age as all of us. But we call him the Fifth Beatle, because he's, you know, straight, so he doesn't fit in with us."

"Yeah, we're worried that he might break up the band," Willie said, laughing, in an English accent that sounded just like something one of the Beatles might have said.

I liked these four young men. For a couple of reasons. First, it was just cool to find 4 young queer guys here in my club, that just happened to be from my hometown. And it was clear they were a tight-knit group. I got the feeling they weren't just friends, and I wondered how they balanced out their feelings among four different guys. Did they all have sex with one another? In my imagination, I was sure that they did. Just thinking about group sex always got me excited, remembering how many times Henry and I had joined in to form a group. It was always fun for me.

The next day, I was happy to see that those same guys, the Four Williams, showed up at the Super Skates skating rink, where Club Sanctuary was hosting another AIDS fundraiser. A location like this allowed us to have an all-ages event, and since it was in Northeast Philly, outside of our regular Center City events, we hoped to attract some new people.

A word about Northeast Philly. When I first moved to Philly, everyone referred to that area as "The Great White Northeast." No, I'm not kidding. And they were referring to the racial makeup of the neighborhood. I'm not sure if everyone called it that, but everyone I knew did. And I have no idea if anyone still refers to the area by that nickname.

Now, Philly is known as a city of neighborhoods, and segregation was a reality, so maybe this surprises no one. I didn't know that part of the city very well, since it wasn't an area I visited often.

On this day, we rented a bus to take people back and forth from the club to the roller rink. I wasn't expecting it, but you know how gay people like to dress up and show off. So, people were arriving at the club in all sorts of costumes to participate in the skate-a-thon.

Drag queens showed up in force. Gowns, tiaras, wigs, make-up, glitter, jewelry...each queen seemed to be trying to be more outrageous than the next. Seeing these queens skating, their gowns flowing in the breeze as they showed off their skating skills was so much fun!

When I saw the Four Williams, I was impressed. They had gotten into the spirit, with two of them renting formal wear and now attired in top hat and tails, skating with apparent skill. The two in their tuxes took the lead as all four of them skated together, the other two dressed like ballerinas, in tutus, tights, and those swan-like bodices topped off with tiny feathery hats. I wished that we had hired a videographer. It would have been fun to watch that event over and over again.

As the music blared, the DJ playing "Tainted Love" by Soft Cell, the skaters having fun, and raising money for a good cause, Henry and I took a break from the action. Resting our legs, Henry leaned against me, closing his eyes, taking a deep sigh.

"You know, babe, this is a lot of fun. But…"

"What is it, Henry? Something bothering you?"

"I was just thinking back to how it was before. Before all this happened. When our lives were so carefree. Hardly any responsibility. No worries, especially no worries about getting sick and dying young."

I leaned against him, always finding comfort in his strength and beauty.

"I get it," I assured him. "It's okay to wish that things were different."

"I know that we can't snap our fingers and just make everything right again by magic," Henry continued. "But right now, I'm feeling the pain of losing so many people, so many friends."

He started crying. Very quietly, not wanting to draw any attention. But I knew the pain. I knew the hurt. It never stopped. It never went away. We had our lives to lead, but we always carried the memory of so many in our hearts.

We watched as the four guys from back home skated by.

What does the future hold for them? I wondered. *Will there be a cure sometime soon? Will all of them be spared?*

Of course, at the time, I didn't know the answers to my questions. I had no idea that 40 years later, after the very first cases were diagnosed, that the world would still be waiting for a vaccine against this virus. Why do vaccines work against some viruses and not others? I don't know the answer to that question either.

As I cradled Henry in my arms, wishing that I could hug the hurt away, I heard what sounded like a crash behind me.

"Oh no, it's Old Man Joe! He fell down!" someone shouted.

Two thoughts raced through my mind. First, *what the hell was Old Man Joe doing out on the skating rink?* I soon found the answer to that one. He had taken the Club Sanctuary bus, and a couple of the gogo boys had been skating with him, apparently in return for all the tips he had stuffed into their jocks and bikini briefs during the past few years. Despite being held in their strong arms, he still somehow managed to slip out of their grasp and take a tumble to the floor of the rink.

My second thought was…and may god not strike me down for this…*I hope he didn't hurt his thumbs!*

Of course, Old Man Joe was known throughout the Gayborhood for his ThumbThing creations, and I admired his skill in that regard. But, I should have been more worried about his wrist, which looked like it might have been badly sprained, instead of worrying about his thumbs.

We called 911 for an ambulance to take him to the nearest hospital for X-rays. We were later told that he did sprain his wrist, which would have to be bandaged for about a week. Other than that, no harm done.

***

Hours later, the Four Williams were at Willie's apartment. As a reminder, Willie had just moved to Philly for school, while William, who lived with his family in my old house, Billy, and Bill were still living in my old hometown, 75 long miles away.

Willie had one of those apartments where most of the rooms were rather small, but for some reason, he had a huge bathroom. With a claw-foot tub, no less. Located on Spruce Street, in the heart of the Gayborhood. Willie would be attending classes at the University of the Arts, located on Broad Street, taking classes in art design, hoping to major in ceramic design.

All four of them headed into the bathroom, stripping completely naked, while Willie filled the tub, adding bubble bath to the water, filling the room with a lavender scent mixed with steam from both the water and the heat from the four boys. Did I mention that all four were very sexy 19-year-old boys?

"Slutty Cunt, put on that latest mixtape you made," Willie said to William. Willie had assigned nicknames to each of his submissive boys. William was Slutty Cunt, Billy was PigBoy and Bill was FagHag. Each had been taught to obey Willie.

The music started playing from the boombox, including hits such as "Ice Ice Baby" by Vanilla Ice, "My Prerogative" by Bobby Brown and "Wind Beneath My Wings" by Bette Midler.

Willie got into the tub, motioning for William to join him. Billy and Bill sat on bath rugs just outside the tub, but close enough to watch and listen to everything going on.

Willie, clearly the leader of this group, told William to open his legs.

"You know I want to see it. Show it all to me. Show me your little hole," he whispered, as William obeyed, opening his legs wide as he sat facing Willie.

Both of their cocks stood at rigid attention, protruding out of the water. Their cock heads were both wet, but not from the bathwater. No, it was their sticky teenage pre-cum oozing out of their thick white dicks that shone in the light from the candles that Billy had lit and placed around the tub.

Bill was moaning as he watched Willie lather up his hands, soaping them up, then sliding two soapy fingers into William's hot, hairless pink butthole. Billy wanted to stroke himself, but he already knew from experience that he had to be given permission from Willie, who from this point on in the ritual could only be addressed as "Master."

"You want anything from me, boy?" Willie asked the submissive William, as the Master kept sliding his slippery, wet, soapy fingers in and out of his willing boy.

"Yes, Master. This boy is asking permission to suck the cock of my Master."

"Yes, boy. Permission granted." Willie leaned back against the back of the tub, his throbbing cock still sticking far out of the water. "Just the tip, boy. Just the tip. Lick it and suck it just like your Master taught you."

Bill and Billy, still sitting on the side of the tub, watched, gasping as they saw William lick and nibble on Master Willie's wet hardness. Keeping two fingers of his right hand inside William's hot, throbbing zone of pleasure, Master Willie took hold of Billy's hand, guiding it to his nipple, nodding, giving permission for Billy to tickle, tease and squeeze the Master's nipple. With that, the slit of Master's cock opened up and more pre-cum was oozing down the side of his shaft, almost reaching the water.

"Get that!" Master Willie commanded Bill. "Don't let your Master's seed go to waste. You know how precious my liquids are."

Bill reached into the tub just far enough to catch Master's precum from entering the water. His fingers were covered in goo. "May I eat, please?" he asked Master Willie, who nodded his assent and Bill slowly licked his fingers clean, enjoying the taste of the creamy gift from his god.

"Switch places," Willie commanded.

William felt the Master pull his fingers from his ass, and he then got out of the tub, dripping wet, sitting on the bath rug, his hard cock aching with desire. Now it was his turn to sit silently and obediently and watch as the Master demanded service from his boys. Willie knew enough that to keep these boys in line, the sex could never be boring, so he always had something new to excite his worshippers.

Billy was the next one allowed to get into the tub, the altar of worship, with the Master. At this point, Master Willie had turned himself around, on his hands and knees, presenting his ass to Billy.

"Do you see anything you want?" Willie asked the desperately horny young man behind him.

"Yes, Master. There's a boy back here, an obedient boy, who's hungry."

"Hungry for what?" Willie asked in a low growl.

Billy sighed, hoping he'd be permitted to eat that beautiful piece of man ass that was dripping wet in front of him.

"Get the fuck outta the tub," Willie commanded, unhappy that Billy had waited too long to answer. "Go over there and kneel with your nose against the wall until you're told to do otherwise. And make sure your legs are wide open in case I decide to come over there and spit in your unworthy faggot ass."

Those words hurt coming from the Master. Billy knew that sometimes a disobedient boy would be forgiven that same night. Other times, that boy might not be so lucky and would be placed in a chastity device for a week or more.

"I hope boy number three can do better," Master told Bill, who was next to enter the tub.

"Does this boy see anything he likes?"

"Yes, Master. This boy sees the hot open ass of my god, who I love and worship as my lord and this boy wants to lick your ass and provide pleasure to the Master."

"Good boy," Willie said, giving permission for Bill to begin, as William watched and Billy listened to the sound of Bill slurping away like a hungry, happy puppy.

Willie used the three other boys for his pleasure for 30 minutes, all the while feeling his passion building to the point of explosion, but always pulling in his desires for a climax at the last minute. Finally, even the Master couldn't contain himself any longer.

"You!" he said to Billy, who still had his nose against the wall. "You get it tonight!"

Billy was surprised and happy to hear those words. He immediately got up, as all three of the submissive boys took hold of their Master, bringing him out of the tub.

Once all four of them were standing, Billy placed his hands on the seat of the toilet, bending over, knowing that he was the one who had been chosen to get fucked tonight.

Soap up his ass, good and slippery for me," the Master told the other two boys, who obeyed as they had been trained to do.

With that, Master Willie pushed himself inside of Billy, thrusting harder and harder, treating his boy to the pleasure that a true submissive will feel when his Master's hardness is stretching his ass wide open.

The other two, William and Bill, were allowed to stroke each other's dicks, pointing them at the sub who was getting dicked, knowing that their cum was not allowed to touch the body of the Master.

"All right boys, let's do this," Willie shouted, feeling his balls get so tight against his body, ready to shoot his godly essence into his willing and hungry fuckboy.

Willie let the boys shoot first, covering Billy's entire ass with hot boyjuice. As he watched his obedient boys squirt their thick jet loads of cream all over the ass of a boy who worshipped him, Willie erupted with the force of a young demigod, flooding the boy's tunnel of love with slippery streams of his pearly god cream.

As soon as he had filled the boy, Willie remembered that he still had a role to play.

"Not you. Not tonight," he told Billy, who was left with the only dick that was still throbbing with desire.

Willie went to the sink, filled a glass with cold water, and threw it on Billy's dick, ending any hope he had of being permitted to cum that night. Billy's dick went limp as all 4 of them headed out to the living room. The worship service had ended.

Later, all four of the boys were lying in Willie's King-size bed. They were chatting, listening to music and watching TV, all at the same time. Typical kid-type behavior.

Also typical was that they were always horny. Sex play was a huge part of their lives. As they talked, it wasn't uncommon for any of them to get a boner, stroke themselves in front of the others, or even to suck some dick. They did this casually, because Willie allowed it. He didn't always play the role of the Master, but when he did, then the casual nature of their relationships ended and everything got serious. Quite serious.

Right now was not a serious time. But Billy suddenly brought up a serious subject.

"I don't wanna leave. I wanna stay here. With you, Willie."

Billy, who had just been humiliated, punished and had his orgasm denied, wanted to stay here in Philadelphia with Willie.

The truth is, all of them wanted to stay. But only Billy had the balls to say it out loud.

"The four of us have been together a long time," Willie finally answered. "We all know we got a good thing going on here. Four of us, always havin' fun times. And I know that as people get older, they drift apart. Are we ready for that?" Willie wondered out loud.

"I bet I could get a job in less than a week," Billy said. "And I'm likin' Philly a lot better than back home. Think about all the fun we had in just a couple days. At the club with Joey, at the roller rink, and well…you know, just now in the bathroom. I just don't wanna lose out on all that."

"You're a good boy, Billy," Willie said, rubbing him on the head, which caused an immediate rush of blood to Billy's dick, still aching for release.

"But don't get any ideas. You ain't gonna get no relief from your horniness tonight. I still have you on punishment, you naughty boy."

"Still, you know how much I like all of you. I don't know anybody who has a better setup than the four of us guys."

Everybody in the room agreed that their arrangement was special and worth keeping.

The next day, William and Bill sadly left for the trip back home. Billy stayed. He was determined to find a job. And he had to do it quickly. He knew Willie wanted him around, but he also knew that Willie wouldn't be able to support both of them.

And that's why Billy was sitting outside the locked club when I arrived for work the following afternoon. I was happy to see him, but I didn't know why he was there.

"Joey, wow, we had a blast with you. Me and all the guys," Billy started, when I reached him at the front entrance of Club Sanctuary.

"Whatsup? I asked him.

"I'm tryin' to stay here in Philly, instead of going back home. I'm lookin' for a job. I thought maybe you could help a guy out. I do know how to bartend. I served drinks at lots of the parties we had back home."

"But never worked in a club?" I asked.

"No, but you remember how we party back home. It might be at somebody's house, but they get pretty wild, and I served lots and lots of guys."

I laughed at that statement.

"I mean I served them drinks," he corrected himself.

"Sure you did," I answered, smiling. I was quite sure I knew exactly what he meant. And he had been right the first time. He had served lots of guys. I could tell just by looking at him.

"Come on in," I invited him. "Let me give you our bartender's test. See what you can do."

In reality, there was no bartender's test. I could hire anyone I wanted. And this kid had promise. As in, wow, he was a looker. He's the type that'll keep guys coming back for more drinks. I was sure of that.

Still, I named a few cocktails and he showed me that he could make them. All of them.

"Let's go in my office and do the paperwork before I make an official offer," I told him.

Sitting at my desk, I pulled an application form out of the top drawer. I swirled in my chair, planning to head for my office fridge and maybe offer him a Perrier, when I saw that he had practically pounced over to my side of the desk and was kneeling in front of me.

"What?" I said, almost involuntarily. If I had time to think about it, I would have known exactly what he was thinking.

I could see that his dick was already big and thick and HARD. It looked like it was ready to pop right out of his jeans. Of course, I didn't know at the time that he had been forced to deny himself any sexual pleasures the night before. But I think I was mostly surprised by how quickly he had moved himself into position – the cocksucker position.

I knew what I was considering was wrong, but I pushed that thought to the back of my mind. I let my passions take over.

"Go over there and lock the door."

I watched in surprise as Billy crawled on his hands and knees over to the office door. As he crawled, he kicked off his shoes, pulled off his shirt, and then he reached up and locked the door securely.

By the time he was kneeling in front of me again, he had shed his jeans and his briefs were down around his ankles. He kicked them off as he got up on his knees, his head wedged between my legs, his tongue already licking at my bulging crotch.

I wanted to close my eyes and pretend that something else was happening, but in reality, I kept my eyes wide open so I wouldn't miss anything that the boy did. He unzipped my pants and stuck his nose inside, sniffing me, then licking me. Raising his eyes to meet mine, he reached under me and slid my pants down.

Next, my bikinis hit the floor. And that's when he started giving me an oral treat, taking my balls in his mouth, sucking them and pulling at them with his lips, then very lightly with his teeth, then slowly working his way up my shaft with his tongue.

"Not so fast," I whispered.

With that, Billy pulled back just a bit, reaching under my ass cheeks and lifting me slightly, raising me into a position where he had clear access to my pucker.

My sighs were all the permission he needed. Feeling his tongue flickering against me, and then into me, I begged him to give me more.

The sucking sounds filled the room as he dug deep into my ass with that hot sexy tongue, and I heard him gasping as he climaxed and shot a mess of man cum onto the carpeted floor.

He reached for my dick that was hard against my belly, and his knee slid just a little in his slippery cream as he was taking my cock in his mouth. Again, he made sure to make eye contact, wanting both of us to know that this was really happening.

His tongue worked its magic on my most sensitive areas until I just couldn't hold back, groaning and pulling at his hair as I blew my hot load into the boy's mouth. And then he swallowed what I had given him.

It took about a minute before I regretted what I had done. I had just betrayed Henry for the first time. I never thought this would happen. What had I been thinking?

I didn't want Billy to know that I was worried about Henry finding out, but I had to be sure that this would be kept a secret, forever.

"Ok, Billy, you got the job. You can start bartending tonight. But I gotta tell you two things first."

"Anything you want, Master," he replied.

"Ok, now I gotta tell you three things. First, you are never ever ever to call me Master. Understood?"

"Yes Sir," he answered meekly.

"Second thing is, you can make a helluva lotta money bartending here. If you wanna keep your job, with all that cash, you cannot ever tell anyone what just happened here. Especially Henry. But not anyone. Are we clear on that?"

"Yes Sir," he answered, agreeing again.

"And third, I want you to know that I have a lot of power in this town. I know everybody. And they all know me and respect me. So, if you ever breathe a word of this to anyone, including the other boys from back home, I won't just fire your ass but I'll also ruin you. No one will ever hire you in Philly after I get done trashing you, if you ever tell anyone. And just call me Joey, just like everybody else."

"OK, I get it. I can keep a secret. But may I say something?"

240

"Sure, what is it?" I asked.

"That was the best ass and the best dick I ever ate. I know you won't let me do it again, but if you ever change your mind, I'll eat you out and swallow your babies anytime you tell me."

And then he stood up and hugged me.

Billy got what he wanted. A job bartending at Sanctuary and moving in with Willie. The other guys, William and Bill, went back home, but they started visiting Philly every weekend. Six weeks later, William found a job at a bakery in South Philly, as he had always excelled in the culinary arts. Eventually, he enrolled in classes to become a certified master baker.

Bill couldn't bear to be away from the rest of the Williams. He found work at a nursing home, located in the Germantown section, providing care and assistance for seniors.

Of course, with Billy working at the club, they became regulars. Eventually, all four of them moved into an apartment together, where they could continue those scenes where the three submissive boys worshipped their Master in secret.

After my encounter with Billy in my office, I spent that whole night at the club with Henry, trying to act normal, like nothing was different. I don't think he ever had a clue. But I knew the truth. I betrayed our love. I swore that I would never allow that to happen again.

That night, when we went to bed, I continued our usual ritual. "I love you, Henry."

"I love you, babe," he replied, rolling over to place one strong leg over me, protecting me, but also claiming me as his very own. I had a hard time sleeping that night.

SEVENTEEN

Sometimes, I wonder what people think about me. I know that some people respect me. I mean, I do a lot for the gay community, providing a place to get away and forget about the stresses of daily life. Besides the club, my building provides space for resources for other community needs.

We used to have a space for Reverend Greene to conduct services, but his ministry had grown too large for our space. His congregation provided the money needed so he could purchase a building on Arch Street, near 10th, where they could worship and build a community within the larger LGBTQ community.

I also know that some people think of me as, well, an under-achiever. Many of them know that I inherited the building where my club is located. I inherited part of the money that was used to establish the club. I'm a high school graduate, who has taken a few classes at community college, and so I don't have a formal education.

I don't deny that I have aspects that are both positive and negative. I think that's true for just about everybody.

But I want to share with you two aspects of me that I think truly define me as a person.

First, I am an advocate for the LGBTQ community. I love Henry with all my heart. I'm married to him. It isn't a legal marriage, but we were both willing to defy the law and have a public ceremony that we consider a valid wedding and a valid marriage. I love my queer friends. I will always fight for our rights. I believe in us. Our right to live. Our right to live our lives just like any other citizen.

When the AIDS pandemic descended upon us, it only increased my concerns and my efforts to be sure that we were treated equally. The need for healthcare, for access to much-needed resources to maintain some semblance of a normal life had become more important than ever.

Besides being an advocate for my LGBTQ community, I also consider myself to be actively anti-racist. You might wonder exactly what I mean by that term. To me, it means that I not only have an anti-racist attitude, but that I'm willing to confront racism when I see it. To be silent is to condone it. And I will not be silent. I cannot be silent.

When I first moved to Philly, I was lucky enough to meet Henry, a young gay Black man, when we were both hanging out one night in Rittenhouse Square. I wasn't afraid of him when he came and sat down next to me. Quite the opposite. I was interested in him and attracted to him.

But knowing one Black person, even being involved with a person of a different race, doesn't make someone anti-racist. I got to know many people, both men and women, both queer and straight, who aren't white. I met people of different races and backgrounds at the club, of course, but also through my work with various companies and organizations. And I learned that these are people of value. I see others as people first, but some people try to dehumanize those who are different. Somehow, that makes it easier for people to hate others, if they deny their basic humanity. I will always confront anyone who thinks of another human, whether straight, queer, older, younger, white, Asian, Black, or any other concept that we construct about ourselves as something less than human. And I will always confront racism to the best of my ability.

Even as I think of myself as anti-racist, Henry will remind me that *it isn't a state of being. It's an act of becoming.*

"You can't just proclaim yourself to be an anti-racist based on past actions," he'd tell me. "It's a continual process, a never-ending path with obstacles constantly being put in your way." And of course, he's right.

Think what you will of me, but I hope that you will not only recognize these qualities in me, but celebrate them and hopefully adopt them as part of your identity.

I just want to provide a few specific examples of what this means. If a bouncer at my club refuses admission to a member and that decision is based solely on race, then that bouncer will be fired. They are informed of that policy when they're hired. Therefore, we don't give warnings, require additional training, or whatever. We do what we tell them we'll do. We fire them.

Or, if we find out that a distributor is charging more for their product at a place like Sharkey's, a mostly Black club in North Philly than they charge us at Sanctuary, we confront the distributor about that. You might be surprised how much power we have when we work together. I know this to be true because I've had to have those tough conversations with people I do business with.

I feel good about those qualities. I think they make me a better human being. But no, I don't think I'm perfect. And of course, those are just two small examples. What I'm really talking about is a lifestyle, about how we treat each other as human beings. I used to think that progress was being made. If I'm being totally honest, from what I see going on right now, I think we're sliding backwards in this area.

One of my imperfections, of course, is that I betrayed my promise to my husband that we would only play with

244

others when we did it together. Though only two people know about that act of betrayal, it was a heavy weight for me to bear. And of course, now you know about it, too.

***

As I look back at the person I was during those times, I now understand that I was consumed by sadness. It was inevitable, I guess, with so many people, many of them very young people, who were getting sick and dying at an alarming rate.

But I wasn't depressed, at least not in the clinical sense of the word. I've been told that clinical depression can be caused by a chemical imbalance in the brain. I was never diagnosed with depression, but I did decide to look for help with my general sense of sadness.

That's why one day, I found myself outside the office of Reverend Greene, waiting for my first therapy session.

It was my first time here at his new office, located in the building which had recently been acquired by his congregation.

I saw the sign on the outside of the door. "Reverend Doctor Elijah Greene, Psy.D., D.Div."

He had two different doctoral degrees. A doctorate in Clinical Psychology and a doctorate in Divinity.

Talk about a man of major educational accomplishments.

"Hello," I said simply, entering his office.

"I feel a little dumb. I've known you for years now, and I don't even know what to call you. Doctor? Reverend? What?"

"You could just call me by my name. My friends call me Eli," he offered.

245

"Well, maybe outside of your office. But I'm here strictly on a professional basis. And no offense, but I'm not here for any religious needs, so I don't really wanna think of you as a Reverend right now. Does that make sense?"

"Yes, Joey. That makes perfect sense. In here, why don't you just call me 'Doctor Greene' and we'll keep everything professional, with a focus on counseling and therapy. That sound okay to you?"

I'm not going to go into detail about our conversations. But I will tell you that I mostly talked about my sadness. And I didn't forget to tell him that I didn't think I was depressed. But after years now of what seemed like non-stop disease and death, well, I was pretty fuckin' sad.

After the first session, we scheduled a regular appointment. Every Tuesday at 1 PM. You know, with my work at the club, I wasn't much of a morning person, so I never made appointments in the AM unless it was absolutely necessary.

I'd have to decide later whether I trusted Eli enough to tell him what was really bothering me. You know, the "B" word – Betrayal.

***

People say if you want to know about someone, take a look at their friends. I considered my best friends to be Henry, who of course is also my husband, though not legally; Alejandro, an excellent resource and event planner at the club; his new boyfriend Kirk, a gay veteran who had sacrificed so much while fighting in a war that he didn't believe in; and of course, Georgina, the most prominent and influential female in my life. Georgie, as everyone called her, was my best lesbian friend, and I knew I could count on her to provide a different outlook than my own on many issues, but also to always have a common-sense approach to handling difficult situations.

Georgie wasn't known for maintaining long-term relationships with her girlfriends. She called most of them her "gal-pals." I always thought that was her way of keeping some distance, not to let anyone get too close.

With that being said, she always had someone that I thought of as her girlfriend or her lover. But those were my terms for those people, not hers.

The five of us had gathered for Sunday brunch at the Reading Terminal Market, where all sorts of foods were available. We ate in the center area, where tables and chairs were scattered, rather than in a booth. That made accessibility easier for Kirk, who still used his wheelchair to get around rather than trying to walk long distances on crutches. Every time we ate there, I always left a donation at the bronze statue of Philbert the Pig, making sure to rub his snout for good luck. Philbert was the official mascot of the Market, and I believe he still holds that position of honor.

We scattered among the various vendors, with a wide variety of Asian, Italian, Greek, South Asian, Mexican, and Amish foods available, among others. No fast foods served here. It was all fresh and made-to-order. Kirk was assigned to hold 4 seats for the rest of us.

As soon as all of us had settled into our seats to eat, Georgie asked for our attention.

"I have something to tell you, but I don't want to spoil anyone's meal," she began.

"Nothing can spoil my meal," I stupidly said, not thinking that she was warning us that she had bad news.

Henry gave me an odd look while Jando and Kirk looked at Georgie with concern clearly showing.

"Ok," she said, starting bravely, but quickly faltering.

"It's me…I have to tell you…"

Suddenly it dawned on me that I had been very self-absorbed with my statement. "Oh, Georgie, I'm so sorry. I didn't mean to make light of anything."

Georgie might normally glare at me for saying something without thinking, and then she'd normally laugh it off and then continue with whatever she had to say. This time was different. Her look softened as she took hold of my hand, gently caressing me and taking a deep breath.

"You know I'm an advocate for women's health. I've been fighting that fight for over 10 years now. But all of a sudden, it's personal."

I already felt my eyes welling with tears. *What could be wrong with her?*

"I get a mammogram every year, because I have family history. Maybe I told you about that before."

Oh my god, mammograms…that means…

"My doctor told me a week ago. I've been trying to find the right time to tell all of you."

No, no, no, was all I could think. *Not her, not this, not now.*

"I have Stage 4 metastatic breast cancer. I think you know that means it's already spreading throughout my body. And it's spreading fast," she told us.

I was in shock. It was always a horror for someone to disclose to me that they had contracted HIV, which was still considered to be a death sentence. Somehow, it just never occurred to me that anything might happen to Georgie.

My reaction was to stand up, right there in the middle of the Reading Terminal Market, and I let out a scream like nothing I had ever heard from me before. Long, loud, wailing, as I stood up, picked up the table, turning it over with a loud, sudden bang, and then turning, lifting my chair and smashing it into the floor. That's when I collapsed to my knees, sobbing uncontrollably.

The only regret I have about my behavior is the look of sudden fear I saw in Georgie's eyes. Maybe she was afraid that I'd accidentally hit her with something I was throwing during my tantrum. I could never forgive myself if I ever did anything to hurt her, whether physically or to cause her any kind of pain.

It was Henry who lifted me up from the floor, walked me away from our friends, and calmed me down. And though I regained my composure and was able to re-join our group, the hurt inside me was so deep it was almost unbearable.

Of course, Georgie's diagnosis wasn't really about me at all. I'm simply telling you my reaction to it.

Georgie was a health care professional, specializing in women's health issues. She already knew better than most, certainly better than I did, that her prognosis was poor.

She fought the cancer as best she could. Seeing her go through the process was a gut-wrenching experience for me. The double mastectomy, the chemo, the hair loss, the weight loss, the nausea, the lack of energy.

The last time I saw her, I already knew. That sparkle in her eye, which she had maintained for a full 15 months after her diagnosis, had disappeared. Lying in bed, so weak, so frail, so filled with drugs to numb the never-ending pain. But at this point, while visiting her, I had to show strength, hoping that somehow she could draw from that. I bent down, leaning in very close to her, whispering gently, "I love you."

Henry, on the other side of the bed, did the same. "I love you, Georgie, I always have." He said in a voice so quiet that I could barely hear him.

As Henry and I left, I turned back for one final look. I watched as Georgie's girlfriend, Layla, whom she had met just 6 months before she was told about her cancer, sat at her side, stroking her hand and whispering to her. Layla had stayed with Georgie for every step of her final journey.

Reverend Greene officiated at Georgie's funeral three days later. The church was packed as hundreds of people came out to show their final respects for a woman who had lived her life giving to her community.

I placed a forever candle in the window of our bedroom. I would keep that candle lit continually, in memory of my beautiful friend.

EIGHTEEN

Over the last 15 years that Club Sanctuary had been open, many things had changed. The music styles had changed. Disco no longer ruled. While still somewhat popular, disco now shared the stage with house music and other genres of pop. Fashions constantly changed. Sometimes a look would come and go in the blink of an eye. Individuals changed. Regular club-goers would eventually move on to other pursuits. Even the décor within the club changed, being re-styled every few years to keep up with changing tastes.

What didn't change was the constant stream of LGBTQ people and their friends, looking for a good time.

We adapted to meet the wants and needs of the people who came out to party with us. For example, the leather/levi bar in the basement of the building, called The Hole, no longer allowed anonymous sex to take place in the area previously known as The Blackout Room. The crowd in that bar, often into kinky scenes with leather, domination, submission, uniforms, and other gear, adapted as well. Now, the bar was still dark, still crowded with men who enjoyed various kinks and fetishes, who could watch their fantasies being played out on video screens that were scattered throughout the club. Video producers were still making new porn, but doing it in a way that promoted safer sex practices. The use of condoms was a requirement on the set of any new production. Watching bareback scenes, even if filmed before the pandemic, was generally frowned upon. Of course, there were always exceptions.

What I hadn't expected was the huge popularity of a new room that we had opened a few years ago.

Remember that Sanctuary was located within a five-story former warehouse, so we always had plenty of room to grow.

"A piano bar? With karaoke nights?" I was skeptical when Alejandro had suggested it. But he made a convincing argument, and the other Board members thought it was a good idea. So, I agreed to give it a try.

That part of the club was closed on Mondays through Wednesdays. Thursday night was Karaoke Night, and let me tell you, these queens loved to get up on stage and show off. Besides that, some guys had real talent.

One night, I stopped in, just to see what was happening in there. To my surprise, Old Man Joe was up on the stage, performing a duet with a much younger man. They were singing "Unforgettable," the version where Nat King Cole magically performed, through the miracle of technology, a duet with his daughter Natalie.

Hearing Old Man Joe singing Nat King Cole's portion of the song was magical in its own way. I had no idea he had such a beautiful singing voice.

I didn't recognize his partner in the song. He was young, very young. Like maybe 18. Old Man Joe, on the other hand, was at least 60, maybe older. Or so I thought.

I mentioned something to Henry, who was with me as we checked out the various parts of the club.

"That's Jerome," he told me, motioning towards Joe's younger singing partner. "I've talked to him before. Including about Joe. I warned him that Joe's a friend of mine, of ours, and I told him he needs to be respectful."

Henry always amazed me. He knew everything that went on in all parts of the club. Nothing ever got by him.

And whenever I thought about Henry that way, I became a little worried that maybe he did know everything. You know what I'm talking about. My little scene with Billy, who was now one of our most popular bartenders.

On Fridays, Saturdays and Sundays, the karaoke bar was converted to a piano bar. Show tunes, show tunes and nothing but show tunes. Packed every night it was open. The crowd closest to the piano swinging, swaying, carrying on, belting out one hit after another. And the tip jar on top of the piano was always overflowing with cash.

Again, I was surprised to see that Kirk, the disabled veteran, and Alejandro, his lover, were regulars here. Kirk knew every song, and I remember watching him, holding onto Jando, singing to him as if no one else in the room even existed. The love between those two was so apparent. No one could miss that each of them found in the other a perfect fit.

***

"Hey, are you even listening to me?" I asked, feeling a little irritated that maybe I was being ignored. I was surprised at the sound of my own voice. Somehow, it didn't sound like me.

"Yes, dear," the voice beside me said. "You were telling me about the club, the piano bar."

"Oh yeah," I murmured, my voice drifting off.

***

People love to be judgmental. Even within the queer community, where being different was supposed to be celebrated, sometimes it seemed to me that people were supposed to be "different" only in ways that had the approval of others.

As an example, Old Man Joe and Jerome were often met with hostility, when they were seen together as a couple. I have trouble with this. In a community that's despised by many members of the straight world, why are we trying to impose rules on those who are already operating on a different playing field?

Are they hurting anyone? I don't see how. Is it unusual? Yes, but that's my point. Just because something is unusual doesn't make it wrong. Both of them are recognized legally as adults, free to make their own decisions about how to live their lives, whom to love, etc.

I started to see them out with each other. A lot. They were at the club every weekend. Having fun. Dancing. Talking with friends. Yet I also saw them getting the side-eye from so many people, and it wasn't like those people didn't have their own ways of enjoying themselves that others might find questionable.

I heard arguments like, "The old man is just using Jerome." Or the opposite, "That young dude is just using that old man." And of course, "They're both using each other to get what they want."

My reply was always the same. "So?"

That was enough to quiet some people, while others went on and on about it being gross or disgusting, or something like that.

Now let's be honest. Isn't that what straight people say about us?

Right about now, I could give you a long, detailed description of the sex lives of OMJ (Old Man Joe) and Jerome. I could tell you that every night, OMJ would stick his thumb up Jerome's ass and kept it there as they slept. But the truth is, I don't really know anything about that.

Or I could give you the juicy details about the rumor that Joe was a collector of paddles. Paddles made from thick pieces of hardwood, sometimes with holes cut into them, which would allow for a quicker, harder smack on the ass of some bad boy. Leather paddles, designed to turn a boy's ass red and hot, with the boy writhing under the strong hands of some Spanking Daddy, taking swats until he was in tears and ready to submit to Daddy's demands.

There was an active gay spanking community in Philly, with many members initially connecting online, a relatively new development in 1991, as pioneers on the Internet quickly found that it could be useful for finding sex partners. Or, for those who wished to avoid sexual contact to keep themselves free of HIV, many engaged in conversations that began with asking for someone's "ASL" (Age, Sex, Location) and claiming to be "DDF" (Drug and Disease Free). The conversation would then quickly turn to sex, called cyber-sex, totally avoiding any human contact and therefore completely safe.

Often, that eventually led to disenchantment and frustration. Gay men were always looking for some sort of alternative, as the pandemic showed no signs of letting up.

The growing interest in meeting other men for activities that did not include actual sex, but did involve physical contact that many found sexually exciting, led to the start of "Spanking Sundays" in The Hole at Sanctuary.

At 5 PM on the second Sunday of every month, maybe 100 to 200 men would gather at The Hole. The Tops would bring their instruments – many preferred paddles, but occasionally you would see someone brandishing a cane or even a whip. Those looking to get spanked were always referred to as "boys", no matter their actual age.

255

The spankees almost always wore a uniform that included white cotton briefs. Sometimes, a jockstrap, but most of them wore those beautiful, sexy white briefs, that many of them remembered from their youth, when they were real "boys."

Barry was one of the regulars, always in his white cotton briefs, looking for a Daddy to bend him over his knee, longing for the hurt from the paddle as his Daddy for the moment would call him a "bad boy," then lower the back of his briefs as the SMACK! SMACK! SMACK! of the paddle could be heard by all present, adding to Barry's feeling of shame and humiliation, which for him was sexually exciting.

Barry seemed to be trying to re-live his childhood. At least, that's how it seemed to me. I know for a fact that when he introduced himself to a new spanking Daddy, he always gave his age as 29. Ten years later, still attending spanking parties, Barry would introduce himself and give his age as 29. Does he really think he's fooling anyone?

As the spanking parties became more organized, Daddies often wanted to only spank their favorite boys, so sometimes, some of the boys would feel left out. And some of the Daddies would walk around without a boy to spank. So, a system was developed for those who wanted to participate, where Daddies and boys would be paired up by pulling names, often aliases of course, out of a hat to match guys up.

The sounds of 50 to 100 boys all getting their asses spanked by their Daddy would fill the air in The Hole. Penetration was not allowed. However, that didn't mean that everyone left feeling unsatisfied. Quite the opposite. Boys would cum while bent over a knee, if Daddy gave permission for the boy to play with his little peepee. Yes, a boy was always told he had a little peepee that he should be ashamed of, again, no matter the age of the boy or the size of the peepee.

And Daddies would take their pleasure, standing over a boy whose ass was bright red, almost steaming from the heat of a hard spanking, releasing their seed all over that bright red butt.

I was telling you about Joe and Jerome and their sex lives. I do know that they attended the spanking parties in The Hole. They both liked to be seen, one giving the spanking and the other getting it. They never switched partners and they never switched positions, unlike many of the guys who would show up for Spanking Sundays.

Who was the Daddy and who was the boy, when it came to Old Man Joe and Jerome? Do you think I would betray their confidence by telling you? Or do you think that might add to the humiliation of the boy for me to tell you? Let me think about that a little. I'm not sure that the role they played is really an important part of the story. Maybe, something should be left to your imagination.

Other than their participation in Spanking Sundays, I don't know anything about their sex lives. I don't even know if sex is part of their relationship. I know that when I see them, they hold hands, they hug, they touch each other in tender ways. And in this case, all I can tell you is what I've observed. I never talked to either one of them about the intimate details of their time together. Disappointed? Sorry.

However, I don't think that Joe or Jerome would be upset if I told you that it was always OMJ who was the one doing the spanking. (Apparently, I'm not very good at keeping secrets.) I could see, as plain as day, that the old man got a huge boner when he was using a leather paddle on Jerome's smooth white mooncakes. And Jerome's dick was hard, wet, oozing, throbbing while he answered

"Yes, Sir, give me one more, please Sir!" when his Daddy asked him if he deserved to be punished like a bad little boy. By the time Joe pulled his boy's white briefs down to his ankles, that boy's butt was burning hot and red as a polished apple. Yes, Daddy enjoyed his sessions with his boy on Spanking Sundays, letting everybody there know who was in charge and who was into being publicly humiliated and shamed.

Joe and Jerome were quickly becoming regulars at every event. Seeing a revival of *The Boys in the Band* at The Forrest Theatre? There they were, chatting with all the right people during intermission. Playing billiards down in The Hole on a Saturday night? Yep, they were there. Walking in AIDS walks? Attending fundraisers? Working on the food line at MANNA? Yes, yes, and yes.

To me, it seemed that they were good for each other.

And speaking of MANNA, I don't know who came up with that name, but talk about the perfect acronym for an organization providing meals for PWAs. Manna, of course, is a Biblical term. As Israelites traveled through the wilderness, manna was food that was miraculously delivered to them.

In Philly, MANNA was, and still is, the Metropolitan Area Neighborhood Nutrition Alliance. Henry and I also volunteered there on a number of occasions. I cannot say enough good things about this outstanding organization.

The bond between Joe and Jerome also was a sign of hope for me. Jerome was a young guy, who should have a long future ahead of him, but in these times, no one could be certain of that. And Joe, already a senior citizen, or at least, close to that age, still had hope for a fun, productive future. The more I think about it, the more beautiful that couple is to me.

258

***

The last time we had an incident at the club that required us to ask for help from the police was when one of three guys who had started a queer radio station with headquarters at Sanctuary had robbed the place of all their equipment. That time, Henry had waited to consult with me before calling in the cops for an investigation.

This time, Henry didn't wait. He was furious about what had happened, and he was determined to find out who did it and make sure they got the punishment they deserved. He was on the phone to 911 as soon as he saw the damage.

It was the mural. Someone had spray-painted over parts of it, covering it with big, ugly, bold strokes of graffiti. Luckily, the damage was restricted to the very bottom section of the mural, which was 5 stories high, covering the face of the old converted warehouse. That meant that the image of James Baldwin was untouched, since that section was on Floors 2 to 4, unreachable by vandals. Of course, the 5th Floor section was the statement "Every Day is a Good Day to be Gay," which was also undamaged.

I was at the club as soon as I could get there.

"Those fuckin' bastards!' Henry hollered at me. "Just wait till they find out we have security cameras outside. I guess they were either too stupid to read the warning signs or they felt so entitled that they didn't care."

Henry and I showed the security tape to the cops who came to take the report of the crime.

"Oh hell yeah," one of them said. "We already know those guys. They've been causing trouble at a couple of places around here."

259

A few days later, we were notified that two teenagers had been arrested and charged with destruction of private property and criminal mischief. Henry, during a meeting with the prosecutor, wanted the guys to be charged with a hate crime.

"That's never going to happen," Henry was told.

"Why the hell not? We were targeted because we're a gay club with a mural of a gay Black man out front. They didn't try to destroy that art just for fun."

"I agree with you about the motive," the prosecutor explained, "but the fact is, there's no hate crime legislation in the Commonwealth of Pennsylvania. So, no one can be charged with a hate crime because it isn't against the law here to commit a crime based on hate."

"What?" Henry was almost beside himself when he heard this bit of news. But the fact is, there was nothing he could do about it in this particular case.

Several months later, when the teens went to trial, they were found guilty of both crimes, destruction of private property and criminal mischief. Henry and I both felt a feeling of satisfaction at the verdict.

That's when the judge in the case announced the sentence.

"I don't think these boys really meant any harm. I don't think they deserve to have their lives ruined after one careless incident. Therefore, I'm imposing a sentence of 3 months in the city jail, with the sentence suspended. I think this will teach them a lesson and they'll never bother you again," the judge said, looking directly at Henry and me.

"Maybe it was just a case of homophobia," he said, as if to explain away the behavior of the young men.

Henry's body was shaking with anger.

"You're both free to go," the judge said to the teens.

***

In case you're wondering, there is still no hate crime legislation in the Commonwealth of Pennsylvania. Why not? The simple answer is that the city of Philadelphia and the rest of the state of Pennsylvania are very different. Pennsylvania is mostly white, mostly straight (of course), and mostly rural and conservative. Things like hate crimes are not part of the normal experience of the citizens there, and that makes it easy for people to ignore the problems of others. That doesn't make it right. I'm just explaining the reality. Most people just don't care. Certainly, they don't care enough to elect representatives who would take action on this issue.

Henry was still livid when we went home after the guys he called "those criminals" were let go scot-free.

"You know what I really hate about that whole experience?"

"Tell me," I encouraged him.

"That judge acted like homophobia is normal behavior. But he doesn't understand. If the courts won't protect us, who will?"

I didn't know the answer to that question, so I remained silent, but supportive of Henry's words.

He continued, saying, "When I first heard that term, 'homophobia', I was told that some people, particularly men, would lash out at gay men because they were afraid that they themselves might be gay."

"Isn't that what it means?" I asked. "Aren't they closet cases who pretend to hate us to hide the fact that they're gay too?"

"That's what 'homophobia' used to mean," Henry said. "But now, the meaning is changing. Straight people are claiming that they're afraid of us. That's what a 'phobia' is. When you're afraid of something. Like people who are afraid of the dark."

"Straight people, afraid of us? That's ridiculous," I told Henry.

"You're right about that. No straight person is afraid of us, not really. But if they claim their actions are based on fear, then they can get away with a lot."

I nodded in agreement.

"I don't like using that word, 'homophobia.' I think it should be called something else. Something that describes what's really going on. Something that means what's really true. They aren't afraid of us. They hate us, plain and simple."

"I don't know what they should be called then," I said. "Homo-haters?"

"That's actually a pretty good term," Henry said, almost laughing at the thought. But this was too serious to laugh about.

"I'm thinking of the Latin word for hate," he told me. Just like 'phobia' is Latin for the fear of something, 'odium' is the Latin word for hating something.

Sometimes, Henry truly amazed me with his knowledge.

So I think the term 'homophobia' should be replaced with the word 'homodium.' They don't fear us; they hate us."

I doubt that word will ever catch on, but I do know that "homodium" better describes what's going on than "homophobia" ever will. And it places the blame for anti-gay behavior on the root cause. Hate. Because I'll never be convinced that any hate crime against members of the LGBTQ community is caused by fear. Those people are motivated by hate. No one calls it a "fear crime."

Henry would admit that there was one problem with his new term for homo-haters. Homodium was a good word when used as a noun. But then it seemed limited if someone tried to use it as a different part of speech.

"If you talk about homophobia, you can describe someone's behavior as homophobic. But if I say that someone is a victim of homodium, how do I describe the behavior? As homodi…"

And then he would stop, because he didn't know how to change the noun to another part of speech. Henry figured that was why the term "homodium" might never really be used by the general public.

As for me, I wasn't very good with words, or math, or anything else that had to do with what I thought of as school subjects. I let Henry and others worry about things like that.

Our mural was fixed, with help from the Mural Arts Program and other community members. The damage to the building could be hidden and then eventually forgotten. However, the wounds from that attack, the wounds that were caused to our minds and emotions, are not so easily hidden away. At some point, people who are wounded on a continual basis will fight back.

The day after our conversation about what to call the homo-haters, I found Henry in the kitchen making brunch for us. Setting our plates on the table, Henry had the biggest grin on his face.

"The answer came to me in my sleep, babe. I know how to describe those bastards."

"What are you talking about, Henry? Those guys who wrecked our mural?"

"Yes, them and all the other haters out there. Remember, they want to hide behind a defense of being afraid of us. But it's hatred, pure hatred that drives them to act against us. And now I know how to describe their behavior. It's homodious. They are homodious people. They act homodiously. Get it?"

I did get it. And I knew this made Henry happy. We both felt we needed the right words to use in this battle against hatred.

Things like this, running into a problem and then solving it, made Henry a hero to me.

NINETEEN

When I look back at the 1980s, three words come to my mind. Anxiety, Anger. Activism.

They describe what I see as the process by which our community dealt with the AIDS crisis.

Of course, individual members of the community went through those stages at different times and to different degrees. And the stages weren't mutually exclusive. You wouldn't stop feeling anxious when you became angry. Clearly, you can have anxiety, feel anger and take action all at the same time.

As the 1980s progressed into the early 90s, I watched the younger generation as they dealt with our new reality of safer sex, less casual sex, fewer promiscuous encounters, etc. Because of course, when the pandemic first began, there was hope that it would be short-lived. Eventually, it became apparent that this disease, AIDS, was going to be part of our lives for longer than expected.

I still believe that homodium played a huge part in that. The government agencies that were supposed to safeguard public health failed our community miserably. There were Presidents of the United States who openly blamed gay people for causing and spreading the disease. Some government officials didn't hide the fact that they considered HIV to be the solution to a problem. They thought that the virus was a gift from God to rid the United States of those hated homosexuals. You might think I'm kidding, but these were the facts of the time.

Henry and I played our parts in the fight. But there were hundreds, thousands of people who joined together to make a difference. You've heard me say before that we had to help ourselves. Straight society didn't care, once they determined that they could consider themselves mostly safe from the epidemic. It was only later, when some "straight" celebrities publicly stated that they had contracted HIV, that a sense of urgency was brought to the government. Of course, they were more than happy to help when the threat was perceived as something that might affect the "right people."

Two young people who caught my eye at the club were Sammy and Christian. They had moved to Philly from a small town in Pennsylvania, just like I had quite a few years ago. They were seeking a safer environment, and they hoped that Philly might be a place where they would feel comfortable being their true selves.

They moved into an apartment in the same building where DJ Thunder lived, in the Gayborhood, surrounded by bars, restaurants, bookstores, etc., that welcomed people who were living the gay life.

No, they didn't walk around appearing to be anxious or angry. They seemed to be carefree. They expressed themselves openly as gay, not hiding from anyone. It made me happy to see them at Sanctuary, carrying on, having fun, dressing up, wearing the cool styles of the day, sometimes sporting make-up, or whatever suited their moods and their budget.

They were clearly activists. They were willing to put up a fight. Remember the motto from ACT UP: Silence Equals Death. Those aren't empty words. It isn't just a slogan. It was the truth. To sit by silently was an invitation to those in power to ignore the needs of the people, the PWAs, who urgently needed assistance in so many different ways.

Just like Old Man Joe and his new boy, Jerome, both Sammy and Christian were present at many events that were designed to provide what our community needed.

Again, that gave me hope for the future. Just knowing that the new generation recognized the problem and was ready to fight for our rights made my chest swell with pride. And I continued to remind myself of my personal motto:

Every Day is a Good Day to be Gay.

***

I found that my therapy sessions with Reverend Doctor Greene were helping me see a bigger picture than I had seen before. I was looking beyond myself. Not that I was exactly selfish before, but I did tend to think of my own needs first. I wanted to be more giving, more aware of the perspectives of other people, more empathetic. And I felt that I was growing and maturing in a good way.

Some people go into therapy for other reasons, even the exact opposite reason. Some people always think about others first, never making time for themselves. I wanted to reach a happy medium. Making myself a priority when it was necessary, while also allowing myself to think about other people.

Reverend Doctor Greene, or Eli, as I now called him, provided methods for me to accomplish my goals.

Remember, I wasn't in therapy because I was sad. I wasn't depressed. I didn't need any medication. I didn't have that chemical imbalance or whatever it is that can cause people to see the world in ways that are called insane or paranoid.

Feeling that I was getting positive results from our sessions, I added another weekly meeting to our schedule. Every Tuesday and Thursday, I would explore my emotions and confide my secrets to Eli. However, there was one secret that I couldn't convince myself to talk about with anyone, including Eli. I thought if I didn't discuss it, maybe it would disappear from my mind. Of course, I'm talking about the day I betrayed my husband, letting Billy, one of our bartenders who was then looking for a job, suck my dick.

On Tuesday, December 10, 1991, Eli told me that he would have to cancel our session scheduled for Thursday, the 12th.

"I have three funerals scheduled in the next two days, so I just don't have the time to meet with you."

It took a moment for me to comprehend the enormity of what Eli had just said. There I was, trying to learn to be more empathetic, and it had honestly never even occurred to me what Eli's life was like. To consider his feelings and his situation. Not only was he spending many hours each week with members of the LGBTQ community who wanted and needed therapy, but he was also working with the community of PWAs, Persons With AIDS, who also needed help. And on top of that, he was the minister for a congregation that was greatly affected by HIV and officiating at their funerals too.

It made me feel selfish. Not that I was utilizing his services, but it seemed that while I thought I was doing better, I was missing the entire point of my therapy. How could I be so stupid?

For a few months now, Eli had been feeling the weight of his responsibilities growing heavier each day. Sometimes, he would have a conversation with someone, maybe even during a therapy session, and he wasn't quite sure what he had just said. He didn't even know if he was making sense. Was he speaking in English? Or in tongues? He was getting confused. He couldn't remember. But he did his best to hide it.

I never noticed that anything was wrong. I don't know if that was because I was too involved in listening to myself, or if Eli was just able to cover it up really well.

Eli felt himself sinking into that deep dark hole of depression. He wasn't just sad about what was happening to his community. It went beyond that. There were days when he would wake up feeling completely numb. And yet he went through the motions of getting through the day because that's what people expected him to do.

On Thursday, December 12, 1991, Eli spent the early afternoon eulogizing at his third funeral in two days. He was speaking about someone he knew, another in a long line of young gay men who had their lives ended much too soon, just being one of the unfortunate ones who had contracted a deadly, incurable virus for which no vaccine had been found, without any effective treatment.

Eli heard himself speaking, but it was as if he was in the audience listening to himself. He thought he remembered describing the deceased man as kind, loving, giving, but he wasn't sure. He hoped he was saying the right things.

When he returned from the graveside service, where he again spoke a few words, blessing the soul of the beautiful young man, Eli went quietly into his office.

He opened the desk drawer where he kept a pistol. "Just in case," he would explain to anyone who knew about the weapon.

He didn't feel anything. He put the barrel of the gun in his mouth and pulled the trigger.

I was devastated when I heard the news that Eli was dead. Not just dead, but having committed suicide. And I wasn't the only one. This was a community in mourning.

I wish I had somehow known to say something to Eli about his worries, his concerns, his condition. But I failed to recognize that anything was wrong. Again, I wasn't the

269

only one to feel that way. Survivors' guilt can be a terrible thing.

I have to take a minute to say that if you're hearing my story, and if you feel anything like Eli was feeling, if you have ever thought about committing suicide, please ask someone for help. There is help available and things do get better. Try to take a step back and save yourself from seeking a permanent solution to a temporary problem. Please.

TWENTY

Time has a way of moving forward. It always does, stopping for no one. Somehow, Henry and I, and so many others who knew and loved Eli, managed to get through the holidays and the calendar changed to 1992.

The hurt was still too raw, too real, for me to enjoy any holidays that year.

I felt like I was coasting along, not doing anything important, just trying to survive and get through each passing day. I felt an emptiness, but I still maintain that I wasn't clinically depressed. But the sadness was sometimes unbearable.

Henry helped. A lot. His presence was always appreciated. I kept thinking about that terrible day when I had given in to a temporary temptation, instead of being true to a man who had provided me with so much joy in my life.

You know what else helped? That beautiful creature known as Zumi, my cherished Boston Terrier. He never failed to bring a smile to my face with his antics. He could be stubborn; he could be annoying, but he never failed to provide a laugh at least once every day. Even the very darkest days.

To look at him was to love him. That face, with his pug nose that caused him to snore like a bear when he was asleep. Those adorable markings, with that distinctive white stripe at the middle of his head. And those ears! Always pointing straight up, standing at attention, always hearing when someone approached our front door, with Zumi ready to enthusiastically greet any guest.

Taking him for a walk was therapy for me. I was unable to bear the thought of going to a different therapist after Eli, so I was content to let the combination of exercise while walking with Zumi and his irrepressibly good-natured pure joy be my therapy. We especially enjoyed spending time at the park located just a short distance from our home, on that very same block.

Zumi was a little unusual in that he didn't like to spend too much time away from home. Undoubtedly, he did enjoy our time at the park, but after a short time, he'd start pulling me in the direction back home.

He always enjoyed meeting people in the park, wanting to jump up to greet them whenever he was given the opportunity. I couldn't break him of that habit. And as much as he liked meeting new people, he generally chose to ignore any other dogs who were in the park at the same time as us.

I loved Zumi and his name, which still fit because he'd still get the zoomies at home, bouncing around the house like he was just so full of energy that he couldn't contain it. Those were some of the funniest times!

As you know, I have a habit of assigning nicknames, and Zumi was no different. I'd call him my little jellybean, my little peanut, even my little potato-head. I thought it was funny. Henry thought it was weird, but he'd laugh when I'd use those little terms of endearment for my little spuddy buddy.

Once winter turned to spring, both Zumi and I enjoyed being outside a bit more. There's something so appealing about the arrival of spring weather in Philly, especially after some winters that were brutally cold and snowy.

While Henry was the rock of my life, the man I could always count on for support, comfort, advice…I thought of Zumi as my silent therapist. When I told him about a problem, he'd look at me with his soulful, bulging eyes, and not say a word. Sometimes, that's what I needed. No advice. No encouragement to consider a different point of view. Just a being who was willing to silently listen, allowing me to think things out for myself.

I liked to take him out to the park where he'd run around for a bit, sniffing around, making friends with different plants, bushes, or trees. Then, as I sat on a bench, maybe reading or listening to tunes on my Walkman, Zumi liked to perch himself directly on my foot. Somehow, he felt that was comforting and you know what? So did I. And after a few minutes of sitting at perfect attention, he'd stretch out, still keeping part of his body against mine, enjoying that special connection between us.

Wednesday, May 6, 1992, was one of those glorious spring days in Philly. There had been a light rain that morning, which served to sweeten the air. The apple trees in the park were in full bloom, white petals scattered along the pathways as the wind swept them from the branches. Squirrels seemed to be everywhere, chasing one another in playful delight.

Always late risers, due to our schedules working late into the night at the club, Henry and I enjoyed our morning coffee together, as he told me that he'd be busy meeting with distributors over in Jersey all day. We planned to meet at the club later, since he wouldn't have time to come home before it would be time for work.

"Is Mama gonna take Zumi to the park today?" Henry asked me.

"Yes, Papa. It looks like a good day for the park," I replied, as we referred to each other by our Zumi nicknames. Yes, we were Mama, Papa and Zumi, the little family.

273

"Ok Henry, I love you," I told him as he headed out the door to catch the High-Speed Line to Jersey.

"I love you too, babe," he replied, which by this time had become both a daily and a nightly ritual.

With that, he was out the door.

"Zumi, you ready for a walk, little buddy?" I called a few minutes later. Just hearing the word "walk" had Zumi twirling in circles, tongue hanging halfway out of his mouth, a look of excitement on his face. He sat quietly as I attached the leash to his collar and we headed for the park. I took the rest of my coffee and that day's copy of the Philadelphia Daily News, a tabloid-style paper, with me.

As usual, the park was mostly deserted at this time of day. Our neighborhood was home to many professionals, most of whom worked in the office towers or hospitals in Center City. From our neighborhood, Queen Village, people could easily walk to Center City, though there were also plenty of buses that ran on convenient schedules for professional people.

Sitting on a park bench, with Zumi seated on my shoe, I looked up from the paper when I heard a skateboarder approaching. I knew that sound from many hours spent skateboarding back in my old hometown when I was a kid.

I smiled when I saw him. *Damn, he's a hot one,* I thought to myself, seeing a young guy about 18 or 19 approaching us, practicing a few flips on his board.

Since the early afternoon sun was warming the air, the boy had shed his flannel shirt, tying it around his waist in that style that the skaterboys loved. That left him wearing only a white athletic shirt to cover his skinny but tight torso. I sighed just looking at him, thinking about all the young dudes, just like this one, that Henry and I used to

274

take home with us for a night of carefree, casual sex, drinking, and drugs.

He was also wearing baggy grey sweatpants, hanging low on his hips, almost falling off as he skated in the area near me. Long blonde hair flying in the breeze, he smiled at me as he skated right up to the bench where I was sitting.

"I love your dog. Is he a French bulldog?" he asked innocently, making a fist and extending it close to Zumi, who sniffed to determine whether this was friend or foe.

"No, but a lot of people think that. He's a Boston Terrier," I replied, trying not to blush at the sight of this sexy young god.

Zumi clearly liked him, jumping up and getting close to the boy's privates as the young guy realized it was okay for him to scratch Zumi behind his ears.

I felt an all too familiar stirring in my pants as the skater sat down next to me, brushing his long bleached blonde hair behind his ears, showing two earrings in each earlobe. His smooth face was a little flushed from the exercise of boarding, and I could see a soft glistening on his skin from just a hint of sweat.

He leaned back, spreading his legs wide, and I could see that he was hanging low. It looked huge from my point of view and I licked my lips, not even realizing that I was staring.

Suddenly, I flashed back to Rittenhouse Square, where I had been sitting on a park bench, cruising for guys. That was the night I met Henry. The night our long relationship had started. The night I had found the man I loved and went on to marry.

But that happened years ago. This was now, 1992. And I felt a yearning, for my youth, for my carefree life before the horror of AIDS had forced me into a life of responsibility. I thought I was happy. But was I really?

I spent an hour talking to Xander, which he explained was short for Alexander. Zumi was getting impatient to go back home, as I talked and talked, all the while moving my glances from his eyes to his cock which looked like it was getting rigid right there in the park. Or was it just my imagination? And as I was wondering about his dick, he'd lean back suggestively, placing his hands behind his head, so I could see his shaved underarms, and then he'd rub his abs, lifting his athletic shirt just enough to give me a glimpse of that beautiful young tight body.

Maybe he was waiting for me to make the first move, but sensing that maybe I was shy or submissive or…something, he finally said what we were both thinking.

"You feelin' horny, Joey? I am. I'm so fuckin' horny. Do you live around here?"

Just mentioning the possibility of this turning into a sexual encounter made my dick swell with desire. And I watched as his cock, clearly long and thick, went from a limp state to standing straight and tall in those sexy baggy sweats, and I wanted him so much. I wanted to taste him, to smell him, to feel his power against me and inside me.

"I live right over there," I said, motioning my head in the direction of my house. *No, that wasn't accurate. It wasn't my house. It was Henry's house too.*

I stood and felt Zumi pulling, wanting to get back home.

"Can I walk him?" Xander asked. I figured there would be no harm in that, so I handed the leash to Xander, who used that excuse to grab hold of my hand. I tried to pull my hand away, but Xander wasn't about to let go.

276

"I hope your neighbors aren't watching," he told me. "'Cause I can't get my dick to go down, especially now that I can get a good look at your hot ass."

As much as I hate to admit it, that was just the kind of talk I liked from a man, especially one that looked as delicious as Xander did.

We walked slowly towards my house. *No, I had to remind myself. This isn't my house. It belongs to me and Henry. What am I doing?* I thought to myself.

But I didn't tell Xander to go on his way. To go back to skating in the park. I took another look between his legs, and I could see that big piece of meat swinging and swaying, clearly rigid with desire, wanting to find itself buried inside a deep manhole.

And I could feel myself getting wet with desire. I pictured Xander on top of me, holding me down with a firm masculine grip, licking my nipples, working his way down as I imagined him turning me over and using his tongue against and inside my pucker.

I let out a sigh.

He heard me.

"You really need it, don't you?"

Oh god, that took me even further back. Back before I met Henry. Back in my old hometown. Years ago, hanging out in front of Uncle Teddy's Tavern, the only gay bar in that town, cruising for sex without even knowing what I was doing. And that's when that boy Tommy, who had been watching me clumsily trying to get attention from any boy, had said those exact same words to me.

"You really need it, don't you?"

When Tommy said those words, I pretended that I didn't know what he was talking about.

With Xander, I knew that wouldn't work. I was too experienced, too obvious.

"Tell me. I wanna hear you say it," Xander said as we got to the edge of the park, with my house…our house…just a few steps away.

"I want it," I whispered. "I want your dick."

"Oh no you don't, you little bitch. You don't get to whisper it like it's some secret. Tell the world. Tell them you wanna get this dick right now."

Somehow, he recognized my need to be dominated, even humiliated. For me, it made it even more exciting because we were outside, in public, and he was forcing me to do something I didn't want to do, though in reality, he was tapping into some of my deepest desires.

"Yes Sir, I want your dick right now," I said, in a normal speaking voice.

I noticed that there were a few people on the street near us. Most of them I didn't recognize, but I did see Zak and Fetu, two guys I had met when they were regulars at The Hole, who lived about two blocks away. If I had been able to think about anything other than Xander's cock in my butthole, I would have remembered that I used to call those two guys Tattoo Lou and Tattoo Too. Before I got to know them, of course. I hoped they wouldn't notice me, walking with a guy who wasn't Henry.

"You ain't gonna get nothin', you disobedient slut, unless you show me RIGHT NOW that you can follow my directions," Xander said, growing annoyed. "I can go right back to that park and have a willing piece of ass for my cock in less than 10 minutes. And you know what I'm sayin' is true. So if you want this dick, like you claim you do, get down on your fuckin' knees right now and beg me for it. And I mean beg, and beg loudly, so everybody within three blocks of us knows that you're a bitch in heat, begging for dick. Do it, boy. RIGHT NOW."

He knew how to play me. He hit all the right buttons. The huge cock in those baggy sweatpants, tempting me, driving me crazy, making me forget everything else.

I got down on my knees. Right there in the middle of the block on Queen Street. My dick was controlling me, as I felt such a rush of desire that I felt like I couldn't control myself.

"PLEASE, YOUNG MASTER! PLEASE GIVE ME YOUR DICK. I WANT IT. I NEED IT. I WANNA GET FUCKED RIGHT NOW. BY YOU!"

Oh god, did I really say that?

Xander smiled, laughing out loud, knowing he had a horny bitchboy under his control, at least for the moment. I watched as a wet spot appeared on the front of his sweats, his dick oozing the passion juices that I craved.

"Ok, fagboy. You earned it. Your Master is pleased. Now let's get inside so I can fuck your wet ass."

As soon as we stepped inside, Zumi was unleashed and he headed for one of his favorite spaces, his daybed in the living room. It took about 10 seconds for him to be sound asleep, snoring loudly.

"Where's the bedroom? Or you wanna get fucked on the couch?" Xander growled, lowering his sweats down to his ankles, then stepping out of them.

My eyes widened. His body was magnificent. So young. So smooth. So tight. And his cock was already throbbing with desire, drops of precum appearing at the tip and sliding down the side of the shaft.

In the bedroom, Xander treated me like a dirty whore. The filthy talk. The commands to lick his feet, suck his toes, swallow his balls, lick the shaft of his dick without permission to suck it until I was almost crazed with desire.

When he turned me over, aiming his wet dick at my hungry hole, I gave no thought to safe sex. No thoughts of Henry. Desire and lust drove me to spread my legs wide so my strong young Master could have his pleasure inside me, to fill me with his seed until his cream dripped out of me, his cock plunging deeper and deeper as I screamed wildly with sexual hunger.

He was cumming inside me as he bit my neck, reaching between my legs and squeezing my balls, making my dick jump as I shot my load on the bed.

***

I had no way of knowing that the vendor who was supposed to meet Henry that morning ended up staying home because he was sick. There were no cell phones, so Henry couldn't call or text me from the car as he drove back home.

I was too busy screaming lustily as my ass was being pounded by the beautiful boy whose dick was deep inside me to hear the key turning in the lock of the front door.

"Babe? You here?" Henry called.

I heard nothing but the moans coming from deep inside my soul.

Just as I was shaking, trembling, as I climaxed on the bed, the door to the bedroom opened.

"WHAT THE FUCK!"

Xander and I both turned and saw Henry standing there.

"You! Get the hell outta MY house!"

Xander immediately got off me, got off the bed, and pulled on his clothes as he quickly headed for the front door. He let himself out.

I had to deal with Henry, the fury obvious on his face.

"This is what you do when I'm not around? You whore around with some stray boy you pick up on the street?"

I was crying. Through my sobs, I tried to explain. To apologize. To beg for forgiveness.

"I never expected this. I never thought were cheating on me all this time. I thought I could trust you," he told me, as I tried to get dressed. I was trembling too much, my fingers unable to grasp anything to cover my shame.

I started to speak again, to tell Henry that I had never cheated before. But of course, that wasn't completely true.

"Don't say anything. Don't talk to me. I don't wanna hear any sorry pathetic excuses," he hissed, then continued, "I'm going out to try to cool off. I don't know when I'll be back."

I spent the afternoon crying, regretting what I had done. I tried to explain it away to myself, trying to find some way to explain to Henry why I did something so stupid. But nothing really made sense. I did love Henry. What made me fall for a few quick minutes of pleasure, risking everything that Henry and I had built together?

Hours later, I was asleep on the sofa. Henry came home, obviously drunk, clearly still angry. I jumped awake, startled, when he took hold of a bookcase in the living room and just shoved it over, toppling it, spilling books and other pieces of art and sculptures that we had collected together. Everything was broken. Just like us.

"I'm going to bed," he slurred. "You're lucky I didn't bring back some whoreboy and fuck his ass right in front of you," he snarled, slamming the bedroom door shut behind him.

I lay on the couch, sobbing and trembling. I wanted to apologize, but I sensed that Henry wasn't ready to listen to me. Not right now.

Around 2 AM, I woke up, remembering everything that had happened, wishing it had been a dream. But no, this was all too real.

I went into the bedroom. Henry was still fully-dressed, sleeping with his back to me. Or so I thought. In reality, Henry couldn't sleep at all. His emotions were a mixture of anger, betrayal and wondering how this could have possibly happened. He just stared at the wall in front of him, ignoring my entrance.

I crawled into bed with him, lightly wrapping my arm around him.

"I love you, Henry," I said, repeating our nightly ritual. "I know you're mad and you're hurt and I'm sorry. But I really do love you."

I was met with a silence that stung me to my very soul. With difficulty, I finally drifted off to sleep.

***

Thursday, May 7, 1992. When I woke up, I could tell it was already afternoon by the angle of the sunlight streaming in through the bedroom window. It had gotten colder during the night, and I was huddled under the comforter, in my usual fetal position. I always woke up slowly, not being the type to jump out of bed, fully awake and ready to face the new day.

It took a minute before I realized that something was different. Then, the horror of the previous day suddenly came back to me in a flash of recognition and regret. I reached for Henry, but he wasn't there.

282

Probably already making our coffee, I thought hopefully. Dragging my head up from the pillow, I made an effort to focus my eyes. I think they were swollen shut because, without realizing it, I had been crying in my sleep. I knew that I had to get everything explained to Henry, set this episode behind us, and then continue with the plans we had for our lives and for the club.

Rubbing my eyes helped bring the world into focus. And then, suddenly, I saw what would ensure that this date, May 7, would be a date that I would never forget.

There, on the pillow next to mine, Henry had left his wedding ring. Nothing else. No note. No message.

It took a moment before I realized that the ring *was* the message. He had never taken it off since the day of our wedding, back on December 25, 1980, 12 years ago.

The ring in which I had the following words inscribed: "You are my Sanctuary" followed by two hearts melded together into one. The initial "H" was inside the first heart, with "J" inside the second. For Henry and Joey, of course.

With a shock, I remembered the words I had spoken, my vows, that I had said in front of Henry, in front of Reverend Eli Greene, and so many of our friends.

"Henry, before I met you, I wasn't sure if love was possible for me. You taught me that I can love and be loved. I promise to share all of life's adventures with you, loving you every step of the way. I will be your devoted husband forever."

The guilt was stabbing me in my heart in a way that I had never experienced before. Yesterday, I had thrown everything away. All the love. All the trust. All the support. Everything that Henry had provided for me had been thrown away for what? For a big dick in my ass?

Oh my god, what the fuck did I do? I moaned to myself softly, sobbing, tears streaming down my cheeks.

Then, because I wasn't the type to be quietly upset, I found myself standing in the middle of our bedroom, screaming, pulling at my hair, beating my chest as the agony of losing my soulmate was dawning on me.

"I love you, Henry!"

I LOVE YOU, HENRY!" I screamed, collapsing once more to the floor in a heap of misery.

To be continued...

EPILOGUE

The lives of Joey and Henry changed dramatically on Thursday, May 7, 1992. That date was not selected randomly.

On that date, my best friend, whom I had first met when we were freshmen in high school, died from complications caused by AIDS.

My life was dramatically changed on that date, which is one that I will never forget.

I still wonder how his life would have turned out if it wasn't for the AIDS pandemic.

And I still miss you.

A Message to Readers
of CLUBBED TWO

Thank you for sharing in the stories included in CLUBBED TWO: Anxiety, Anger, Activism.

If you enjoyed the book, please give it a rating on Amazon. If you would be so kind as to also write a review, well, that would be awesome!

I like to show photos of my book in various locations. You can help me with this promotion. Just take a photo of the book in some cool location in your city/town/area.

Send the photo to me by email at robert.karl.author@gmail.com. I'll post it on Instagram using the tag #wheresmybookwednesday. I'll give you credit for the photo, of course. Or, if you're on Instagram, you can post a photo of the book yourself, using the same hashtag. You can follow me on Instagram @robertkarl_inpr.

Again, thank you for reading CLUBBED TWO. Remember, every day is a good day to be gay.

Other Books By This Author

CLUBBED: A Story of Gay Love: Trials, Tribulations and Triumphs (Book One in the CLUBBED: Stories of Gay Love series)

Made in United States
Orlando, FL
02 March 2022